LITTLE
LOST
SOULS

BOOKS BY STACY GREEN

LITTLE LOST SOULS

STACY GREEN

bookouture

Published by Bookouture in 2023

An imprint of Storyfire Ltd.
Carmelite House
50 Victoria Embankment
London EC4Y 0DZ

www.bookouture.com

ISBN: 978-1-80314-956-1
eBook ISBN: 978-1-80314-955-4

ONE

Blowing snow blinded me as I careened down Interstate 81. My jaw muscles throbbed from clenching my teeth for the past five hazardous hours, and the truck stop was still four miles away. The icy roads made me late—the exchange was planned for 9:15 p.m., exactly eight minutes ago. Unless my luck had been blessed with a major traffic accident, I wouldn't be catching the seller. But maybe saving the child and interrogating the buyer were still within reach.

"If I don't die before I get there, it'll be a miracle." My tires hit yet another packed-down section of snow and sent the car sliding. I wrenched the steering wheel into the skid, my stomach burning as if I'd lit it on fire. Gently pumping the brakes and cursing the polar vortex, I saved the car from skidding onto the shoulder. The kid I was trying to save couldn't afford my slowing down.

Pain burned my bottom lip; I dug my teeth out of the tender flesh. Two hazardous miles to go. The windshield wipers were on high, their annoying swish-swash giving me another reason to cuss.

After discovering Kailey Richardson had nearly been sold

into an online sex trafficking ring, I'd decided to take my operation beyond old case files. Child sex trafficking was running
rampant in this country, and law enforcement often found its
hands tied by our legal system.

I didn't.

Kelly and I spent weeks searching online classified ads,
learning the code words for selling sex. There were thousands
of readily accessible ads, and most of the sites had IP addresses
that simply bounced back to a server in another country, making
law enforcement's job nearly impossible. Kelly created our ad,
posing as a twelve-year-old girl. We read through the hundreds
of replies very carefully. We needed a weak opponent, not a
pimp looking for another child to destroy.

Our choice was the right one. The guy cried when I showed
up instead of a little girl, and he begged for his life when I gave
him the overdose of ketamine. Not before he bargained away a
few online accounts and passwords, however.

It didn't take long before Kelly found deeply embedded
groups selling kids. Tonight was the first verified hit—our first
chance to save a kid and glean some new information in the
process.

I couldn't erase the memory of the video. A little boy with
dark brown skin, a little skinny but overall healthy looking,
stood naked in the middle of a nondescript room. A disem-
bodied voice ordered him to turn in a circle, to raise his arms
over his head, to bend over. He obeyed with a glazed look in his
eyes and tears running down his cheeks. A price was named
just before the video ended.

I would kill someone for that little boy tonight.

"Stupid snow." My eyes watered just looking at the
cascading white flakes. I glanced at my bag. Injection loaded
and ready. Cash for the kid. Pepper spray just in case. Kelly
discovered the sale so suddenly I'd resorted to running around
my apartment, throwing things in a bag and hoping I had what I

needed. I promised the cat I'd be home to feed him in the morning, and I didn't intend to let him down.

I peered through the sheet of snow to see Hagerstown 81 truck stop's bright red sign.

"Please, God, don't let me be too late." As I turned to take the icy exit, I felt the tires lose traction. "Give me a break!" Blood pounded in my temples as I half slid onto the iced-over exit. For one blinding second, I saw nothing but the snow-covered metal guardrail and braced myself for impact. Beyond the rail appeared a snowy abyss with a drop sharp enough to break my neck. Not ready to face the brain-numbing fear of death, I rapidly tapped on the brakes, pulled the steering wheel to the left. The tires had nothing but snow to grip, my small car careening down the exit ramp. All I could do was follow the curve until somehow I bottomed out and hit the next patch of clearish pavement.

Back in control, my head damp with sweat and my fingers cramped, I turned into the truck stop.

A few short months ago, this moment was unimaginable. Watching a man die by my own hand—not the first time I'd administered death, but the first I'd witnessed—left me cold and guilty and shattered. The man I'd killed deserved to die. He was the worst kind of monster, but he was still human. I wasn't sure I realized that until I saw the life fade from his frightened eyes. Someone would grieve him, and that was my shame to bear. My brand of justice needed to be re-evaluated. I couldn't take another life.

And then I found out about little Kailey Richardson being sold for sex. The part of me I'd started to think of as evil rose from the secret corner I'd buried it in and screamed for vengeance. I probably should have been nervous, but instead I felt as if I'd rediscovered my favorite pair of jeans. A match made in the blackest of heavens.

I used to think I was special, that I had a calling. That only I could deliver much-needed justice. A martyr, to be honest: risking my own freedom for the greater good.

Those were just my first round of lies.

With the seller likely long gone, I'd go after the buyer. Spun from the same cloth, anyway. Kelly discovered he would be driving a lime green Freightliner with a flatbed trailer. Code name Sand. No other information. We'd assumed the traffickers had a private CB channel. I didn't have time to run out and buy one.

"He said go to the west side of the truck stop," was the last information I had from Kelly. Since Hagerstown 81 was the largest truck stop in the state and one of the biggest in the country, the west side meant several acres and more semis than I could count.

The parking lot was partially cleared, and I managed to drive the Prius between drifts and not get stuck. Bringing my own car was a risk, but everything happened too last minute for me to get a rental. On this terrible night, the massive parking lot was loaded with semis, and most of them were at least half covered with snow. With so little to go on, I'd have to rely on instincts.

Fortunately my instincts were as incessant as an aggressive tumor. Always there, never quiet.

Privacy would be essential. Even in a truck stop with a lot of comings and goings, kids attracted attention. A psychologically damaged, physically abused kid would probably obey, but the seller wouldn't want to stand out. With the increase in human trafficking, truck drivers were becoming more perceptive and forming their own groups to help protect children. Extreme caution was needed to accomplish the trade.

I stayed on the outskirts of the west lot, gaze panning for the truck I so desperately needed to find.

The buyer came early, excited and prepared. Eager to test out the merchandise.

The winter storm could have held him up, so he'd plan his day accordingly, and snow provided a great cover. If he had any smarts, he would have let the snow pile on and then cleared only a small portion of his cab so the seller could see the color. I needed to look for a flatbed semi whose cab had mismatched snow covering.

I found it in the far west corner. I parked twenty feet away, shut off the lights, and watched. The rig didn't move. But inside the cab, a pinpoint of light flashed.

Whatever racing nerves I'd been battling now smoothed into calm. The malignancy extended its veiny fingers, shuttering my heart and wrapping itself around my nerves until they were snuffed out. I didn't think about what the buyer was likely doing to the boy. Doing so would only invite my locked-up emotions to take control. That caused mistakes.

I slipped my bag over my head, settling it across my thick coat. Double checked to make sure my tools were inside. Opened the door, shut it. Keys in pocket. Squinted my eyes against the stinging snow. I didn't feel the cold.

Anyone watching would assume I was meeting the driver for a good time. Maybe a local girlfriend ready to warm him up. My inner voice hushed, my conscience shrank into its corner cage as I approached the large truck. I kept an even pace as I crossed the front of the semi to the partially hidden passenger door, each movement with precise purpose. The bright green cab shuddered. *Movement inside.*

This is the time most people would step back, afraid of what they were interrupting. Afraid of what they might see, what could damage them for life or even worse, embarrass their delicate sensitivities. I stayed on autopilot, my actions as familiar as breathing. I reached into my bag, feeling the cold of the metal emanating through my thin gloves.

I slipped the magazine into the receiver, then pulled the slide into place.

I hated guns. They weren't my weapon of choice. Too messy and loud. But I didn't intend to use this one. Controlling a person is all about showmanship.

And the metal made a nice sound when I slammed it against the cab door.

The cylinder of light inside the truck—probably from a small beam flashlight—blinked out. I banged the Glock on the door again and then hid it in the folds of my coat.

Only part of me heard the howling wind or felt the miserable cold that had plagued us for weeks. My eyes and ears lasered in on the truck door. The handle clicked; I brought the gun around.

The door opened slowly. Stepping my left foot back, I reinforced my footing and moved my finger to the trigger. Chris had only taken me to the range twice, but I figured I could hit a man from five feet away no matter how lousy of a shot I was.

A narrow-faced white man peeked out of the slightly open door. His cheeks were hollowed out and flushed red, his pupils dilated from either fear or arousal or drugs. Maybe all three. Despite the cab's engine not running, the guy's collarbone was soaked with sweat that stained the collar of his already dingy white T-shirt.

With the speed of light and the force of all my unanswered anger, the pictures of the scared, naked boy Kelly discovered this afternoon flashed through my mind. I leveled the gun at the man.

"I'm here for the boy."

His eyes popped open. His body shifted. I caught sight of a bare knee.

"If you're going for a gun, rest assured I'll put a bullet in your head before you reach it. Show me your hands."

"Who are you?" He didn't deny the boy.

With my left hand, I showed him the FBI badge I'd painstakingly crafted. "FBI, Human Trafficking Division. I know you're holding a nine-year-old African American boy purchased less than half an hour ago from a seller out of Ohio. The transaction took place here, and you're under arrest."

Lying came naturally to me, even easier than breathing.

"Please." A tear formed in the man's eye. "I was just trying to save him."

My finger twitched. Liar. We can spot our own kind, and men like him all have the very same sob story. Trying to save the child, bringing him home to a frantic family. All lies. "Is that why you're sweating and half dressed in this cold?"

"My truck's real warm."

"The engine isn't running."

He shifted again, backwards as if he wanted to slam the door, but I was too quick, and the ice-caked snow worked in my favor. I stepped forward and slipped right to the door. Shoved the Glock under his chin. "Show me your hands."

Shaking, he stuck out first one hand, and then the other. The fingers of his right hand were bloody.

"Having a problem?"

He didn't say anything.

"Open the door, slowly."

The man did as he was told. He was down to the T-shirt, blue paid boxers, and dirty socks.

"Step down onto that top step." I retrieved the handcuffs from my messenger bag.

Shocked by the cold and my presence and the gleaming Glock, he obeyed. Confidence is everything. And the fear of others—fear caused by the power of one's own actions—can be as exhilarating as the best narcotic. "Turn around."

"What about my rights?"

"I'll read them after I secure you."

Snotty and shivering, he stumbled on the step, nearly sliding off. He jammed his hands behind his back, and I quickly snapped the cuffs on him.

"Inside the truck."

He craned his neck over his shoulder. "My rights?"

"Inside. Too cold." I pressed the Glock against his flaccid penis. "You know how easily I could shoot off your dick from this angle? Guarantee you the review board would say I was justified."

"My hands are behind my back. I'm freezing!"

"Make like the snake you are and move."

He pitched forward, his chest thudding against the interior of the cab. Using his right knee and then his left, he wriggled inside and into the driver's seat. He flopped around to face me. Gun in front of me and overloaded on the power that came from his compliance, I hefted myself into the cab and slammed the passenger door shut.

"Aron?" I kept my voice soft and kind, a feat considering the rush surging through me.

A shuffling came from behind the curtain of the cab's sleeper bed.

I kept the gun low but ready. The thought occurred the seller might still be here, or another accomplice, but I'd already entered the lion's den. "My name's Agent Rex with the FBI. I'm here to take you to safety. Are you alone back there?"

More shuffling followed by a small, terrified voice. "Yes."

"Good. Why don't you come out so I can see you? I promise I won't hurt you. That's over. And this man is going to jail for a long, painful time."

The coward in the driver's seat began to cry. His fear stank, polluting the entire cab. Another ruffle of the curtains, and Aron's young face emerged. Fine-featured and dark-skinned, with dulled brown eyes, he stared at me. "I don't have bottoms on."

My eyes flashed to the coward, my teeth clenching. Another sliver of my heart broke off and disappeared. "That's okay. You go ahead and get dressed."

Aron moved to do as he was told, and I reached into my bag for the final solution. Still pointing the gun, I angled myself over the man like a lover would.

"You're sick," I whispered.

"I can't help it." His hot breath wafted across my cheek.

"I know." Carefully, I slid the needle between his skin and the thin material of his T-shirt. "That's why this is the end for you." I jammed the needle into his armpit until he yelped and then shoved the plunger down.

He cried out as the lethally high dose of insulin shot into his system. One hundred units was likely all I needed, but as a precaution, I'd injected two hundred units. Less than a minute passed before he lost consciousness. He'd likely be dead soon after we left the cab. A medical examiner probably wouldn't notice the injection site. Twenty-seven-gauge needles don't usually leave a large mark, and his body hair concealed it. Low blood sugar would be found on autopsy, and assuming the man wasn't a diabetic, the red flags would rise. But I'd covered my tracks well.

I sat back in the passenger seat. Breathing rapidly, hands no longer steady. Heart banging in my ribcage and pulse thundering in my neck. I found my reflection in the rearview mirror. Flushed from cold, yes, but my fair skin was also dotted with excitement. My pupils looked as if I'd actually taken a mind-altering substance.

Aron poked his head out of the curtains. He stared again, with awed and frightened eyes.

"I just put him to sleep for a little while," I said. "That way when the jail truck comes, he won't fight." I eased the slider off the Glock and put it away. "Let me take off his cuffs, and then we'll go."

Aron watched as I reached underneath his tormenter's quivering body and unlocked the cuffs. I brought his hands around to his chest and laid them across his stomach so it looked like he'd fallen asleep. "There. Now he's comfortable. And the jail truck will be here soon. We should go."

Inside my knit cap and thick, blond wig, my carefully tied-back hair was dripping wet. I quickly glanced over the inside of the cab. Gloves worn. Hair covered up. Skin cells no doubt left behind, but that couldn't be helped. Maryland didn't have my DNA on file anyway.

I held out my hand to little Aron. "Ready?"

Warily, he took it. He'd likely learned he couldn't trust a single adult, but he didn't have the ability to say no. I might be the first person who didn't let him down. "You going to take me back to my foster parents?"

I smiled, wishing I could run my hands over his little cheeks and give him a mothering kiss on the forehead. "No. I'm going to take you to some real heroes. Firefighters. And they'll get you home."

His sad eyes brightened to a glimmer. "Like a real fire station? I didn't know they could do that."

I opened the door and climbed down into the worsening storm. Snowflakes with the consistency of birdseed rained down on us. "Firefighters can do anything, Aron."

He took my hand and allowed me to help him climb down the steps. I zipped his thin coat to his chin and pulled his hat down past his ears. Silently, we walked to my snow-covered car, hand in hand. Perhaps a mother and child, retrieving the boy from a trip with his dad.

"Aron?" I asked once I'd buckled him into the Prius. "Do you know where that bad man was taking you? Or were you supposed to stay with him for a while?"

He looked down at his lap, shame taking over his face. With the worst over, my emotions began to war with my instincts. I prayed this child would receive the counseling he needed, that he wouldn't be thrown back into a corrupt home. Sometimes I thought if I could house them, I'd keep every child I'd saved for myself. And then I'd know they were safe.

"I think he was taking me to some place in Pennsylvania. The city with the big bell."

Exactly what Kelly had managed to hack from the file she broke into. "Do you know where?"

"The man who brought me here." Aron looked like he was about to cry and then gave himself a little shake. "He kept saying 'exhale.' That I'd be going to exhale. People there were interested in me. That's all."

Exhale. A business name? I'd have to get Kelly on it.

"Thanks." I started the car and then reached into the backseat. "I've got a ham and cheese sandwich and a bottle of water if you want them."

He looked unsure and then grabbed the food, ripping the plastic wrap off. His first bite was big enough to nearly choke him. My heart ached.

"Well, Aron..." I put the car into gear. "We're going to go see those firefighters, but first I need you to make me a really important promise."

Eyes wide, he nodded so fast he should have given himself whiplash. Little Aron would be no problem at all.

TWO

This is a bad idea.

I read Chris's text again and then stuck the phone back in the pleather bag I'd picked up from Goodwill. Cold breezed through the thin, black leggings I wore, and my feet felt like frozen bricks in the cheap, calf-length boots. I pulled the too-short and much-too-thin coat tighter around my waist and tried to look like I belonged.

"That your pimp?" The girl standing on the street with me couldn't have been more than eighteen, and I'd be willing to bet my apartment she was younger than that. Short, dark hair framed her angular face, her fake eyelashes heavily made up to accentuate gray-blue eyes.

Thick foundation a shade too dark covered a rash of acne on her chin. Her nose had once been pierced, but the empty hole had a nice scab, indicating a healing infection. I wished she had something on her cracked fingers. Her stick-thin figure gave her no extra body fat to keep her warm.

"Yeah," I said. "Ain't even my phone. He's going to be pissed I didn't answer his text, but I'm working, right?"

She nodded over a full body shiver. "Took me forever to get a phone, and he checks it every time I come in."

"Same here."

She eyed me with the dull gaze of a much more experienced person. "You're new. Haven't seen you around."

I tugged at the blond curls of the scratchy wig. "Yep."

"But you can't be new to the game. No offense, but most pimps don't want women your age no more. Although you look real nice. You even have all your teeth."

I ducked my head, trying to look embarrassed. "Thought I got out of this a long time ago. Things happened."

"Who's your pimp?" She asked the question easily, as if she were asking about my shoes, but the set of her hardened face gave her intentions away.

"Not supposed to give that information out."

She shrugged. "I'm just asking because mine is real territorial. He don't like to share the area. He sees you, he'll be in your face. And he won't like it. No offense."

I adjusted the glasses and wished their fake lenses gave me the ability to read the girl's mind. "What's wrong with my face?"

"It's too old. No offense. But you aren't going to get picked up around here." She gestured to the slow traffic on Kensington Avenue. The elevated train tracks above us on Somerset Street blocked the weak winter sun and made for a perfect wind tunnel. I tried to keep my teeth from chattering.

"You got your addicts down there, the heroin guzzlers looking for their next fix," the girl continued. "They won't care if you're old, but they can't afford to pay you. And they aren't trading their buzz for sex."

I'd passed the crowd of addicts on the walk down here. They huddled in a small group, stinking clothes covered in weeks of grime. Several stumbled toward me, offering needles. Since leaving Aron at the fire station in Hagerstown, I'd done everything I could to avoid this particular area of Philadelphia, choosing instead to run my fake prostitute scam on safe corners. But I was getting nowhere, and this was a hotbed of activity. I needed to find out about "exhale."

"What about the nice cars that drive by?" I nodded to the sleek silver Toyota cruising past us. Chris rented it for this occasion, and seeing it gave me a rush of warmth.

"They're not looking for someone your age, honey." The girl shrugged. "You're too old to be an escort too."

I shook my head, wondering how this young girl knew about anything more than this life. "Your pimp into that?"

"He's into a lot of things." She dug around in her pocket. I tensed. I'd left my various weapons at home on the off-chance a cop decided to make an appearance. Unlikely, since this area had been nearly forgotten by the city's finest. But it was a chance I wasn't willing to take.

She pulled out a stick of gum and popped it into her mouth. "I can't think of anyone with any real money who'd want to bang you. Unless you want the junkies, you might want to try some other gig."

"How long have you been on the streets?"

She shot me a dark glance. "I'm not on the street. I've got a place to live. And I've got my own johns. My pimp's got me out here today looking for new girls. And you ain't it."

"Too old." For once I was thankful to be in my early thirties. "He send all his girls on the street?"

"Nope."

"Escorts," I guessed. *Probably finds runaways either pimping for others or out of desperation and then cons them into the life by promising a sweet deal with expensive men.* How long before this pimp made it clear the girl didn't have a choice? "I didn't know pimps were into that nowadays. I thought that was something a businesswoman did. Like the girls trying to put themselves through college."

"Times change." She popped a bubble. "Tell you what. You give me your pimp's name so I can pass it along, and I'll give you $40. Something to take back to him so he doesn't whale on you."

I met her cool, gray eyes. "I don't want money."

She looked me up and down. "Sorry. I don't go that way. But I can hook you up with someone who does."

"That's not it." I caught sight of the Toyota, knowing Chris had me in view. If I pulled my scarf off, he'd know I needed help. Worth the risk. "I'm trying to find a friend of mine. She didn't follow me out of the game, and now I think she's in big trouble."

The girl popped another bubble. "What's her name?"

"Charity." I said the first thing I thought of. "The last time I spoke to her, she said she was going to a place called Exhale. She didn't give me any information. I don't even know what that is."

That wasn't exactly true. Kelly and I had found three different businesses with the name Exhale, but we had no idea which might be serving as a front, or if any were. For all we knew, it was another code word.

"Exhale?" The girl's eyes narrowed. The dark instinct that served me so faithfully made the icy hair on my arms stand up. "How old is your friend?"

"Nineteen." Getting the age right was crucial. I couldn't directly ask about minors without alerting this girl. She'd be onto me in a second. Or so disgusted she'd clam up. Either way, I lost out.

"Too old. Exhale likes their clients younger." She pushed her blowing hair out of her face.

"What is it?" I asked. "Is it like a group of pimps or something?"

She cocked her head, popping her gum in a way that made me want to yank it out of her mouth. "Seriously? No. It's a business with something on the side. Don't you know anything about how we do it these days?"

I looked down at my miserable boots. "I guess not." I sank my teeth into my tongue and felt the tears well in my eyes. "I just need to find her."

"She's not at Exhale, I can tell you that."

I wiped a tear and snuck a quick glance at her. She stared straight ahead, a muscle working in her jaw. "Is that where you're out of? I mean, you're so young and pretty."

The compliment didn't faze her. She turned steel eyes on me. "Don't worry about my business. Now, I gave you information. You give me yours. Who's your pimp?"

"You didn't give me anything I could use."

"That's not my fault. Trust me, looking for your nineteen-year-old friend at the spa ain't going to get you anywhere. And she's probably long gone, anyway."

I thanked the cold for keeping my expression static. This girl, who I'd pegged for street-savvy, had just given me the information I needed. *Guess there's something to be said about the wisdom of age versus the impatience of youth.* "All right, I'm sorry."

"Pimp's name?"

My fingers ached as I untied the scarf, shook it out, and wrapped it tightly back around my neck. "Andrew Parks." I almost laughed at giving her the name of the man who molested my sister so many years ago. "Goes by Andy P. and is staying at the Johnson Motel a few blocks down."

"I know the place." Her eyes drifted to the silver Toyota rolling to a stop. "Well, looks like I might be able to make some extra money today."

The passenger window rolled down to reveal Chris's handsome face and expensive Burberry jacket. I heard the girl's whisper of appreciation, thinking she'd hit the jackpot. He smiled. "You got some time for me, blondie?"

· · ·

As soon as we turned the corner of Kensington Avenue, I cranked up the heat and stuck my face in front of the vents. "My skin will never be the same."

"I never should have let you do this." Chris's eyes were on the road, his hands tense on the steering wheel. "Did you see the crackheads gathering not one hundred feet from you?"

"First off, you didn't let me do anything. Let's get that straight. And I saw them." The crackheads were harmless. The other girls were the worry. Things got territorial, especially when times were tough.

"Yeah well, I'm not doing this again."

I pulled off the wig and poor excuse for a winter coat and tossed them into the backseat and then snuggled into my own wool jacket. "We don't need to. Kelly owes me coffee. Exhale Mind and Body Salon is the place we're looking for."

Six weeks later

Breathe in, breathe out. Inhale, exhale.

This was the mantra I had to repeat as I sat behind the receptionist's desk at Exhale Mind and Body Salon, a swanky place in the heart of downtown Philadelphia that caters to the city's wannabe New Yorkers.

The day after my street gig, Chris and I staked out Exhale. All day long, women of all ages came in and out of the spa. Nighttime brought the jackpot: a black SUV rolled up the back door, and a classy-looking blond emerged from the driver's seat, followed by a boy and a girl easily under the age of fifteen. The salon was empty, locked up tight. The blond had a key, and when she emerged with the kids minutes later, they were dressed in new, stylish clothes.

Chris managed to tail the SUV to a craphole motel on the

north side. The woman ushered the kids inside. Within minutes a young, black male arrived and was allowed into the room. The blond left without the kids.

I applied for the receptionist's job the very next day, and after weeks of hearing the dullest conversations and being assaulted with a cacophony of supposedly relaxing sights and sounds, I was ready to make my move.

My cell beeped with an incoming call. One look at the screen and I considered not answering. He'd just keep nagging. But he did pose as my john during my street gig, so I owed him some tolerance.

"Chris."

"Lucy."

I pictured the full-mouthed smirk and the crinkling around his eyes. But I also caught the tone in his voice. "I'm at work."

"Guess that's one way to think of it. Still planning on staying late?"

"Yes."

He sighed, long and drawn out and superior. "You know she probably has security cameras?"

I forced a smile as the last masseuse waved to me on her way out the door. "Of course I know that."

"And if the police are called?"

We'd discussed this last night. And the night before that. I wanted to tell him to stand down and mind his own business, but then again, he'd made me his business, and I'd allowed it. The pretend sociopath and the magnificently damaged vigilante gravitated toward each other like self-igniting magnets, white-hot sparks burning us. Sometimes I hated Chris. But I couldn't imagine my life without him. Not after the past few months.

"I'll deal with it." I was a licensed private investigator, after all. I might be risking a suspension but probably not an arrest. Not after I shared the information I had. But I really didn't need any more attention from the Philadelphia police. I already had one detective watching me.

"You're making a mistake. This isn't what our focus should be right now."

"Your mother can wait." I hated saying the words. Mother Mary was cruelty personified. But I couldn't go after her. *Not yet. Not with these kids being carted out like produce.*

"You promised me." Chris sounded like a petulant child, and in some ways, that was exactly what he was. After being rescued from his nefarious and heartbreaking early childhood, he'd grown up the treasured nephew of a prominent attorney and pediatrician. He was used to getting what he wanted when he wanted it.

"I plan on keeping that promise. Just not yet." The front door opened, and our last client walked inside, bringing a rush of dark, winter air with her. "I've got to go. I'll call you later."

I smiled at the plump, middle-aged woman squeezed into a calf-length leather coat. She reminded me of a sea lion. "Ms. Rollins, welcome. Can I get you anything?"

Before she could respond, the classy blond Chris and I had tailed to the hotel swept out of her office. Sarah Jones was the owner of Exhale, and she was all sweet fragrance and physical perfection: silky, blond hair shining; skin glowing; nails mani-cured and perfectly applied mascara. Tall and slim as a movie star, Sarah's understated beauty made her both classy and intimidating. She never lost her cool, her poise a byproduct of being beautiful in a materialistic society. And the customers loved her.

"Amanda, it's good to see you." Sarah set her business cell down on my counter, its red-sequined case making my eyes hurt. "Thank you so much for staying, Lucy. You can head home now. Just make sure to lock the door."

I smiled my sweetest smile. Sarah enjoyed being boss and didn't like to be argued with. She also enjoyed being the prettiest woman in the room, a fact I'd picked up on during our interview when she'd called my red hair flashy and asked if I'd like a facial. Since my hair and complexion have always been my best traits, I took the hint and made sure to keep my hair pulled back and to be dressed in frumpy clothes. "Sure thing, Sarah. I just have some paperwork to finish up, and then I'll be out of here. Enjoy your stay, Ms. Rollins."

"Don't forget the door," Sarah reminded me before following Amanda. I gave my boss one last smile, the gesture melting as soon as I heard the door shut. I glanced at the clock. Although Sarah never left her room after a client arrived, I'd give her a few minutes just in case she forgot something. She'd taken her phone with her, but it wasn't the one I was after.

Sarah had a different phone, one that she used in the back alley when she slipped out for the cigarette she didn't smoke. The one she texted on when she hurried to her car long after the salon closed. One that she used the night we followed her to the motel.

I wanted that phone, and I'd take it tonight.

I rolled my neck, the tendons popping. I had no doubts about searching Sarah's office. I'd made the decision and wasn't going back on it. I'd probably get fired, but any information I found would no doubt lead me to my next scumbag.

Maybe you like killing.

Chris's words from last night blasted in my head. I pushed them away. Five minutes had come and gone.

I gathered my things, dumping everything essential into the big, leather bag I'd recently started carrying around. Now empty except for Sarah and her client, the silence of the spa made me feel like a criminal. I choked back a giggle and slowly made my way to Sarah's office. Tucked in the far corner of the building, away from everyone's rooms and stations, it was off limits to most employees. We were told to never enter without knocking, as Sarah needed her private space.

The lock was easy enough to pick. I checked behind me before slipping through the black door and shutting it quietly. The room was dark with only the light from the street pooling in the window. I flicked the switch, the click spurring my adrenaline. Sarah's office was sparsely decorated: her computer on the black desk, two stylish but uncomfortable-looking chairs, and a fake plant in the corner. A set of shelves was loaded with sample creams, cleansers, lotions, and other work items, but there were no filing cabinets to search. Sarah didn't like paper, she told me during my interview. Her salon was environmentally friendly, and her employees were expected to follow her lead.

I sat down in her chair and tried to log in, but the screen remained locked. Kelly had taught me a little about password hacking, but nothing I tried worked. I started going through her drawers, but they were littered with lip gloss, sample lotions, other skin products, and nail files. Sarah had nothing business-related in this desk. That alone was a red flag.

"Where is it, blondie?" Frustration mounting, I felt underneath the main section of wood, hoping to find some sort of secret compartment or, even better, everything I needed nicely typed and tucked in a manila envelope with my name on it in Sarah's loopy script, along with the mysterious black phone. No such luck.

"God forbid anything come easily. Just once."

No bag of any sort. Her coat hung on the back of her chair. Hope renewed, I dug into her pockets but found only gum and tissues.

Damnit. I didn't see any sign of cameras, but that didn't mean they weren't there. If I got caught, I'd end up fired and losing my in with Sarah for nothing. I rested my elbows on the desk and dropped my head into my hands.

"Let's reassess. It's got to be here."

The desk hummed.

I looked around for the source, but there was nothing on the desk to make that noise.

I dropped to my knees and checked the underside again. Bare.

Another hum, this time with a vibration.

The phone was somewhere in the desk.

Trying not to be loud, I attacked the drawers again. The wide, thick bottom drawer didn't pull all the way out. I hadn't bothered to check why earlier because the drawer was nearly empty. Flattening myself to the floor, I wiggled my hand underneath the drawer. The soft material of my black sweater snagged on the edge, but I kept fumbling around. And then I felt the smooth, thin lines of what was unmistakably a cellphone. I snatched it free of its hiding place.

Squishing my racing nerves and the desperate desire to look at the phone's contents, I dropped it into my big bag. I took a deep breath, smoothing my sweater and hair, and then patted my damp forehead with the back of my hand. Calm enough, I exited the office, quietly closing the door.

Soothing music drifted down the hall from Sarah's room. A lullaby.

I shrugged on my coat, shouldered my purse. My desk was nice and tidy, no personal items left.

I locked the door behind me.

I hated the early darkness of winter. The lack of sun made me feel run-down and perpetually stuck in slow motion. And the bitter cold seemed to seep right through my skin and bones and settle into my very core. *Maybe I'll become a snowbird one day. Disappear to someplace warm, maybe Florida, and lie on the beach all winter drinking fruity liquor and admiring the male scenery. No dark memories lurking around the street corner— just warm sand and the sound of the ocean.*

Bowing my head against the freezing wind, I hurried toward Kelly's building. Rittenhouse Square looked lonely; it was too cold for the breakdancers and dog walkers. The trees were bare, all of the flowering bushes stripped of their greenery and vibrant blooms. But in a few months, the plants and trees would come back with brilliant vigor, their blossoms likely more abundant than before. If only humans were so lucky. What if we could go dormant for a while, hide away in the earth and replenish, and then come back for a fresh start? Would any of us really do anything differently, or would we just continue on whatever course we'd carved out for ourselves?

Once, I might have said yes to that question. But not anymore. I don't believe we ever really change, not in our hearts. Human wants and desires drive us all, and that's it. But it was nice to pretend we could always do better.

Kelly buzzed me into her building, and I shivered the entire elevator ride to the fourth floor. Inside her apartment, I hung my coat on the rack and pulled my sweater tightly around me.

"Your cheeks are red." Kelly handed me a cup of steaming coffee. "Make sure you put something on them before they crack."

In these moments I envied her ability to live most of her life in the confines of this apartment. At least she didn't have to deal with the Arctic blast.

"I will." I held the cup to my face, breathing in the warmth, before taking a sip. "Thank you."

Kelly sat down in her large, overstuffed chair, folding her legs beneath her. The flat-screen television on her crate-style coffee table droned on about a murder in Trenton, New Jersey, forty minutes away. The killer had left dimes on the women's eyes in some pathetic cry for attention.

That's the difference between me and those kinds of people. I don't do it because I have an urge that must be quelled—at least not a physical urge. Killing doesn't satiate me, and I don't want

the police marveling and confounded over my brilliance. I just
want to cleanse the filth.

"Kind of stupid to leave such a brazen calling card," Kelly
said. "Silver is deeply rooted in mythology. He's only helping
the cops out."

"Trying to make a statement, I guess. Hopefully he left a
fingerprint."

She swiveled around. Her wispy black hair contrasted
sharply with the white chair, and her tiny frame looked like it
had been swallowed by a marshmallow. "So. Did you get it?"

I pulled the cellphone out of my purse and handed it to her.
"It was hidden underneath the desk. I didn't even try to decode
the lock screen. I'll leave that up to you."

Her slim fingers moved easily over the smartphone, trying
varying arrangements of numbers. I soon heard the click of the
phone giving her access and eagerly leaned over her shoulder.

"This thing is really well protected," Kelly said. "It's got
separate passwords for email and Internet access. I can't even
mess with the settings."

I slumped against the back of the chair. "Can't you get
anything from it? That's got to be where she keeps her
information."

"How do you know she's the one running this sex ring?"

"Why else would she have hidden this phone, Kel?"

She shrugged. "Maybe she's got another identity. Or she's
having an affair and her boyfriend is possessive. Who knows? I
just have trouble understanding why she's working through this
phone when the dark web is a lot more protected."

The dark web. I hated the term. It belonged in the Middle
Ages, especially since many of the things found on the deepest
layer of the Internet—the one normal search engines can't touch
—are barbaric.

"I mean, think about it," Kelly said. "All you need is software that allows you to access the hidden domains. And then

you're in with your own username and passwords, and the best part is you're anonymous."

I rubbed my temples. Tech-speak usually gave me a headache. "I still don't understand how it works."

"Think of it like this." Kelly's hands started flapping around like they always did when she got nerdy. "Normal search engines, like Google or Yahoo, use things called spiders. They crawl around looking for keywords, which lead to active links, domains, and so on. But the sites on the dark web are too hidden for those spiders to find. You need passwords. It's the same kind of technology that protects your online banking."

"And it's not all child porn, is it?"

"No," she said. "Plenty of people just want their privacy. They don't want the government watching them regardless of whether or not they're doing anything bad. And I've run across watchdogs who try to report these kid porn sites, but it's impossible to find many of them."

This was the point my headache started. "Why? That's what I don't understand."

"Because of the encryption and the sheer number of domains. And everything bounces off foreign servers in Timbuktu or some other obscure country. Look, these people spend their lives online and in a half-paranoid state. They're on the lowest level of the dark web, like the deepest layer of trash at a landfill, and they know how to cover their tracks."

"Maybe Sarah's not smart enough to figure it out," I said. "Or maybe she is, and we just haven't gotten that far. But I have no doubt she conducts business on this phone. Maybe it's just her top layer. We won't know until we break into it." I sat down on the couch across from her. "Anyway, you don't really believe she's innocent, do you? Not after everything I've seen and heard."

"By stalking her," Kelly said.

"Following her," I clarified. "Like I've done plenty of times on cases. And Chris helped."

"But this is different," Kelly said. "You're getting so up close and personal. She nearly saw you the other day. And the whole finances thing, calling the credit card companies and fishing for her information?" Her voice rose, adding to my headache. "Lucy, that's illegal. You could lose your private investigator's license if you get caught."

I laughed. "As if that's the most illegal thing I've done."

"You're deliberately ignoring my point."

Of course I was. She wasn't about to change my mind, and we didn't have any more time to waste. "Kel, I don't have any choice. This isn't just some released offender we're tracking. We're trying to bring down a well-organized sex trafficking ring."

"But that is your choice," she said. "You could easily walk away from this. Go back to all the dirtbags we're keeping track of. If you're focused on the guys trolling online, we can find them on the dark web. You don't have to focus on these trafficking rings."

She was wrong. Ever since discovering Kailey Richardson on the auction site, my entire focus had shifted beyond the everyday creep. As bad as these creeps were, the big networks were far more sinister. It wasn't just one sick monster trying to consume a child's innocence. It was pedophiles helping pedophiles, justifying their behavior as if they had every right to breathe the same air as the rest of us. But that wasn't even the worst of it. That honor belonged to people like Sarah, who had no physical interest in kids but saw them as a product to capitalize on. If I thought I could have gotten away with it, I would have killed her my first week on the job. But that wouldn't stop her organization. I needed as many details as possible: names of associates, clients, partners, victims. So I endured watching her elaborate act, submitting to her insecurity and allowing her to feel the power she so obviously craved.

I still planned to kill her. When the time was right.

I couldn't muster the words or the energy to explain myself to Kelly. "I can't walk away from this."

"I know, and that's what scares me. It's about more than justice now, and I'm afraid that's going to be your downfall."

She was probably right, and I was powerless to stop. "If it is, hopefully I'll take some of these people with me."

She stared at me with those big, doe-like eyes that had experienced too much in her young life. I didn't want to cause her worry, disappointment, or fear. If I wasn't so selfish, I'd walk out of her life tonight. Let her find her way without the help of a jaded killer who didn't really know who she was more afraid of —the people she hunted or herself.

"Kel, I need your help." I'd like to say I felt shame for asking, but I didn't. I only felt desperation and determination. "If you can't get anything off the phone, I'll return it and walk away from Exhale, okay? We'll go back to the repeat offenders, maybe do some searching your way. But I've at least got to try to get to Sarah."

She sighed and turned her attention back to the phone. "This thing has a really good password protection system. It's a paid app that provides different passwords for as many programs as you want. I got lucky on the lock screen. But with the email and the other applications? After the fifth failed attempt, it will take a screenshot of my face and then lock me out. You've got to go on the website and enter a special pin code to reactivate the phone."

I dragged my hands through my hair. "We've got to at least try."

"Let's try the calendar. What are the last four digits of her social security number again?"

"9065."

Kelly typed in the numbers. The phone beeped, signaling the wrong code. Next were her birth date and then a combination of her bank account numbers. "We've only got one try left." She leveled a hard stare at me. "Have you stolen any other numbers that might be useful?"

"No. But I did hear her give out a phone number the other day, and it didn't match the cell she'd given to employees or the salon number. Do you think she'd be foolish enough to use the last four digits?"

Kelly debated. "If she thinks no one else knows about the phone but her, it's worth a shot."

"5834."

She typed in the numbers while I waited with a sinking stomach. "Holy shit, you were right."

I jumped up from the couch and sat on the arm of the recliner, almost forgetting Kelly didn't like physical contact. "What do you see?"

"Appointments." There were only four in the month of January, each coded the same way: in blue, with letters representing what I assumed were client and victim names, followed by time and place.

Today, January 10, was shaded blue. I read with a turning stomach. "R for L. Eight-thirty, Rattner Hotel."

I took out my own phone and did a quick search. "North Philly, a few blocks off Temple's campus."

"Lovely neighborhood," Kelly said sarcastically. The area had been rough for a long time, but thanks to fentanyl-laced heroin and other drugs, it looked more like an episode of *The Walking Dead* than a neighborhood.

"Good thing I've got my pepper spray and bottle of kill juice." I dropped the phone back into my purse. "If I'm lucky, I can make it in time."

"What the hell?" Kelly jumped up. "You're not going out there alone at night."

"I'm always alone at night," I countered. "And this is my chance. If I can interrupt this... transaction, I might be able to get all the information I need."

"What about this?" Kelly held the phone up. "We can still keep trying."

"Until we're locked out. We won't get lucky again." I grabbed my coat off the rack. She stared at me with stricken eyes. "What did you think I was going to do?"

"I don't know," she said. "But I think you should leave this with the police, Lucy. This is bigger than you."

I zipped my coat up to my chin and tugged on my hat. Chasing a creep in this cold sounded as appealing as an enema. "That's exactly why the police are the wrong people to handle it. It's happening right under their noses, and they don't have a clue. Besides, I don't need a warrant or have rules to follow. My world moves much faster."

Her shoulders sagged. "This *will* be your downfall." She repeated the words from earlier in a small, broken voice. "Please be careful."

I couldn't allow myself to feel badly about her fear. Intercepting this meeting was the right thing to do for everyone involved, including me. I mustered a smile. "I'm always careful, Kel."

THREE

Despite being below zero with dangerously cold winds, traffic was still thick and most drivers were exceptionally stupid. Driving like they walked, whipping in and out of lanes, cutting people off and cruising as though they were the only people on the road. It was no different than walking a busy sidewalk or department store aisle. By the time I made it to North Philly, it was nearing 9 p.m. I parked four blocks away from the motel and ran down the sidewalk, the cold air ripping through my lungs like a frozen knife.

The Rattner Hotel sat on a rusting corner of an older area of the city. Three stories of weather-beaten, cracking brick with a drooping marquee and faded lettering, it was a throwback to the storefront hotels of fifty years ago. Time had literally shrunk the place, the wood framing of the door splintering under the building's weight. The "A" in the vacancy sign in the window blinked on and off like a creepy tic.

Inside, the smell of old, dusty carpet and the faint scent of mold greeted me. A balding, middle-aged man sat behind a yellowed counter. He perked up from his wrinkled copy of the *New York Times* when I blew through the door. "Help you?"

Breathless from the freeze, I gathered my thoughts and then sneezed, barely managing to shove my face into my elbow in time. "Excuse me. I'm looking for someone."

"Can't give out information." His gaze flickered between me and the paper. His oily skin left him with a smattering of blackheads across his nose. A blush dotted his cheeks, and his eyes bore a look I recognized and could use to my advantage.

Toes burning as they began to warm up, I approached him, pulling my hat off and letting my hair fall around my shoulders. I leaned across the counter, trying to ignore the years of stickiness. I licked my lips, pitched my voice low, into the sort of breathy whisper so many men loved. A college friend called it the "porn whisper." She wasn't far off. "Sure you can."

He scratched his thinning forehead. "Against the rules."

But farming out young kids to predators is okay. I swallowed the words. This guy might not have any idea what was going on, although the more likely scenario was that he probably just told himself he didn't know because then he didn't have to deal with the facts. We all lie to ourselves.

If I had all the information, I could probably wheedle a room number out of this guy. But all I had were initials and zero time.

"I'm looking for a man sharing a room with a teenager," I said. "They might have arrived at different times. Her dad is from out of town and visiting."

"All I can do is call the room, if you've got a name or room number."

I thought back to the calendar. R for L. "First name starts with an L."

"That's not enough." He went back to his paper. Moisture shone across his forehead. The index finger on his right hand tapped the paper, making it rustle. He didn't strike me as the sort who would still read a newspaper, much less the *New York Times*.

Irritated and short of time, I decided to take a chance. "Look. Either you tell me where this meeting goes down, or I call the police in here and let them know what's really going on behind closed doors. They'll never believe you weren't aware of it."

He messed with his bald spot yet again, his eyes shifting from me to the paper.

"So." I rested my chin on my hands, smiling like we were old friends. "Either you tell me where to look, or I call the police. Your choice."

He shook his head. "This is bullshit."

I took out my cellphone. "Have it your way."

He slammed the paper down on the counter. "You're pretty late. Check the back alley." He jerked his head to the left. "Guy you're looking for will be leaving through the back door."

I followed his direction and bolted down a dingy, musty hallway toward the door with the blaring red "exit" sign. I should have taken the time to make a plan, but all I could think about was the late hour and that I'd probably lost my best chance. I shoved at the door, fighting the force of the wind. At first there was nothing but more icy air and wind so strong my eyes stung, but then my vision cleared. Several feet to my right were a tall man with a thick overcoat and a teenage girl a few inches shorter. She wore a dark knitted cap, but the street lamps provided enough light for me to see the telltale signs of youth in her profile: vibrant skin with some errant acne, a smidgeon of baby-fat still left on her cheeks, and hands devoid of lines and wrinkles.

The man's face was turned down and shadowed—all I saw was a beard and part of a smile. He put his hands on the girl's shoulders, and the girl looked up at him not with adoration but resignation. The man leaned down, my stomach shifted, and my feet moved before my brain caught up.

"What the hell are you doing?"

FOUR

Wind blasted down the alley. The force sent me back on my heels; I dug them in and strode forward, ignoring the windsicles pelting my face. If only the cyanide were nestled in my pocket. But my fingers were probably too numb not to kill myself.

The man recovered quickly, drawing himself up straight. He kept his face turned away, only allowing me to see his very generic profile. "My daughter and I were talking."

"In the freezing cold in a back alley in a dangerous part of the city?" I asked. "Strange place for a chat."

His head twitched like he wanted to turn, maybe get in my face. The girl stepped back, her body language both defiant and desperate. I got my first direct look at her face. My sex worker friend from Kensington Avenue. She glared at me, but I didn't see the telltale flash of recognition. Hopefully my wig, glasses, and heavy makeup had done the job.

Cocking her head, she looked up at the man and reached out her right hand, rubbing her fingers together. She'd yet to get paid.

"So." I stepped forward, trying to get a better look at the man. "Which one of you is R and which one is J?"

In true cowardly form, the man bolted down the alley, his long legs quickly carrying him out of sight. The girl turned to me, her cherub-like face twisted with rage. Short, dark hair peeked out from her hat. She was even prettier without the heavy eye makeup she'd worn on the street. Her delicate features reminded me of Kelly in the worst way, and the surprise left me vulnerable. Before I could react, she struck, slamming both slender hands against my shoulders.

"What did you do that for? He hadn't paid me yet!"

I stumbled backwards, the heels of my boots sliding across the sheen of ice. Teetering, I regained my balance. "You don't have to live this way. I'm here to help you."

Her black eyebrows knitted together, the movement thinning the baby fat on her cheeks, making her face look strikingly beautiful. "I don't need your help, bitch. This is my job."

Her anger didn't surprise me. Kids like her are usually abused most of their lives, and working for sex is a natural transition. Even more were convinced prostitution was their only direction, and their loyalty to their pimps was unquestionable. Shuddering against the cold wind, she looked thin in her insufficient coat. "Why don't you let me buy you some supper, and we can talk about it?"

"No thanks. But you can pay me the seventy-five bucks you just cost me."

I debated. Giving her the money made me a hypocrite, but that certainly wouldn't be the first time. It might earn enough of her trust to glean some information. And I didn't want to be responsible for her getting a beating from her pimp because she failed to deliver.

"Tell you what," I said. "You walk down to the diner on the corner with me and have something to eat, and I'll give you a hundred cash. Plus the meal. You can't beat that."

She snorted, looking me up and down. "You want something. Like everyone else."

"Just information."

She folded her arms, stuck out her jaw in the rebellious way teenagers excel at. She'd lost all of her self-assured attitude from the street. "Don't have any."

Cold settled into my jaw, making speech a struggle. I wiggled my toes to make sure they weren't frozen. "What's your name?"

She held out a bare, exposed hand. "Give me the money now, and maybe I'll tell you."

I fumbled in my coat pockets for the cash I'd withdrawn earlier. I held out a wrinkled bill. "Here's fifty. Answer some questions, and you'll get the rest."

Her ruby lips pouting, she snatched the money. "Riley."

"How old are you?"

"Fifteen." Her narrowed eyes challenged me to tell her she was too young. "Do I know you? Your voice sounds familiar."

I bet on her memory being too full of the destitute women she likely saw every day. "Trust me, I'd remember if we'd met before. What was your friend's name?"

"Can't say."

I nodded. "How'd you meet him?"

"Mutual friend." She smirked, trying to be cocky, but the effort failed. Shame flashed through her eyes.

"Her name Sarah?"

Riley couldn't hide her surprise. She rocked back, mouth falling open, and then snapped it shut. "Don't remember."

Another hard gust of wind whistled between the buildings. Both of us shook with cold. I cut to the chase.

"Just tell me if she's the boss, or if she's working for someone else. And their name—that's all I need."

"I can't give you no more names, lady. And Sarah don't have anything to do with tonight." Her voice cracked. She wrapped her arms around her thin waist. "I'm just trying to make a living. I don't need to get my ass kicked. And that's what happens when the boss gets crossed. If you don't get out of here soon, my friend'll be making an example out of you."

"You mean your pimp?" I gave her a quick once-over. My surprise attack had taken away the bravado she had on the street, and she was too young and inexperienced to know how to recover. My advantage.

She looked past me, glaring down the alley. "Whatever."

"I can help you start over," I said. "And I can help any other kids being used by your boss. Just give me his name." I rested my shaking hand on her rigid arm, hoping the human contact would breach her walls. Before I even registered movement, her forearm shot out, slamming into my chest. I lost my footing this time, landing hard on my butt. My elbows hit the pavement hard, and tears sprouted in my eyes. Shock and pain and sheer cold paralyzed me. I gazed up at her, trying to catch up. "Riley—"

"Shut up." She planted her feet on either side of my hips and reached toward me. I remembered my pepper spray too late. She grabbed my arm, fingers digging through my coat and into the flesh, and fished into my pocket with her free hand. "You owe me money."

"You owe yourself more than this."

She faltered, but only for a second. Then she drew out the rest of my cash—over two hundred dollars—and took another fifty. She shoved the rest at me. "I'm not a thief."

I took the money, locking eyes with her. "My name is Lucy Kendall. I'm a private investigator. When you're ready, I can help you."

Footsteps halted whatever she might have said next. A tall man rounded the corner, his expensive winter boots thudding against the concrete. Chris's heavy, wool coat was at least twice as thick as Riley's, and his head was covered with a designer knit hat.

"Get away from her." Chris bore down on us like a bull. Riley sprinted down the alley, disappearing into the freezing, black night.

Chris knelt beside me, his warm hands on my cold arms. "How bad are you hurt?"

"I'm not." That wasn't entirely true. My tailbone throbbed. My pride singed. I took Chris's hand and allowed him to haul me to my feet. He grabbed my shoulders, pulling me toward him. Even in the below zero weather, his cologne wafted over me, the familiar scent comforting. I fisted my hands against his chest in a half-assed attempt to push him away. He leaned down, his face too close to mine. "Lucy." His soft voice sent a wholly different kind of chill down my spine.

"Go ahead and say it."

The corner of his mouth twitched. "You're such an unbelievable dumbass."

I didn't say another word as I stalked behind him to his waiting car. I let him rant, knowing it was better to get it over with. "I can't believe you came down here, in the freaking Arctic weather, at night, by yourself, to Shitville, with only some creep's initials to go on." Chris yanked open the car door, and I fell into the leather seat. I wanted to soak up the blissful heat. He ran around to the driver's side and planted himself next to me. "Are you trying to get yourself killed?"

He glared at me, and I tried to think of what I wanted to say. His damn eyes always did me in. Every time I decided to stay angry with him, or to tell him to get out of my life, he looked at me with those eyes. It wasn't their bright blue or the way they always looked flirtatious. Good-looking men I can handle. But Chris's penetrating stare, his keen ability to see through every layer of my bullshit, rattled me. I hated that about him, and yet I craved it like the worst kind of addict. "That's me. Always looking for new ways to die."

He rolled his eyes, slamming the car into drive, and then merged into traffic. "Right. Where are you parked?"

With every second of warmth came fresh irritation. I didn't need him sticking his nose in my business, trying to play hero. "Three down, off Pear Street. For your information, I had it under control, and you ran off my best lead. Jackass."

He didn't say anything, instead making a derisive noise from somewhere deep in his throat. The sound only torqued me off even more. "Seriously. If I wanted help, I would have asked."

"There's a difference between need and want."

"Fine." I gave him my most insincere smile. "I don't need your help. Nor do I want it. Happy?"

He ground his teeth, making his full lips even plumper. "In your obnoxious presence? Not a chance."

"Pot, meet kettle."

Chris skidded into the small parking garage, his Audi handling the slick surface like a race car. "Level?"

"Two."

I tried to make my exit as soon as he found the Prius, but he hit the child locks—a favorite trick of his. "Come on. I want to go home."

"Kelly told me about the phone." He spoke as if I wanted to listen to him. "She'll never get all the information you need out of it."

"She already got something. You lost it for me." I shivered, wondering if I'd ever be warm again.

"That kid wasn't going to tell you anything." He turned the heat on high. "What's wrong with letting the police handle this? Give them the tip and move on."

"That kid was the same girl who gave me the information about Exhale," I said. "She's got a pimp who's in this up to his neck. And as far as handing information over to the police, it's not that easy," I said. "Riley is a teenager, and in Pennsylvania, minors fourteen and older can give limited consent to sexual activities. Kids over sixteen can give full consent. If I call her in, Vice gets the tip. They won't want to arrest her, but if she doesn't give up her pimp, they will. And then she'll never trust me, and I won't get the information I need."

"Yeah, well, she looked like she was fine with consenting."

I turned a furious glare on him. "Really? Because a sixteen-year-old girl has the emotional capacity to consent to sex with an older man, in a seedy hotel, for money? Because she just up and decided one day to sell her body for sex? Yeah, that's exactly what's going on."

"You don't know—"

I cut him off. "You're the one who doesn't get it, Chris. In the vast majority of trafficking cases, these kids, even the older ones, have been abused from a very young age. They don't know their own worth, and they don't see themselves as human beings because they haven't been treated as anything more than property or a toy that will eventually wear out." I took a deep breath. "If I call the police, they'll bring Riley in. She'll tell them the same story she told me, and guess what will happen? She'll be charged in the hope she'll give up her pimp." These were truths as old as the profession of prostitution. And the men doling out the girls made my manipulative streak look tame. Some spark of instinct drew them to the vulnerable girls—the ones who needed acceptance and security, even if those things turned out to be smoke and mirrors—and they knew exactly how to entwine their prey so deeply into the net the girls became too afraid to leave.

"She won't do it," I said. "These guys keep their girls good and brainwashed. So she serves some time, goes out and does the same thing, right back with the pimp. Meanwhile, this big network keeps right on trafficking kids. And make no mistake, they stretch further than we realize."

"Why do you think that? Right now you're looking at prostitution, not trafficking." He shrugged his broad shoulders like we were talking about the unending winter weather. I wanted to shake him for his lack of compassion.

I shook my head. "Any cop worth their badge will tell you that's a gray area. A lot of times this starts off consensual, with a runaway thinking hanging out with an older man is heaven. Then they're in over their heads and can't get out. But I think there's more to it than that. I think some of these kids are local, but there are also others being brought in, like Aron. And they all go back to the same person. Someone is running a major trafficking ring. I'm sure of it."

"I don't understand why you can't let it go." Chris slouched in the leather seat, not looking at me. Even in profile, he had a way of looking like a beautifully sad puppy that wasn't getting its way.

And I couldn't give him the concise answer he wanted. Chris lived his life by simple cause and effect. If certain bad things happened to a person, then he must be destined for a specific fate. That's the same thinking that caused him to believe he was a sociopath for so many years, when it was actually just his inability to deal with trauma and repressed memories. I knew he wouldn't like my response. "Riley's afraid of someone other than Sarah. Most likely a man, and most likely a man who believes he's all powerful."

"And you know this how?"

I scowled. "I just told you."

He shook his head, stubborn to the bitter end of the building argument. "You're just guessing. And fixating on something you can't change."

And so we came full circle. "I can too change it. Maybe only for a handful of kids, but I'll change their lives for the better."

"Unless they end up in jail or back on the streets in worse

situations." Chris heaved the same sigh I heard every time we had this conversation. "You're right about one thing: this is bigger than you realize. But not because it's some kind of massive network. It's bigger than you realize because you're not going to kill just one guy and move on. You kill one, there's more to deal with. Some who might want revenge. And who knows how many kids that have been brainwashed into thinking they only have one option in life. You can't just drop some poison and then move on to the next with this one. Are you really prepared to deal with the collateral damage?"

"I'll deal with whatever comes my way." His warming anger electrified the car's already hot exterior. I loosened my scarf, pulled off my winter hat. His tense posture latched on to my nerves, alerting my defenses until I was primed for battle.

He snorted. "Except the promise you made to me."

And there it was. We'd gone around about this so many times. He thought he could convince me to see it his way, and every time he pushed the issue, I stepped farther back. But I didn't want to argue. "There hasn't been any sign of your mother in months. I can't just make up leads to follow."

"You're not really looking." He wasn't entirely wrong. But I had Kelly keeping an eye out. We'd hacked into Mother Mary's last known credit card account, but it hadn't been used in nearly a year. We didn't even know if she was still in Pennsylvania, and the police weren't faring any better. Mother Mary knew how to disappear.

"If we get a tip, we'll follow it."

"No you won't." His eyes darkened. "You're too fixated on this trafficking thing."

I probably was. But he didn't have any room to talk. His obsession with his mother invaded every conversation we had, even when Chris said nothing. I saw it in the shadows that passed through his eyes. Heard the sudden exhaustion in his tone, as if a memory had walloped him and he needed to rest.

But I didn't think finding Mary would give him the peace he longed for, and some part of me wanted to protect him from going down a road he could never escape.

"Have you talked to your brother?"

Justin, the younger brother Chris had only recently discovered, was the only person who could truly understand the shame and hatred Chris endured. And that was exactly the reason Chris avoided him. As I'd expected, he slammed his hand down on the child locks. He stared straight ahead while I exited the car.

I leaned into the still-open door. "Listen, even though I didn't need your help tonight, I appreciate your being there for me. Really."

He grunted, still not looking at me.

I sighed. "I'll call you tomorrow." I shut the door, and he peeled off.

The biting cold wedged my guilt aside as I fumbled with my keys. The car's cold engine turned over three times before finally grinding to life. Wrapping my arms around myself, I waited for some sign of warmth.

Tomorrow, I'd go to work like nothing had happened. Imagining Sarah's reaction made my blood pump a little harder. I hoped she was scared, pacing, wondering where her phone had gone and waiting for the police to knock on her door.

The police would be a blessing for Sarah.

FIVE

Our justice system is a convoluted mess of red tape and personal agendas. Every politician I've encountered—no matter the level of government—was staunch in his belief that his plans for change were vital to our government's survival. He championed his platform everywhere he went, and the really good ones managed to convince the masses they weren't after power and glory but were just trying to help the little guy. Middle America, as the latest catchphrase goes. And some politicians really meant that. But every single one had a pet cause attached to their docket. Most of them were of little use to me, but Senator Mark Coleman was a man who could help my own agenda. After weeks of asking for a meeting, I'd finally been given my shot.

Most people didn't intimidate me, but sitting across from a man like Senator Coleman wasn't an everyday occurrence. A middle-aged, Democratic dynamo, Senator Coleman was equally loved by the press and the voters, and he appeared to possess more of a moral center than most politicians. Hopefully that was just more than a political shell.

Still nearly as fit as his days as a star high school quarterback, Coleman's Nordic ancestry was obvious. Thinning, wispy blond hair and fair skin the winter hadn't been kind to. His left cheek peeled from windburn. But his fine features were pleasant to look at, and his voice had the ring of authority that every good politician has.

"I'm sorry you had to wait this morning, Miss Kendall." The senator's smile seemed meant to set me at ease.

"Please, call me Lucy. And it's fine. I know you're a busy man."

"I appreciate your understanding." He rested his arms on the tidy desk, giving me his full attention. "I understand you want to talk about my human trafficking task force."

Two years ago, the senator formed PCAT, the Pennsylvania Coalition Against Trafficking. His efforts resulted in the state passing a bill to create a cohesive legal definition of human trafficking, something Pennsylvania had been sorely lacking. Now PCAT consisted of over one thousand volunteers—civilians, federal and custom agents and law enforcement officers—across the state, and Assistant District Attorney Hale had heard rumblings of the group expanding into Maryland and West Virginia.

"Yes." I put my carefully practiced speech into action. "Senator, you've done amazing things for trafficking victims. The bill you lobbied for now gives victims a better chance at putting their abusers behind bars. And that's incredibly admirable. But up to this point, most of your investigations have focused on adult women. You've barely touched the tip of the iceberg of child sex trafficking."

Senator Coleman nodded vigorously. "You're absolutely right, and that's something I've been working on with Customs and Immigration."

"It's not just immigrants being trafficked, sir. There are children born in this country who end up in this horrible situation. I've seen it with my own eyes."

"The Richardson case," Senator Coleman said. "Assistant District Attorney Hale apprised me of your perseverance in saving Kailey Richardson from being sold online to predators a few months ago. Considering your involvement and your work as a private investigator, I'm willing to share some information. I checked in with the federal agents handling the case, and they're making progress with the trafficking ring. Thanks to the information found on Steve Simon's computers, they've infiltrated a group working well below the surface web."

Steve Simon had kidnapped the little girl with the intent of selling her. His computer history was likely worse than anything I could imagine, and I'm pretty damn dark. "The dark web?" I asked. "I thought law enforcement didn't have much hope of infiltrating thanks to privacy laws."

"Yes and no. The National Center for Missing and Exploited Children has been a great resource," Coleman said. "And getting into Simon's personal files allowed us a starting point. The FBI were able to encrypt several of his images with technology that tracks active downloads. They've been able to arrest a few of his cohorts, and we're hoping it's just the beginning."

"I'm happy to hear that. Kailey deserves more justice than Steve's arrest." Now was the time to tread carefully. Waltzing in here and telling the senator to change up his task force required finesse. "I've been doing a lot of undercover work lately, and I've discovered additional trafficking here in the city. That's the reason I'm being so presumptuous and suggesting changes to your task force."

The senator raised his eyebrows. "Your methods?"

"I'm a private investigator." *And not the first one to cross the lines of my profession*, I wanted to add. *I just do a better job of it than most.* "I can't share my resources, which I'm sure you understand. But I think after my assistance in finding Kailey Richardson, I've proved I've got the sources."

"Which may be illegal." He gave me a well-oiled smile.

I returned the savvy smile, but I could feel the corners of my mouth drooping down, unable to hide my disdain. "The same could be said about many government operations."

Coleman's pale blue eyes became unsettling the longer I stared. They reminded me of the watery eyes of my sister's corpse, blank with death. He used this to his advantage. He gazed over the desk at me with a pleasant, if not slightly vacant, expression. Those eyes that looked as if a mortician needed to sew them shut. I finally conceded and looked away.

"Point taken," Coleman said. "You're suggesting changes to my task force because of your findings?"

This time, I focused on the bridge of his nose, where his glasses had left a nice indentation. "I think if you look at the information I've gathered, you'll see a Philadelphia-centered location is warranted."

He scratched his chin, looking at me with those murky eyes. "It's not a bad idea. What are your leads?"

"Four different businesses." I gave him the list I'd spent half the night organizing. Three months' worth of research by Kelly and me, all handed over to someone I still wasn't entirely sure I could trust. The act made me feel slightly sick, but I didn't have the time or resources to track them all down myself, and the needs of the victims came first. "Senator, if you got behind this, we could make a difference in the city."

He read the list, his forehead wrinkling, making his winter-abused skin look even worse. "Exhale Mind and Body Salon has asterisks. Why?"

I retrieved the bagged phone from my purse. Last night, Kelly had gotten all the information she could off it. I explained to him about following Sarah and the two kids to the hotel. "I admit to going undercover at Exhale because of the leads mentioned in the list. After several weeks of careful observation, I realized the owner of the salon conducted private calls on a cellphone she never allowed anyone to see. Last night, I took the phone."

Another raise of his bushy eyebrows, a glimmer of appreciation in his creepy eyes. "You stole it."

"I did. And I was able to intercept an exchange between an adult male and a minor female at the Rattner Hotel in North Philadelphia. The man ran, but the girl confirmed the owner, Sarah Jones, was a go-between for a much larger network."

"Sarah Jones." The senator scribbled on the printout, his fine-point pen making rough scratching sounds. "And the girl's name?"

"She refused to give it." I wasn't ready to hand Riley over yet. "Inside the phone is a very complex coding system. I was lucky to figure out enough to intercept the meeting last night. I'm hoping your resources will have better luck."

He turned the phone over in his hand. "I've got a specialist who might be able to find more information. But what you're talking about is the prostitution of minor children. An abomination and criminal offense to be sure, but defining them as sex trafficking victims is difficult. Not to mention you've given me stolen merchandise."

I did my best to look contrite, glancing down at my folded hands. "I realize that, and I understand if you don't want to get involved, but I assure you, I've done my research. This phone is part of an active network I believe can be traced back to the African American boy left at the Greencastle Fire Department a couple of months ago. Are you familiar with that case?"

The senator nodded. "Very much so. How are you tying the boy with this thing at Exhale? The little boy didn't have any idea who brought him to Maryland, or who purchased him, or where he came from. He'd been blindfolded during the entire journey."

Sweet Aron. After promising to keep our secret about putting the man to sleep, Aron had been mostly silent on the drive to the fire station, eating his sandwich and staring at me with those big eyes. I smiled and played the radio, chattering about kid things. He seemed content, even waving goodbye to me as he walked the remaining steps to the station. The satisfaction of doing the right thing lingered with me for a few days, and a fresh wave surged over me. I sat up straighter, bringing myself back to the senator's questioning eyes. "After I received my first tip about Exhale, I was still trying to decide what to do. Then a friend with connections in Hagerstown told me the boy found at the fire station talked about going to Exhale. Given the evidence I've just given you, I'm not sure that can be ruled as coincidence."

"That's still a stretch. The child could have misunderstood." Senator Coleman balanced the slender pen on his large, farm-hand-looking fingers. "You have a lot of connections, it seems."

He should have just stamped the question on his forehead. My connections could be useful to him, so why don't I share them? I diverted the implication and pushed ahead. "He could have misunderstood, I suppose. Is it possible to question him?"

Another pretend smile, acknowledging the unspoken no in my answer. "His foster parents are being investigated, and he's been removed to another part of the country." The politician reared his head as I assumed he eventually would. "It would take some doing, and I'm not sure it's worth messing with the red tape."

"I accept that," I said. "But I won't accept you don't have enough evidence to warrant your attention."

Coleman ignored the direct challenge. "This information wasn't in the papers, but the boy claimed a female FBI agent by the name of Rex left him at the fire station." He leaned back in his chair, regarding me with an eel-like smile. "There's no record of that agent."

"Really?" I pretended to be surprised and not disturbed by

the innuendo in the senator's voice. "Did he give any other information?"

Kelly had scoured every law enforcement source she had in the tri-state area. There'd been no mention of the boy talking about the agent putting his captor to sleep. But I'd like to be sure little Aron had kept his promise.

"No. Just that the agent retrieved him from a bad man and brought him there. Since the boy was brought across state lines, the FBI took over the case."

I waited. Bob Stewart's body had been found nearly frozen solid in his semi two days after his death. Last I'd heard, Hagerstown Police and the Maryland State Police considered Stewart's death as suspicious due to his extremely low blood sugar. Two overworked counties in two different states had yet to match their cases together.

Senator Coleman lifted the papers and stared at them for a long, silent minute. Finally, he set them back down on his desk and looked me in the eye with a direct gaze that sent chills up my spine. "God bless whoever tracked down that child and delivered him. She clearly isn't afraid of the consequences."

I said nothing, nodding in agreement and preparing to volley back if the senator outright confronted me.

He nudged the phone with his pen. "I can't say you're wrong about the local situation. But creating a team for something like this doesn't happen overnight."

I nodded in understanding like I knew he wanted me to. "Of course. But this is your pet cause. And you're up for re-election in less than a year. Think of what cleaning up Philadelphia would mean to voters."

He looked away, debating again. "All right. I've got some customs agents in Philadelphia who will hopefully have time to look into these allegations. I'll give them your list, and if they find anything at these locations, I'll start pushing for the task force. But it's going to take some time. As for this phone, you realize I'm taking a risk keeping it."

I took the chance to say what we both already knew. So easy to read, even easier to manage. In less than five minutes of conversation, he'd revealed to me that politics were at least as important as his pet cause. He'd practically handed me my best bargaining chip. I rose to leave. "You're an upstanding politician. If you say you didn't know it was stolen, the police will believe you. And we're talking about the greater good here."

Senator Coleman stood as well, extending his hand. "Duly noted. Thank you for bringing this to my attention, Lucy. It's people like you who will make the difference in the war on these horrific crimes."

People like me. What if there were more people like me? What if zero-tolerance laws were finally passed against sexual predators and actually enforced? How different would the next generation grow up?

The senator escorted me to the lobby. He touched my elbow —an old-fashioned gentleman's gesture. "I'll be in touch."

"Sir." A pleasant-faced twenty-something man waved from behind a desk loaded with odds and ends. "I need you to sign these forms for the budget meeting." Offering me a shy smile, he hurried around the desk and handed the senator the forms.

"Thanks, Jake." Coleman swiftly signed the papers without reading them. "Lucy, this is my top aide, Jake Meyer. He's a grad student at Penn State and the most organized person on the planet. My life would be a mess without him."

I smiled warmly at Jake. Shorter than me, with soft brown eyes and olive skin, he looked like he still belonged in high school. Then again, maybe I was just too far removed from his age group to realize I was the one looking older while they stayed the same. "Do you work with private citizens? I could certainly use some organizing."

He glanced between the senator and me, tugging uncomfortably at the carefully knotted tie resting snugly beneath his burgundy sweater vest. "I'm sure a lady like you doesn't need my help."

"Only a lady on the surface, Jake. The rest of me is a mess."

He laughed, a breathy trill that wasn't at all masculine. "Well, the surface is sparkling." Realizing his cheesy line, Jake flushed to the roots of his dark hair.

I played with my earring and smiled. "Thank you. That's the best compliment I'll have today."

Nodding, he flushed again.

"Here you go." Senator Coleman handed back the signed papers. "Again, Lucy, I'll be in touch. If you need anything else, call my office directly. I'll make sure Jake and the others know to put you through."

"Thank you." I buttoned my wool coat, shooting a still-embarrassed Jake one final smile. My mind was already moving on. Time for the big show.

SIX

Dressing for success was key to being taken seriously. That was one of the few useful things I learned from my mother.

Sarah was bound to confront me over the missing phone, and nothing intimidated an insecure woman like a confident, attractive rival. My auburn hair fell in loose waves around my shoulders, and the dark green, figure-hugging dress made my eyes pop. Topped off with a little mascara and no glasses, I knew I'd have the eye of everyone in the spa as soon as I walked in the door.

I blew into the spa with the blast of frigid air. Making sure to keep my back to the front desk, I smoothed my hair and slipped off my wool coat. Tension—or perhaps it was finely honed instinct—crawled up the back of my neck with legs as thick as a hairy tarantula's. Instead of the usual morning bustle —idle chitchat, stations being cleaned, coffee being made—the spa was quiet. Whispers crawled past me, as if my coworkers were collectively waiting to witness the impending storm.

The anticipation of Sarah's confrontation came as a blitz attack, making my scalp tingle and my fingers twitch. Was this what drug addicts felt when they needed a fix? A dazzling, hot fire that spread throughout every inch of their bodies until they wanted to scream or pass out?

"Lucy." Sarah's voice was colder than the Arctic weather.

Center stage now, the spotlight blinding and intoxicating. Slowly, I turned and approached the front desk. where Sarah leaned against the counter. Satisfaction forced the corners of my mouth up. Her hair looked less smooth this morning and her makeup not quite pristine. Fine wrinkles around her eyes, and bags beneath those. Her gaze flashed over me, taking in my drastically different appearance, and like a rippling stream, her stance subtly changed. She swallowed and then shifted in her heels. Squaring her shoulders, she jutted her chin, smoothed her hair and then her silk blouse. She picked at one of her manicured nails.

One lioness formally challenging another, in the subtle way that only human females can accomplish.

"Good morning, Sarah. How are you today?" Chris would have laughed at the singsong tone of my voice. I supposed my love of confronting people like Sarah meant a far deeper neurosis, but I'd think about that another day.

"It's not very good." Her sharp voice reminded me of my ninth-grade English teacher. My friend Kenny used to say the woman desperately needed to get laid or none of us would pass.

I feigned concern. "What's wrong?"

"Why don't we speak in my office?"

Interesting move. I hadn't been entirely sure she would know I was the one who took the phone, but since she'd been in the office with the door shut just before the last client arrived, it was a good bet she'd used it. Common sense pointed to me being the logical suspect, but how exactly was she going to accuse me of stealing a hidden cellphone without calling herself out? She'd have to rely on my not challenging her, and that was a gamble she'd lose. Pulling me into her office was a way to regain power, bring me to her territory.

I trailed my hand through my hair, pretending to watch the red strands glowing in the soft light. Sarah huffed. "I don't really feel comfortable being in your office right now. You're very angry. Why don't you just tell me what's going on?"

Her left eye twitched. My lips begged to lift into a smirk, but I held back. Out of my peripheral vision, I saw the other women crowded around the beverage station. The weaker lionesses waiting to see who would be their new queen.

"Something is missing from my office," Sarah finally said. Her eyes searched mine, the unspoken words sizzling between us. She realized I had to know something to search for that phone. But how much? And was I a cop? The questions plaguing her were embedded into the lines across her forehead and the deep creases between her eyes. "It was there when I took the last client last night, and then it disappeared. You were the only one here."

Every jittery movement telegraphed her fear, bolstering my ego. I put my hands on my hips. "I'm sorry? What are you talking about?"

Sarah glanced from me to her employees. Her narrowed eyes, coupled with the soft yellow light, made her look reptilian. She snapped her gaze back to me, shoving her chin high. "If you needed money, Lucy, you should have asked. Stealing my purse and cellphone was foolish."

So that's how she'd decided to play it. Throwing her purse into the mix. I made my eyes go wide. "Excuse me?"

"They're missing. You were the only one here."

"Then you must have misplaced them."

Sarah shook her head. "Give them back, and I won't call the police." She smiled a fake smile that reminded me of Senator Coleman's oily politician grin.

"I don't think so," I said. "Did you look at the security footage? I'm sure your cameras will catch whoever snuck into your office and stole that phone." I emphasized the last word and leaned against the counter.

She stood straight as a twig. Her forehead glimmered with a light sheen of sweat. "I don't have security cameras."

I made an obnoxious sound between a snort and a laugh, honestly surprised. "You're running a high-end business, and you don't have security cameras?" I looked around the plush lobby. All the other employees watched now, not even pretending to be doing something else. I pointed to one of the massage therapists. "Does that sound right to you? What company in this day and age doesn't have security cameras?"

"I don't believe in them." Sarah's voice warbled. "Until now, I haven't had to worry about this sort of thing."

"That makes no sense to me." I crossed my arms over my chest, still directing my words to the others. "As an employee, don't you feel unprotected? She can accuse anyone of anything, and so could a customer."

Sheri, one of the manicurists, shrugged. "Sarah treats us well. We've never questioned it."

Sarah's head bobbed up and down. "Lucy, I'm a nice person. And I don't want to get anyone in trouble. There's no reason to get the police involved. Just give my things back." So she'd decided I wasn't an undercover cop. Not a hard conclusion to make. But it fascinated me how this woman thought she had the upper hand. Only someone with knowledge about what she was hiding would know to look for that phone. She wasn't ignorant. But then again, she was used to control and privilege and didn't mind farming out children. I suppose some redhead off the street didn't faze her.

"Lucy?" Sarah's voice bore the faintest hint of nerves.

I pushed myself off the counter to stand straight. My pulse battered against my chest; I felt light and airy and in complete control. Almost manic. "How do you know the police don't already have that phone? By the way, L is a total coward."

The flush that had reached her forehead evaporated as though I'd thrown white paint at her. Even her lips looked like chalk. The stronger, more cunning lioness taking her rightful place, I stepped forward until I was in her personal space and out of earshot of the shocked employees. I'd love to be a fly on her pretty walls and hear what story she gave them after I left.

"Yes, I hacked into it." I pitched my voice into a whisper. "If I can find L, I can find another man. And what if I get him to talk?"

"We should speak in my office." Smelling of breath mints and fruity perfume, her voice was as pitiful as a newborn kitten's.

"If that helps." Letting her have this small victory would give her a false sense of security. Easier for me to manipulate her. And I didn't need to worry about the peanut gallery butting their noses into my plan.

I followed her into the office, which looked as boring as it had yesterday, save for the mess on her desk. She'd torn it apart searching for the phone. Shutting the door, I faced her hard gaze.

"I'm not quite sure what you're accusing me of—"

"Spare me," I cut her off. "Last month, I saw you take two teenagers—a boy and a girl—from here to a seedy motel in North Philly. After you made a pit stop here and got them cleaned up, that is. You left them there with a black male who arrived on foot. How much did that transaction earn you?"

She stared.

My entire body felt light, as if I'd just downed a shot of whiskey. I loved seeing her squirm.

"You're the middleman," I continued. "That much is obvious. And your boss is pissed off because I've got information on his clients—or he will be when you tell him. Here's the thing. I don't care what sort of side business you guys have going." I lifted my shoulders and then let them fall. "I just like a certain lifestyle, and since my man left, I don't have it. You understand where I'm going with this?"

Sarah's nose curled. As if she were any better than the blackmailer she believed me to be. As if she weren't a trussed-up, female pimp. "You want money."

"Oh no, not from you. I'm not interested in dealing with the help." I dropped the word like lead, enjoying the flicker of anger on her face. "I want to speak to the boss. Is he the person you left those kids with?"

"I don't know what you're talking about."

"Sarah." The name rolled off my tongue in the most conde-scending tone I could muster. Mentioning what Riley had told me was out of the question, but I didn't need to. Sarah's weak-ness shined as bright as a red-light district at midnight. "You run a profitable business that's rocketed to success in the past year in a high-end part of the city. You're a high-class lady with a repu-tation to uphold. What do you think would happen if word of your side jobs got out? I may not have enough to hold up in court, but I could tell some pretty damned good stories, and I'd have your phone to back me up. Something like that would cost you clients."

The cords in her neck stretched tight. "He won't see you."

Easily as that, my suspicions confirmed—someone else ran this show. But how many more people like Sarah were out there? "And you're afraid he'll cut you loose. Pretend like you never existed."

She flinched, giving me the answer I needed. "So either you accept the position you're in right this minute and do what's best for you—what it takes to keep your business running—or you allow yourself to be squashed."

Sarah crossed her arms, but her shoulders sagged. Gray pallor still colored her skin. "What are you saying?"

I was taking a big risk, but at worst I'd end up right back where I started. "Tell me everything you know about him. Who his other associates are, what other businesses front his operation."

She barked a laugh. "Why would I do that?"

"Because you have two choices: tell him you lost the phone to some redheaded broad who gave you a false identity, which means he cuts you loose and I get no money and then I go to the press, or work with me to gather as much dirt as we can and split the profits."

"You gave me a false identity? How? I put you through a background check."

I almost laughed at the surprise on her face. "Honey, I'm a con artist. I know how to protect myself. So, what do you say? Are you going to help yourself or lose everything you've worked for?"

"What if I call your bluff and say your assumed information won't affect me in the least?"

"You could do that." I ran my fingers across the framed picture of Sarah at her ribbon cutting two years ago. "But is it worth the risk?"

Sarah considered this. I waited, letting her finish the picture I'd started. Her imagination would do much better work than any story I spun. "You'll need to come back tonight. I can't do this here."

"And I'm not dumb enough to meet you by myself in your building. Let's pick a quiet, neutral location. I'll even let you choose."

Sarah rocked on the balls of her feet, her jaw muscles clenching. "Maisy's on Twenty-Second. It's a busy place but we can get a private table."

I wanted to dance. Or better yet, call Chris and tell him I knew exactly what I was doing and maybe he should have a little more faith in me. Instead, I extended my hand. "I'll be there at seven."

She closed her eyes and nodded, the defeat on her face almost making me feel sorry for her.

I opened her office door. Her employees were all steadily working, but their straight backs and jerky movements made it clear they were on edge and waiting to pounce. "Thanks so much for the day off, Sarah. I'm glad we got this misunderstanding worked out." I sauntered to the coat rack and pulled on my heavy winter garments.

The only downside in my plan was that I'd have to leave Sarah unharmed, but she was a valuable pawn in a much bigger game.

As long as she didn't stand me up.

SEVEN

My head buzzed with the high of confronting Sarah and bending her to my will. A part of me didn't like what that meant —it made me too much like my mother, too cold and manipulating, feeding off the miserable energy of others. But seeing the fear I'd elicited in Sarah had my blood pumping so hard my head throbbed. It was a dangerous rush that could get me into serious trouble if I wasn't careful.

I needed to eat. Located in a popular business district, Morning Glory's Diner was consistently busy. I squeezed into the doorway, my stomach growling at the smells of frying bacon and hot coffee, and craned my neck to see if Kenny had already secured us a booth.

He waved to me from the back corner. Just the sight of him cooled my simmering nerves. We'd been friends since high school. Two damaged people finding each other—he with the abusive drunk of a dad and me with the sexually abused, dead sister—and he was the brightest part of my life. He was a pot-dealing mechanic who helped homeless kids and was always upbeat and smiling. He didn't know my dark secret, but Kenny was well aware of my twisted personality and never judged. He was just Kenny with a smile, and most days there's nothing better than that.

"Goose." He grinned as I slid into the booth and rolled my eyes at the nickname. A cup of steaming black coffee waited for me.

I took a careful sip. "You know me so well."

"Of course I do. Ordered you a breakfast sampler, too. Should be here soon."

I could have kissed him. Funny that was something we'd never done. My feelings for Kenny were deep but uncomplicated, a blessing in my life.

"So what's the emergency favor?" Kenny wasn't one to mess around. Another quality I loved.

"I need you to track down a kid for me. Actually, she's a teenager and a resourceful one." Kenny knew I was trying to infiltrate the trafficking ring, although he assumed that as a PI, I'd turn my information in to the police. I told him about the confrontation with Riley last night, omitting the danger and Chris's semi-rescue. "Do you think you can find her?"

Kenny rubbed his round cheeks. His two-day-old scruff did little to make him look any older. "Well, if she was at the Rattner in North Philly, there's a decent chance she lives somewhere nearby. Unless she's got higher-end clientele, too, and takes city transit." He stared into his coffee, thick eyebrows knitted together. "How do these kids become so complicit to the point of thinking it's their choice?"

The sadness in Kenny's voice made the reality of these kids' lives all the more real. I searched for the right answer even though I knew there wasn't one.

"I mean," Kenny continued, "my dad whipped the shit out of me, told me I wasn't worth the dirt on his shoes. And I believed him for a long time. But to make the choice this Riley has—"

"Sexual abuse is a different kind of beast," I said. "I think it affects the soul, you know? Especially when it starts really young. These kids don't know anything else, so earning money off the abuse can seem like a positive thing. And probably makes them feel like they have an element of control, even if it's all false. The pimps who live off girls like her know how to use her pain to their biggest advantage. They can spot these girls a mile away—it's a nasty talent."

The server appeared with our food, and Kenny waited until she was gone. "I just can't get my mind around it."

"Because you're not in their shoes." I picked at my eggs. "All we can do is try to help."

"What if they don't want it?"

Riley certainly didn't seem to want my help. And maybe she was beyond it at her age, already too hardened. But I had to try, and if I was lucky, I might be able to save some younger kids too. "All we can do is try and see what happens."

"You're right." Kenny popped a sausage link into his mouth. "I won't be able to sleep unless I try to help find this kid. Don't suppose she is in the system?"

"I checked into every database I could." Meaning every one Kelly could hack into, but Kenny didn't need to know that. "No one matching her first name and description are listed as missing children, and she's not been arrested. Which means she's either very good at staying under the radar or really lucky."

"Or the dude running this operation knows how to keep things on the down-low."

"That definitely crossed my mind." I couldn't explain it, but everything in my gut insisted that no matter how many blocks were holding up his filthy pyramid, the man at the top was powerful. Somehow, he moved like a shadow between his various storefronts. How did he pull people like Sarah in? Blackmail? Was she in serious debt? I didn't think her business was doing badly, but that didn't mean she spent her money wisely. Or was she just greedy with no moral center? Her big boss might just be the kind of perceptive person who can practically sniff out those willing to close their eyes for an extra buck. Some people's biggest skill was their ability to read others.

Hopefully she'd tell me more tonight, if she actually showed up.

"So I guess the best thing to do is to hit the streets, talk to my kids," Kenny said. "I've got some contacts at a couple of shelters in North Philly."

"I don't think this kid is working out of a shelter. Even though her clothes weren't warm enough, she was well put together, and most of those places keep a pretty strict eye on kids' comings and goings. They won't allow them to stay if they think something weird is going on." Not to mention she had an air of authority on the street. She'd wanted information for her pimp, which meant she knew exactly where to deliver it.

"Yeah, but maybe they know her. Streets are a big place, but word gets around, you know? Kids talk. Know who to stay away from. I'd say it's your best shot other than just walking the area around the Rattner, and it's too cold for that. Not to mention dangerous for you." Kenny's mouth hung open as if he meant to say more, but he snapped it shut. He knew I wouldn't listen.

I agreed, for now. But if we didn't find Riley in a few days, I'd have to layer up and brave the cold and whatever dangers North Philly had to throw at me.

EIGHT

The thing about a city like Philadelphia in the winter is that the snow and cold weather never really slow it down. People adapt quickly, especially those who've grown up here. The weather is a part of life, and nothing stands in the way of having a good time after work.

Sitting in the middle of a crowded Maisy's, I waited for Sarah, who of course was late.

No hidden corner tables were available, which put me nearly in the middle of a murmuring after-dinner crowd. Part bar, part coffee joint, Maisy's served an eclectic crowd of all ages and provided fantastic people-watching. Another night, I'd be enjoying myself, making up stories about whatever person caught my eye, but my mind stayed on a single track. Would Sarah show?

Chris bet me $100 she wouldn't. Stubborn and forever nosy, he'd positioned himself at the end of the bar where he could discreetly keep an eye on me. His presence was the end result of a very short-lived argument an hour earlier.

"You have no idea if she's coming alone. She might have someone waiting to ambush you." How Chris thought he could prevent that from the bar, I wasn't sure, but I relented. I wished I'd just kept my mouth shut, but a secret part of me was glad he was here. I wasn't exactly a normal girl. A crowd like this made me feel like I had a giant sign flashing "fraud" over my head. The proverbial sore thumb in virtually every situation. Seeing Chris in his wool pea coat and black glasses, broad shoulders slightly rounded, head down as if he were lost in thought, made me feel less like the lone speck of black sand on an otherwise perfectly white beach.

A lithe, blond woman wearing a dark blue, knitted beret skirted around the tables. Sarah and I locked eyes. Gone was the confidence I'd always associated with her, along with about half her usual makeup. She looked worn out and downright nervous.

I cocked my head and smiled as she sat down. "Glad you could make it."

"I didn't have much choice, did I?" Her voice sounded unusually throaty.

"We always have a choice."

Sarah said nothing, sitting down without her usual grace. Lips drawn tightly against her teeth, her entire face looked thin and sallow. She folded her hands across the gleaming wood table and stared at me with a mix of hostility and curiosity.

"Did you want to order something?" I didn't expect to liquor her up, but a little alcohol might work in my favor.

"No."

I swirled my untouched club soda. At the bar, Chris shifted to slightly face me, making conversation with the brunette next to him. I bit the inside of my cheek and smiled at Sarah. "Let's just get right to it. What have you got on your boss that we can use to make some easy money?"

She actually laughed, but it didn't reach her eyes. "Not much. He's got a system of checks and balances to rival the government. I'm just one part of it."

"So how'd you get started?" I made a show of looking her up and down. "You're not into those"—I dropped my voice to a harsh whisper—"kids, are you?"

She screwed her pert nose. "No. I would never do such a thing."

Nodding, I eased back in my seat, as if I agreed that pimping kids was perfectly okay as long as you didn't dip into your stash. Indignation boiled my veins. "Then how did you get involved? I mean, you're risking a lot, especially with such a successful business."

"It's hard to start a business nowadays." She shrugged, her shoulders looking bony beneath her blue wool cape. "My business is really competitive and takes a lot of startup capital, plus word of mouth to succeed."

"So you were in financial trouble," I surmised. "But how does a girl like you find out about this... organization?"

"They found me." She snapped the bracelet on her wrist. "Six months ago, this kid swaggers into the salon just before close, when I was alone. He knew I was the only one there, and he knew half my life history and my financial situation."

I tried not to balance on the edge of my seat. Out of the corner of my eye, I saw Chris mirroring my body language and inwardly rolled my eyes. He still had so much to learn. "Did he tell you how he found all that out?"

"No. But he offered me a position." Sarah swallowed hard, her eyes suddenly coming to life and searching mine. "A business proposition. I couldn't refuse."

"Because you needed the money to save the salon? Don't you have any family who could have helped? Most people would turn to them before jumping into a situation like this."

A shadow moved in her eyes as she chewed on the corner of her mouth with her perfectly aligned, white teeth. Shoulders drawn, she looked at the bar, seemingly catching her reflection in the mirror behind the bar. "No."

"He's the one you delivered those kids to, isn't it?" I'd known it the moment she mentioned the swagger. His ego had radiated across the parking lot the night Chris and I followed her.

She nodded.

"So why couldn't you refuse and deal with bankruptcy, if that's what it came to?"

"Because this kid—and I'm telling you, he wasn't more than twenty-five—wearing genuine Armani and a Rolex waltzes in with more than just general information. He knew explicit details, including my application for a bailout loan at the bank. He knew... things no one should." She chewed on a nail, slightly rocking in her seat. "He said his employer could make it all go away."

"What other things?"

Her glance came and went so fast I barely caught it. "Personal things. I had no choice."

"You had no choice, really?"

"Not with all the information he had." She didn't elaborate further. "So after a few negotiations"—she rolled her eyes—"I accepted."

Whoever this guy was had more than financials on Sarah, but right now wasn't the time to hammer her on that. Pushing the wrong issue too hard would make her close up. "This kid, he give you a name? Anything we can use?"

She snorted. "Yeah, and that's when I knew he was no more than a street kid riding the coat tails of some rich sugar daddy. He strutted around like he owned the place. And while he tried to speak eloquently, every once in a while he'd slip up and sound like he came straight from the ghetto. Preacher."

I didn't recognize the nickname, but I'd have both Kelly and Kenny check on it. "Wow. Sounds like a well-established pimp."

"Exactly. He's arrogant and bossy, but he's good at keeping things secret."

"Come on. You've got to have something we can use."

Sarah gazed at the bar, the seconds ticking by. Finally, she turned back to glare at me with steely eyes. "I've been blackmailed once already. At least I'm getting something out of it. I still don't know what you're going to do to help me."

She'd already given more than I'd hoped for. Was she looking for a way out of the mess before I interfered? "You really want to keep this life up? It's got to be stressful." I appealed to her base needs. "Stress ages a girl, you know. Fast. And if you're dealing with an actual network, it's only a matter of time before someone slips up. Then you're really going to lose everything. Including your freedom."

"You think I haven't thought of that?" she snapped, leaning forward so quickly I barely kept myself from jerking away. "My question is, what are you going to offer me that I'm not getting now? Preacher might be a pimp, but he takes care of me. Where am I going to go without him?"

"I can help you find shelter," I said. "If we take your boss down, we can milk him for enough money to keep you going and get you out of this mess."

"And I need your help with this because?" She raised her eyebrows.

I smiled. "Haven't we established that I'm especially talented at getting what I want? And I still have the phone. Which only points to you, not Preacher or the big boss. Is that fair?"

Her lips quivered. "Can you protect the clients?"

This time, I couldn't stop the quake generating from the disgust rippling through me. "You want to protect the... men?"

"Everything is done with consent." The lights cast shadows on her hardened face, and for a moment, she looked like the monster of nightmares. "If those guys are busted, I'll lose half the salon's clientele."

It took me a minute to catch on. "The wives?"

A single nod.

Meaning the salon was essentially a front for child trafficking. The clientele was supplied by the creeps lusting for little kids, and most of the wives likely had no clue. Anger coursed through me so strongly I had to turn away, letting my hair fall around my face. As if we were connected, Chris's head jerked up and his gaze caught mine. His eyebrows raised in question, and I gave the slightest shake of my head.

"All right. So if we're going to protect those men"—my jaw clenched on the words—"we need something exceptional on your boss."

"I don't have it," she said flatly. "Preacher is the go-between. I'm a facilitator. There are more like me. Don't know how many."

"Who finds the kids? The clients?"

Another noncommittal shrug. "I don't know for sure. Maybe Preacher. He gives me client names, has me match them up with... you know. I set the appointments."

"How about payment? I'm assuming these dudes are paying premium." Riley only expected seventy-five bucks. No way was that the real fee.

"All handed via a secure account on a foreign server," she said. "Client pays. Once a week, I get my thirty-five percent cut."

"Out of how much?"

She looked down and then across the bar at the other patrons. I wondered if she was thinking how sick and selfish and robotic she seemed. Dress it up all she wanted—she helped kids sell themselves for money and took a cut. She was a pimp.

"Starting fee is $3,000."

I didn't blanch. "But you don't handle transactions."

"I'm paid in cash."

"How much does the boss get? Or Preacher?"

"No idea." She shifted, her right hand drifting for her bag.

"Look, I've honestly told you all I know. I get the sense Preacher is the guard dog. He's never given me any idea who the boss is. Preacher refers to him as 'he.' That's the best I can tell you."

I searched her drawn face. Liars are usually easy to spot, especially if you're one of them. Sarah was telling the truth. "He's cocky, thinks he's in charge of the world. We need to shock his system."

"What do you mean?"

I took a drink of the club soda, letting the cold liquid slide down my throat. Keeping my eyes on her nervous face, I smiled. Let her worry. "There's only one time we'll know for certain where he'll be. When's your next payday?"

Her eyes narrowed, face again thinning into a malevolent caricature of herself. "I suppose you want a cut."

My smile widened. "What else am I in this for? Fifteen percent will do."

"He'll never pay me with you there."

"Oh, I know. I'll be waiting in a safe spot down the street. I'm good at hiding, and I'll have backup, so don't think of doing anything stupid. I'll pop by after I see Preacher leave." I rested back in my chair. "So, day and time?"

She wanted to slap me. I saw it in the way her skin turned red, her hands gripping her bag tightly enough to turn her knuckles white. "6:15 tomorrow. Just after close."

"I'll see you then."

More gleaming hate as she rose to leave. She shouldered her expensive bag, buttoned up her fashionable cape. Adjusted her pricey bracelet. Perhaps her materialistic needs had a part in her business failure, but people like Sarah don't want to be held accountable for their choices. It was much easier to lie to herself, to convince her guilty conscience that she'd done what she had to do, that she was desperate. No other choice. That's the only way she could sleep at night.

It's the only way I can close my eyes.

"Preacher isn't a nice person," Sarah said. "He might be playing rich boy now, but he came from the streets. He's a modern-day pimp with better clothes but an even more vicious streak. If he realizes you're involved, we're both in trouble."

"Thanks for the warning."

She shook her head. The corners of her mouth were drawn, her eyes not quite meeting mine. "Your decision." She turned to leave.

I snatched her wrist. "Don't stand me up. Or tell anyone about this. You're in just as much trouble as me if you do." Sarah's head whipped around. Her slitted eyes flashed between my grip on her and my face.

She dug her nails into my hand until I released her. "How dare you put your hands on me."

"Don't play any games with me tomorrow." My low voice still seemed to carry over the chatter. "Or I'll have the police and the press at Exhale before you know what hits you."

"Fine." Sarah stalked to the exit. She might call Preacher and warn him, but I doubted it. Her hatred of him was too obvious. She wanted out.

Chris and I would stake out positions separately, and hopefully one or both of us would be able to follow Preacher home.

A martini appeared before me. "Can I buy you a drink, and we can talk about that garbage you're dying to take out?"

Chris's grin and his cheesy throwback to our first meeting almost made me smile. Instead, I motioned for him to sit. He obliged, taking the seat Sarah had vacated.

"You okay?" he asked.

"Right as rain." I took a long pull of the martini. "I love hanging out with the scum of the earth. Energizes me, you know?"

He ignored my sarcasm. "You could always walk away from this."

"This scum, that scum. They're all the same."

"Maybe." He finished his beer. "But don't you think about it?"

"About what?"

"Leaving all of this behind. Pretending this life never happened and starting over somewhere new, where you don't have to hide who you are."

"I'm not sure that's possible. There's evil everywhere. I'd manage to find it."

"Because you seek it out."

I didn't argue the point because I had nothing worthy to combat it with. "What do you want me to do? Head out to the country and become Amish?"

He started laughing. "Nah. I'd miss you too much, so I'd have to follow. And I don't want to be Amish."

I rolled my eyes, but I was grateful for the brevity. I needed time to breathe before thinking about the next step, and Chris knew exactly how to lighten my mind, if only for a minute.

"I need your help tomorrow," I said. "It might get danger-ous." My anxious fingers drummed the table as my toe tapped an uneven beat.

Chris's fingers brushed mine, stilling the movement. "That's fine. If you promise me—"

"I promise. When this is over, I'll devote all my attention to your mother."

NINE

Snow rained down in fat flakes, making for a miserable evening commute. I pulled my wool cap down to my chin and knotted my scarf. Tucked under the awning of the homemade candle joint two businesses down from the salon, I made a show of typing on my phone. Just a cold woman with her hair hidden by a dowdy winter cap and wearing tortoiseshell glasses too big for her face. I ducked my head, letting the prescription reading glasses slip down my nose so I could see clearly over the rims.

A few minutes before six, the snow started coming down thicker. Hopefully Preacher wasn't late. I'd been out here for twenty minutes, and the cold had already seeped through my heavy clothes. I squinted down the street, searching for Chris. He'd snagged a parking spot with a decent view. My car was in the parking garage five blocks down.

The spa's windows were dark, but Sarah closed at five on Tuesdays. I'd always thought that was strange, but now it made sense.

I scanned the bustling crowd for someone matching his description. Most were late shoppers or store employees hurrying to get home before the roads got worse. Six o'clock came and went. Despite my winter boots, my toes ached with cold. Needing a distraction, I called Chris.

"How's your warm car?"

He laughed. "You're the one who wanted to be on the street."

"Doesn't mean I can't complain about it."

"I'll take you for a hot toddy after this."

"A hot toddy? What are you, an Irish grandpa?"

He laughed again. "Maybe. Any sign of this guy?"

"Nope. I'm assuming he'll stand out." A particularly bulbous snowflake dropped into my eye. Cursing, I rubbed out the moisture. Good thing I wasn't wearing mascara.

"Luce." Chris's voice was no longer playful. "Twelve o'clock."

"I see." A lanky man strode toward the spa. This time, instead of jeans and a heavy jacket, he was decked out in a shiny suit and trench coat, as if he were a lawyer or an accountant. But it was the walk that gave him away, and only to those paying attention. He didn't walk with the fast pace of the harried businessman with too many clients and not enough time. No, this kid had a long stride that could only be described as a rhythmic swagger, a dance reserved for only the coolest of the cool kids—the same one I'd witnessed the night of our stakeout. He reached Exhale's door and knocked.

Without a word to Chris, I ended the call. Like most overconfident young people, Preacher's serene expression quickly twisted into one of impatience. He shaded his eyes and peered into the locked door, then knocked again. Checked his watch. Mumbled.

Chris was out of his car now, casually leaning against it, looking like a stupid model in the falling snow.

Preacher's knocking grew louder as he took out his cellphone and made a call. I couldn't hear what he said, but judging from the short amount of time he spoke, he left a message.

The door remained locked.

Finally, Preacher shrugged, pulling up the collar of his coat, and headed back in the direction he'd come from.

I followed, motioning for Chris to stay across the street and mirror us.

Past the coffee shop and the organic food store, around the corner and past the local art gallery. Preacher's strides were more meaningful now. He was angry. He wasn't used to being stood up.

He headed for the subway station.

I glanced at Chris, still across the street and keeping pace. He shook his head.

Of course he didn't want me to go on the subway with Preacher.

And of course I was going to do it.

I checked the route. This was the Broad Street Line, taking us into North Philadelphia. The subway stop wasn't four blocks from the Rattner hotel.

My phone rang as I bought my ticket. I hit end and boarded the car. It smelled vaguely of stale sweat and fried food, but it looked relatively clean. And packed. Preacher took a seat next to an older woman, and slumped down with his knees apart in the slouch typical of today's youth. My phone vibrated in my pocket as I wedged my way toward Preacher. Forced to stand, I grabbed the rail nearest him.

Up close, I saw his blue silk tie and his gold watch. His nails were nicely manicured, his fingers flying across his phone.

Pushing my glasses up on my nose, I made my move.

"Nice watch." I pitched my voice higher than my usual husky tone.

Preacher barely glanced up. "Thanks."

"And your suit. A man with good taste."

He shrugged. I twirled the blond lock of hair around my index finger, cocking my hips to the right. "I usually hate riding the subway, you know? But this is one of those days I'm grateful for it. Is that why you're riding today?"

Preacher finally glanced up. His eyes were a pretty shade of hazel, with long lashes. Nose a little too squat for his long face, his features slightly off-kilter but not unpleasing. "What?"

Now that I had his attention, I gave him my best smile. "This is my usual route, and I don't remember seeing you. And I'd remember."

His turn to analyze me. Still in my early thirties, I looked close enough to his age to warrant his interest, but old enough for him to feel flattered at my interest. "I only make this trip once a month. Business." He said it with pride, his chin rising a notch.

"Ooh." I licked my lips, still twirling my fake hair. "A successful businessman at such a young age? Impressive. What do you do?"

"Human resources."

The words were spoken so smugly, layered with conde-scending humor at an inside joke Preacher believed only he understood, that I struggled for my next response.

"Liking hiring and firing people?"

"Something like that."

My phone vibrated again in my pocket. I ignored it. "That's very cool. I always thought it would be awesome to have that kind of power. Instant respect, you know?"

"Damn right." He gazed at me again, brazenly looking me over from head to toe. "What about you?"

"Me?" I tried to sound surprised he'd ask. "Nothing special. Just a working girl trying to make ends meet."

He grinned and sat up straighter. "Working girl, huh?"

"Oh God, not like that." I wished I could blush on command. "I just meant I don't have a career. Nothing like you. I've just a got a job that barely pays the bills."

He waited.

"Cashier."

"Honest work," he said. "But not exactly middle class."

"I wish. I still gotta live at home with my parents. It's embarrassing, but it's where I'm at right now. Some days I think I'd do about anything to get out." I looked down at my boots, pulling my shoulders up toward my ears. I didn't know why I'd led Preacher this way. I needed to get his name, find out where he lived. If I was lucky—or really stupid—I'd get him to invite me over for a drink.

He crossed his long legs, still studying me. My skin crawled, my muscles rippling with the urge to walk away from his scrutiny. I'd been ogled by plenty of men, but Preacher's brazenness had a feral quality that set my nerves on edge. I forced my mouth into a tight smile and managed to maintain eye contact.

Preacher nodded. His pink tongue slid across his bottom lip. There was a freckle on the corner of it. "Anything, huh?"

I glanced down at my shoes, tucking a lock of the wig behind my ear. "Pretty much."

"I might be able to help you." He glanced down the aisle and then stood up. He was taller than Chris, and I found myself staring at the knot on his tie. It was perfect. "Here." He handed me a generic-looking business card that read Meretrix Consulting, with a local phone number. "My company is thinking about expanding into a new market. Different age bracket." He smiled. "I think you'd do nicely. Men love red hair. It's natural, right?"

My mouth felt as if I'd eaten sand. "Yes. You really think I'd work out?"

"Sure." He touched his index and middle finger to my chin and turned my head to the right. My blood pressure skyrocketed not with fear but with fury at his audacity. He was checking out his potential merchandise. I kept perfectly still. If I moved, I'd end up laying him out on the dirty subway floor.

"Yeah," he said. "You're just about right, with some training."

The car slowed. We were stopping in North Philadelphia, and my gut told me Preacher would exit.

He dropped his hand. "You decide you want some extra work, you call me. You could make some real money."

"I didn't get your name."

"Ryan."

"Ryan what?" I fluttered my eyelashes and tried not to puke.

"Ryan's enough. What's yours?"

"Lily." Shame at using my dead sister's name flared. At least the blush on my neck would play off as attraction.

Another wide smile from Preacher as the car stopped. "I think I'll be hearing from you soon."

He strutted off the train and onto the platform. As the doors snapped shut, I caught sight of a familiar face waiting to greet Preacher: Riley, the fifteen-year-old prostitute. Still looking cold in her thin leggings and threadbare coat, she gave Preacher a careful hug, as if she were afraid of dirtying up his suit. He patted her back, and she held out her hand. He grinned so arrogantly I nearly charged off the bus, and then he handed Riley a few bills. The young girl with the wispy black hair and cheekbones a model would envy gazed up at Preacher with adoration. He motioned for her to walk, and they headed down the street just as the train jerked into motion. He was the pimp she wanted information for.

Nauseated, I sank into his vacated seat. During my years with CPS, I saw the same thing over and over again. Teenage girls, and sometimes young women, brought in for prostitution. None of them trusted me or the police, and all of them wanted to get back to their pimp. In their muddled heads, he was the only ally they had. It didn't matter if he beat them or didn't pay them. He gave them a place to live, and he played their vulnerabilities until they were in his control. It wasn't a whole lot different than a domestic violence situation. The battered wife just wants to stay with her husband, and the beat-up prostitute wants her pimp.

Without talking to Riley, I had no idea if Preacher had coerced her or kidnapped her or she'd stepped willingly into the life. I knew she wouldn't want to talk, but I had to find a way. If she was that close to Preacher, she'd know more about his life than Sarah.

My phone vibrated again, and I shook myself, pulling my phone out of my pocket. Three new voicemails and two furious texts from Chris asking me to check in and let him know I was all right.

I asked him to pick me up at the next stop.

He didn't look at me as I dropped into the warm Audi. I said nothing, instead watching the fresh snowflakes fall. Chris jumped onto the interstate, the scenery changing as we drove toward the higher-income areas of the city. My mind wandered, wondering what Preacher was doing right now. Did he treat the boys like he'd treated me? Did girls like Riley realize how degrading Preacher's actions were, or did they see him as the good guy? Or was he like the street pimps, demanding obedience through physical threats?

What would he expect of me when I made the inevitable call?

The car slid to a stop, and I realized we were in front of my building. Chris hadn't spoken a word. I unfastened my seatbelt. "Listen, I did what I had to do, okay?"

He closed his eyes, shook his head. "See you."

That's all I was going to get. I sighed. I'd call and try again later.

TEN

I'd rather be at home in pajamas, eating a can of Spam with the cat trying to sneak a bite, than sitting in my mother's dining room. But she'd been nagging at me for a family dinner, and the exhaustion of playing Preacher's game finally broke my will.

My mother's identity was wrapped up in her public persona of perfection, which meant her house must be full of beautiful things and be perfect at all times. Dirty dishes weren't allowed to sit in the sink, nor could there be any clothes waiting to be laundered. Much less children with sticky hands or muddy feet or soiled faces. What would the neighbors think if any thing or person in Joan's life was less than pristine? Why, that would make her look bad.

Sitting in one of her ornate and expensive and miserably uncomfortable dining-room chairs, I banished the diatribe I'd listened to my entire life. Dwelling on things did nothing but make me even more bitter. I had enough of that to go around.

And my stepfather had me worried. Once a solidly built, ruddy-faced general contractor, his retirement had brought nothing but health issues. Atrial fibrillation was the latest issue, combined with high blood pressure. And the man was shrinking, I was sure of it. Once over six feet, he'd lost at least an inch in height and more in girth. Even worse, his skin had the waxen, gray cast of someone sliding toward the grave.

"Mac." I nudged his outstretched foot with mine. Somehow he'd never quite fit into my mother's immaculate presentation. He slouched when he wanted, put his elbows on the table, and walked around in day-old socks. His arms were dotted with the scars of skin cancer removal—a hazard of too many years of hard labor in the sun—and he was missing the ring finger on his left hand from a gruesome electrical accident. When I first met him, he insisted he'd lost it picking his nose. I was a miserable high schooler with little use for my mother's latest boyfriend, but something about the earnestness of Mac's face and the cocky lift of his chapped lips endeared him to me. That and his licking his fingers instead of using the dainty napkin my mother handed to him.

"You look tired." I bobbed my head in the direction of the kitchen, where my mother toiled over something that probably tasted like sand. "Joan of Me-land wearing you down?"

He chuckled at the dig at my mother. "Ah, Red. Your mother's been real good to me these past few months. I get tired so easy lately, and she don't complain nearly as much as you'd expect."

My forced smile made my cheeks hurt. Inside, I sank into a familiar drowning pool. My mother's skill at making a person grateful for her faults was second to none. I should know because I spent years searching for the problem within myself before finally realizing the truth.

Arguing the point with Mac wouldn't change things, so instead I focused on him. "What's the doctor doing about your lack of energy?"

"Says there's not much we can do if I want to keep my heart regular. He's got it slowed way down so it stays steady. But that means I don't have no get up and go." He shrugged. "But only sometimes. Good days and bad days, and that's part of life, isn't it? Just have to find the positive and keep going."

I rested my hand on my chin. Mac couldn't be more different from my mother. With his cheery outlook in the middle of a shitstorm, he reminded me of Kenny. My mother was all downers and criticism. Despite her self-obsession, she excelled at identifying a person's flaws and weaknesses.

A shudder slithered down my tensed back. I'd done that very thing to Sarah. A skill learned from Mom.

I couldn't be like her. I refused.

"Dinner will be ready in a few minutes." My mother breezed into the dining room looking like a modern version of Martha Stewart. Not because it came natural, but because June was the perfect hostess, mother, and wife. Traits my mother was deluded enough to believe she shared with the fictional character. The navy scoop-neck dress she wore boasted a large, white bow in the center of the chest, and its knee-length skirt was hemmed in matching white. Very cute and far too sweet for my mother.

"It smells delicious," Mac said.

It did smell edible, which made my stomach growl. Mother sat down at the end of the table. Her dark red hair, once as brilliantly auburn as my own, was cut in a stylish pixie that softened the angular planes of her face. In the last few years, her once round, full cheeks had thinned, the bones more pronounced. An effect of aging, she lamented.

"Lucy, I still can't believe you're finally joining us." Mother crossed her legs and gazed at me. She still wore blue contacts, giving her eyes an unnatural glowing effect. "I'd say it's a small miracle."

I grinned and matched her dry tone. "Well, I thought it was time I graced you with my presence."

Her smile thinned. "I don't know that 'grace' is the word I'd use." She let her stony gaze slide over my jeans and cable-knit sweater. The gray cashmere fitted my curves nicely, as did the jeans. "You could have dressed for dinner."

I looked down at the sweater. "This is one hundred percent cashmere, Mom. And it's comfortable."

She lifted her right shoulder in a half-shrug. "I suppose. But the color isn't right for your red hair. Are you putting on weight?"

My face throbbed once more. Joan had always been consumed with her body, trying every new diet and exercise fad. Her obsession paid off, and her figure remained svelte even as she got older. I didn't take it that seriously. Happy as a size ten and nursing a love affair with pasta, I wasn't going to starve myself to make her happy. My phone suddenly vibrated; I slipped it out of my pocket and read Kelly's text. She had new information on Preacher. I wanted to excuse myself, but disappearing now would give Joan even more to complain about.

"Lucy." She'd taken her affronted tone, the one she used when she didn't have full attention. "Answer me."

"Nope." I spoke through gritted teeth.

"Well, you need to choose more flattering clothes, then." She fingered the ends of the bow on her dress. "I wish you could get down to your college weight. You looked so perfect then. I got so many compliments on how pretty you were."

Now, she watched me with bright eyes, wanting an argument. Wanting me to agree and to tell her I'd watch myself.

I didn't engage.

Instead, I grabbed a dinner roll and slathered it with butter. "When's dinner going to be ready? I'm starving."

Joan's nose curled, and Mac's mouth hitched in a satisfied grin. Before she could answer, my phone vibrated. Grateful for the break, I snatched it out of my purse without bothering to look at the screen.

"Hello?"

The caller cleared his throat. "Lucy, it's Detective Todd Beckett."

Beckett's younger brother, Justin, had been a suspect in Kailey Richardson's kidnapping. Justin had a history of violence —or I thought he did at the time. He'd been used as a scapegoat by his evil mother, who'd let him spend years in juvy for a crime she'd committed.

More than two decades had passed since Chris's father was sentenced to life in prison for murdering five women. At the time, authorities believed Chris's mother, Mary Weston, was a victim of her depraved spouse. As we searched for Kailey Richardson, Chris and I had discovered Mary Weston was Martha Beckett, he and Justin were half-brothers, and Mary had been very much involved in the killings. The woman's web was terrifying and complicated, and Chris harbored immense regret. Growing up safe in his aunt and uncle's home, he'd had visions of Mary's involvement. He'd hoped they were his mind playing tricks on him.

Whatever energy my verbal sparring with Joan had dredged up evaporated. I hadn't spoken to Todd in weeks, and greeting me with his official title had an ominous edge.

"Well, long time no speak." I kept my tone light. "How are things?"

"This isn't a social call." His businesslike voice set my teeth on edge. "I need you to come into the station."

"Why? What's happened?"

"Do you know Sarah Jones?"

In retrospect, I wished I'd said no. Bought myself some time. "Yes. I worked for her."

"Right," Todd said. "She was found murdered in her salon."

ELEVEN

Sarah was dead. Fury sent my left eye into a maddening twitch. She'd been my best shot at getting to the source of the trafficking ring. With enough time, I could have wheedled more information out of her, perhaps even isolating her until she felt I was her only ally. She'd known more about the operation than she'd told me, and now that knowledge was gone.

I felt very little for her as a person. The choices she'd made stripped her of her humanity, and so I saw nothing to mourn.

Todd Beckett. No doubt he started salivating with glee as soon as he heard I'd been employed at the salon. He believed I'd killed at least two known pedophiles, and of course he was right. Thankfully, he lacked the evidence to prove it. Sarah's murder meant a new chance for him to dig into my business. But it was hard to feel any animosity toward Todd. He'd treated me fairly in the end, and he was a good cop. An honest one. That probably spelled eventual trouble for me, but I still admired him.

At the police station, the desk sergeant was clearly waiting on me. I gave my name, and her eyes flashed wide for a brief second before she fixed her expression into one so stony it was obvious she knew my name and was trying way too hard to hide the fact.

I don't spook easily. But the layers behind her reaction made me jittery. She'd acted as if a wanted criminal had accidentally walked into her precinct, and she was about to make the arrest of her life.

You are a wanted criminal.

But she doesn't know that.

Right?

"Lucy." My name rolled off Todd's tongue much more warmly than it should have. He stood at the end of the gray carpeted hallway. His charcoal dress pants and black shirt made him blend in with the carpet and cubicle walls. He'd shaved his mustache. New girlfriend or shaving mishap? Either way, the effect was pleasant. His decidedly average face wasn't suited for facial hair. "How've you been?"

I smiled at the show of manners. "Busy, but good. You?"

"The same. I can't complain."

A beat of awkward silence. Shuffling of feet—mine, as I waited for his direction, and his, as he let the moment pass in an effort to establish control. I'd come at his calling, and I would follow his lead like a good little helper. I didn't much care for the idea, and if he were any other cop I probably would have tossed my hair over my shoulder, cocked my hip, and started asking why I'd been called down here so late. But I gave him the lead.

"Let's find a quiet place to talk." He motioned for me to go first, an acknowledgment of not only manners but a subtle jab that I'd been here before in a similar position. I stopped at the same interrogation room he'd used after Chris and I saved Kailey Richardson. Nothing about it had changed. Still a hot box with uncomfortable chairs. Avoiding it would make me look insecure.

"How this?" I asked.

"Just fine."

I sat down first, in the very seat I'd occupied last fall. The leather now had a small tear that made it even more uncomfortable. Crossing my legs, I deposited my bag on the floor, carefully folding my coat over it. I clasped my hands over my knee and gave Todd my full attention.

"Justin's doing well." I stayed in touch with Todd's younger brother, the boy whose life Mother Mary had nearly ruined. He worked full time and still volunteered at the homeless shelter. Even better, he'd met a girl his age, and their fledging relationship gave the kid a new lease on life. If anyone deserved it, Justin did.

"So." Todd rested his folded hands on the table. "Sarah Jones."

I shook my head, made a clucking sound I hoped sounded sympathetic. "What exactly happened to her?"

"We'll get to that. First, tell me about your relationship with her."

"I worked as a receptionist at Exhale. I didn't know her much beyond that."

"I thought you were a private investigator. Gig not paying the bills?"

We'd come to the first crossroads. Lying has its time and place, but this might not be the place for it. If Todd thought he had the whole story, I'd have a better chance at not being considered a suspect. And I could use his help.

"Actually, I was undercover."

He cocked his head. "Really? At a spa?"

I nodded. "I had solid information children were being trafficked out of the salon."

His eyebrows shot up. First surprise and then agitation across his plain, pleasant face. "You do know we have a special victims unit that handles that sort of thing."

"I'm aware."

"Why didn't you alert them? Or me?"

I caught the brief wobble of disappointment. "Because I wanted to get as much information as possible before I reached out to the authorities."

"Your client?"

"No client. This was a personal job."

"You're the only private investigator I've encountered who just goes out and does a job for free." He jotted something down in his notepad.

"That's why I got the job at Exhale," I said. "It worked out perfectly."

"How long did you work there?"

"Six weeks."

"And did you find any evidence of this supposed sex trafficking?"

"Yes." I told Todd about seeing the kids arrive in the late hours, Sarah's depositing them at the motel, and my decision to go undercover. "Sarah had a cellphone hidden beneath the desk in her office," I said. "It had more security than the salon itself, but I managed to get some information."

Todd grabbed the file he'd been ignoring and flipped through its contents. "Yet there is no record of you turning said phone in to the police."

"That's because I gave it to Senator Coleman."

He looked like he'd swallowed a lemon. "Excuse me?"

"Senator Coleman is dedicated to stopping sex trafficking. I gave him several leads I'd gathered, as well as the phone. He's got better resources than I do."

"So do we. And you gave the phone to a third party when there's evidence of a crime. What the hell were you thinking?" His feelings were hurt, I realized. Hurt that I hadn't trusted him enough to call him. He'd given me a pass on the way I'd barged into Kailey's abduction. I guess he felt I owed him. I struggled to fuse that fact with his threat to investigate my involvement in the Harrison brothers' deaths. After all, he could arrest me for stealing the phone, and that would definitely mess up my plans.

"Don't take it personally," I finally said. "You're Major Crimes, first off. If I'd given the information to the police, mostly likely Vice would have taken first shot. I don't trust these kids to give up their pimps. I thought the senator would have a better method for handling it. And he's got the funds. Plus, I stole it. Not exactly the thing to admit to a cop."

"You've got a real problem with assuming the police are incapable. And that you're still in my good graces."

"It's not that at all." Todd's frustration with me right now wouldn't earn me any brownie points. "The police are over-loaded. And this is bigger than prostitution. Right up the senator's alley. I thought the task force was the better option for the kids. They've got to come first."

Todd traced the skin above his thin upper lip—a habit no doubt perfected with his mustache. "Coming from anyone but you, I'd call that a crock of crap. But you're twisted enough to think that's the right way to handle things. So I'll give you the benefit of the doubt and assume you believed you had the kids' best interests in mind. You know I can arrest you."

"I know. I'm just hoping my honesty will appeal to you. I'd just be more paperwork." Todd rolled his eyes, but I knew I was right. Every cop detested paperwork, and he was no exception. He didn't want to mess with arresting me for theft—not unless he had ironclad evidence on a bigger charge.

"The only reason I'm not charging you is because you're too good of a source if this trafficking thing turns out to be the real deal. And I can get the information from the senator. Petty theft isn't worth my time. But I can't make any promises the next time this happens." He tapped his pen on the table. "What information did you get off the phone?"

I'd come prepared. As long as I didn't give Todd Riley's name, he wouldn't be able to track the kid. And I needed an olive branch. "Unfortunately, not much. Sarah used a coding system in her calendar to indicate the kids' appointments." My mouth curled up in distaste. "She used the initials of both the client and the kid. The Rattner Hotel is a known meeting place. That's as far as I've got."

Todd scribbled the information down, barely acknowledging the phone. "I assume Senator Coleman knows you lifted the phone?"

I shrugged.

"I'm surprised he'd take it if it were stolen."

"You'd have to ask him about that. But given the information it had on it, Sarah's right to privacy was probably low on his list."

"Because you stole it," Todd said, "the phone is inadmissible in court. Not to mention any information gained from it. This situation seems very familiar."

Referring to me and Chris breaking into Mother Mary's house last fall and busting that case open—with information we couldn't exactly use. I ignored the bait. "The task force is still going to move more quickly to save kids and catch these people," I said. "They're dedicated."

Todd looked like he wanted to argue the point, but thought better of it. "I'll have to contact the senator's office about the phone. What did Sarah do when she discovered the phone was missing?"

"She confronted me."

"Is that when the two of you had your altercation?"

As expected, he'd already interviewed the other employees. "I wouldn't call it an altercation. We had some civilized words and then took the conversation into her office."

"What happened?"

"I told you once that I know how to manipulate people." My detachment surprised me. All my life, I'd fought against becoming my mother. But now I'd begun to embrace it without even realizing it. *But I use it for good*, I reminded myself. *I'm trying to help people.* "It was obvious Sarah was just a worker bee, and I wanted the top guy. So I conned her into thinking I'd help her blackmail him. We met up at Maisy's and discussed it."

Todd jammed his tongue into his cheek, obviously wanting to rail on me for my choice of action. I appreciated his thinking better of it. "Did Sarah admit her involvement in this alleged ring?"

"I got the distinct impression she didn't go into it willingly." I recounted my conversation with Sarah, including the information she'd given me about Preacher. "Honestly, I think there's more to her story with him. She might have been in financial trouble, but that didn't strike me as the reason she started working with him."

"So he's the link between her and the big boss of this trafficking ring?" Todd asked.

"According to her," I said. "He recruits the kids and the clients. Preacher was scheduled for a money drop the next day, and she agreed to approach him with me. I didn't expect her to go through with it. Anyway, he showed up and she didn't answer. Maybe she called Preacher and tried to play both ends, and it backfired on her."

Todd lazily tapped his fingers on the file. "Perhaps. But Sarah wasn't the victim of a hit."

I waited. As we talked, the heat had kicked on, bringing the smell of stale air into the room. The back of my throat itched. I cleared it and wished I had a glass of water. But I didn't want to look nervous.

"No signs of forced entry to the salon," Todd said. "And using your theory, I'd expect Sarah to have a single bullet wound to the head. Easy and out quickly. One second." He stood and crossed the room, popping his head out of the door to talk to someone. I cleared my throat again and hoped I didn't have to sneeze. A minute later he sat a bottle of water in front of me and then opened one for himself.

"The vents need cleaning," he said. "Every time the thing runs, I feel like I haven't had a drink all day."

I caved and eagerly took a long drink. "Why do you say Sarah wasn't the victim of a hit?"

"Because—going by what you've told me—this Preacher appears to be an enforcer type of guy. If Sarah broke the rules or threatened him, he's not going to waste time on her. He'd do the job and get out. That's a hit."

Chewing the inside of my cheek, I debated. Todd was a good enough cop to hang me with the right information, but I wanted to be cooperative. "Well, I showed up for the money drop yesterday, and I waited in the car, trying to decide if going in alone was the right idea. I wanted to check Preacher out for myself."

"What time was this?"

"Around 4:30. Traffic was thick."

"And?"

"Preacher sauntered to the door and expected it to be unlocked. It wasn't. He knocked for a while and then left pissed."

Todd rolled his eyes, already figuring out where this was going. "Where did you follow him?"

"The subway. He headed into North Philly. He was greeted by the same kid I intercepted at the Rattner. I also saw her working the street last month. No doubt in my mind he's her pimp."

Todd regarded me in silence, looking for telltale signs of dishonesty. Another reason to tell a version of the truth when it counts: much easier to get away with omitting information than completely altering it. He grunted and slid the file toward me. "Just for the record, I'm not playing the whole cop trick of looking for a reaction when you see the pictures. They're gruesome, but you can handle it. And showing them is the best way I can explain why she wasn't the victim of a hit."

I wanted to be repelled, to tear up and slam the folder shut. I pinched my inner thigh until tears welled in my eyes and then briefly closed them for good measure.

"Wow." I looked at the wall beyond Todd, counting to ten. Then I took a deep breath and grimaced as I looked back at the pictures.

Sarah had been beaten and stabbed. Most hits were made by some sort of long object and seemed to center on her once beautiful face.

I covered my mouth with my right hand.

"As you can see, whoever killed her was pissed. Hit her hard on the face and back of the head, enough to daze her but not to lose consciousness. She was alive when she was stabbed."

So she'd suffered, which likely meant her killer knew her. Preacher certainly knew Sarah, and if he thought she'd given him up, he might be capable. Still, the idea felt wrong. This looked more personal. But maybe their relationship was more complicated than I'd realized.

"I'm sorry to hear that," I said. "Hopefully there's some physical evidence."

"We're working on it," Todd said. "Lots of hair and various fibers, as you can imagine."

The air in the room changed. Not the air we breathed but the atmospheric energy that lingered around us, feeding off whatever emotions we emitted. The stuff that caused butterflies in the stomach and put the weight on our shoulders or made the hair on the back of our necks rise. I took another drink. "Tough to use hairs found at a salon."

His mouth twitched. "A long red hair was found near the body."

I glanced back at the pictures. Sarah lay prone less than a foot away from the receptionist's booth. Given the blood on the corner of the booth, the killer had probably slammed Sarah's head against it. "I imagine so. That was my workstation until a few days ago. I shed."

My explanation didn't seem to affect him. "We've got witnesses who claim to have seen you two arguing pretty heatedly at Maisy's. Sounds like things might have gotten a bit physical."

"Sarah grabbed hold of my arm during the argument," I said. "I told her to get her hands off me. That was the extent of it. Like I said, she agreed to stand up to Preacher with me."

"I see." He stared down at the file as if the grisly photos would start talking to him. "Coroner puts her time of death as early Friday morning. Where were you Thursday night and Friday morning?"

"At a friend's." Lie. This one so easily told it came out before I considered it.

"I need a name."

"Chris Hale." Stupid, stupid. Chris would back me up, but his high-rise in Center City had about a dozen security cameras. Todd would know I'd lied in a couple of days, if not earlier. Too late now. Chris and I would have to think of something better.

"Really?" The detective laughed. "Seems like you've used Chris as an alibi before. He wasn't your boyfriend then, either."

"He's not my boyfriend now." I didn't elaborate. Todd didn't press me.

"I'll have to confirm that with him."

"He's on shift right now." Chris was a paramedic with the Philadelphia Fire Department. If I got lucky, he would get my cellphone message before dispatch put Todd through to him. "Until midnight, I think."

"Good to know." Todd put his elbows on the table, letting his chin rest on his interlocked hands. He stared back at me the way a cat watches an intruding mouse, biding its time until the mouse got close enough. Then the cat would launch its attack.

"You know I think you've got a screwed-up sense of justice," Todd finally said. "And someone like Sarah is right up your alley."

I said nothing. Todd had gotten everything he would from me. He realized this and nodded. "I'll check into this Preacher, see if I can get some information from SVU or Vice. But in the meantime, I'm just going to be honest: you're on the suspect list."

"I'm sure you'll eliminate me quickly." I reached for my things, making sure to stuff the water bottle into my purse. "Did you need anything else?" Todd would put much effort into finding Preacher. He already believed—and rightly so—that I'd killed Brian and Cody Harrison for molesting kids. He'd love the chance to hang Sarah's murder on me. Then he'd be able to have the other murders reopened.

Todd shook his head. A lock of his hair brushed his eyebrows. He'd grown it longer, I finally noticed. I liked it. "I'll be in touch."

Forcing my mouth into my tightest smile, I nodded and then escaped the room. Head up and calm, I kept my pace even as I walked through the station. Cold night wind smacked my cheek until I fell into my car seat. One glance at the station told me Todd's department had a full view of the parking lot. My fingers itched to call Chris, but I waited until I merged into traffic.

His voicemail picked up immediately. "It's me," I said. "I just lied to Todd Beckett and told him I was at your place Thursday evening and all Friday morning. So yeah, call me."

My stomach growled. I hadn't gotten around to eating any of my mother's subpar dinner. But dinner would have to wait. I needed to find out what Kelly had on Preacher. Hopefully her kitchen was stocked.

TWELVE

Kelly had given me the code to her building a long time ago, but I still buzzed to let her know I was coming up. Although she'd made huge strides since I'd first met her as a badly abused child, Kelly still had serious social anxiety. Showing up and banging on her door felt like tormenting her.

She answered right away as always. "Please tell me you have an alibi for Sarah's murder."

I didn't answer right away. The pink streaks in her raven-colored hair distracted me. "Wow." Each streak was carefully blended into her natural color. "Did you do that yourself?"

Kelly beamed. "Nope. Went to the salon this morning."

"That's amazing." Kelly had been going out more and more on her own, but this venture was her biggest yet. "I'm so proud of you."

"Thanks." She blushed and looked down. "You like it?"

"I love it. It's a great look for a new beginning."

Her smile accentuated her delicate, birdlike features, making her even more beautiful. "If you're hungry, I've got some pizza left over. Help yourself."

I grabbed a slice of sausage and green olives and then

followed her into her work area. Two large monitors came to life, along with the quiet buzz of her computer. "First, what does Todd have on you?"

"Nothing." My voice sounded harsher than I intended. I took a deep breath. "Employees knew we argued. A red hair that's probably mine was found near the body, but that's a joke. My desk was right there, and he'll never get that to stand up in court. Someone at Maisy's saw us arguing. But"—my nervous stomach rolled—"as long as Chris cooperates, I've got an alibi."

Kelly twirled a pink-tipped lock of hair. "You think he'll lie for you?"

"I don't know."

"His building has cameras."

My shoulders lifted and then fell limply. "I'll think of something. And I didn't kill Sarah, so he's not going to pin it on me."

"The suspicion might be enough to get the Harrison brothers reopened."

"Let's worry about that if it happens." I pointed to her now glowing monitor. "What did you find out?"

She curled her legs beneath her in a way that looked miserable. "Since we really didn't want to call the number and ask for information, I had to go old school," Kelly said. "I searched the White Pages, and then two different search engines, and then an invisible web search. That's basically a search engine that goes a lot deeper. I also went on Facebook. The number doesn't come up in any public databases, which means it's a cellphone like we thought."

"How can you trace a mobile number back to its owner?"

"There's a reverse call lookup, but you've got to pay, and we don't want to put in any identifying information."

"What about cellphone pinging?" I asked. "You said you were going to look into that skip tracing company that helps private investigators ping."

"I didn't want to use it unless I had to," Kelly said. "Even if it's not illegal, it's unethical. You'd lose your license if you were caught."

"So would half the PIs operating in this country."

Kelly nodded. "Anyway, since it's winter, I decided to go with the weather alert. Remember how pinging works?"

I rubbed my temples. "You send out an alert to a mobile number. It pops up on the phone and continues to pop up. Then it asks the user if it wants to opt out of receiving alerts. When they do that, their location is sent to you."

"As long as the cell user has their location services turned on—which most people do so they can use GPS—then yes." Kelly made technology sound so simple. I wish I understood it half as well as she did. "It goes to the server owned by the skip tracing company and they'll process it for us."

"And they got a hit."

Kelly tapped her keyboard, bringing up a Google map. "You're going to love this. 2021 Lehigh Ave. In Strawberry Mansion."

"You're kidding me." I sagged down into the straight-backed chair. "Preacher is operating out of the most dangerous area of Philadelphia?"

"He's a sex trafficker," Kelly said. "Are you really surprised?"

"He's making some serious money," I said. "His clothes were nice. Expensive suit and shoes—business dress. Not the kind of thing you'd see in that area. I can't see him strutting around looking like that without getting his ass kicked at the very least."

"Maybe he changes before he gets home. His subway stop was away from Strawberry Mansion, right?"

"It was. But what's keeping him there?" I tapped my chin. The sociology of poverty-stricken areas is complicated. Preacher was likely loyal to some sort of family, perhaps supporting many family members with his earnings.

Kelly seemed to read my mind. "I know there's all sorts of murder and violence there, but it's sort of one side of the neighborhood against the other, isn't it? It's about being poor and drugs and vendettas."

I decided to address the elephant in the room. "Riley is white. But the latest research into human trafficking shows that forty percent of victims are African Americans. And black children make up fifty-five percent of the prostitution arrests in this country."

"So in an area like Strawberry Mansion where a lot of kids are unsupervised, Preacher's got options."

Adrenaline pumped through me. "You need to dig into the statistics in the area over the last few years. How many kids have been reported missing and not found?"

"How many do you think were actually reported?"

"Depends on why the kid went missing. If the mother didn't suspect anyone in the neighborhood, she'd call the police. You got any contacts at that precinct?"

Kelly worked as an independent contractor for the Philadelphia Police Department. "That's Central District, Precinct 22. I might know a woman in records, if she's still there. I can see what I can find out."

"Do that." I thought of Riley standing on the street corner on Kensington Avenue, recruiting. Had she been ordered to look for desperate young girls who needed a savior? She'd known exactly whom to choose. Kensington Avenue wasn't all that close to Strawberry Mansion. "My gut tells me Preacher isn't going to poop where he eats, but there might be kids in the area who've been propositioned who have some idea what's going on."

"And you think you're going to waltz in and chat with them?"

"Not by myself. First things first, I've got to find out if Preacher's in the area. Get a lay of the land."

"Chris is working, right? You'll have to wait."

I didn't to want to wait. The urge to act surrounded me. I wasn't good at sitting around and waiting. It wasn't powerful or in control. Waiting put me at someone else's mercy.

"Lucy, please." Kelly didn't waste much energy on her plea. She knew me too well. "I wish you had a firearm."

"I do," I said. "I just don't like carrying it around. Accidents happen." Not to mention, guns made it so easy to kill, and they were easier for the police to trace.

"I'll call Kenny," I finally decided. "He can't resist giving in to me."

THIRTEEN

I'm a brave woman. I've traipsed through some nasty areas of Philadelphia alone, my pepper spray and self-defense moves at the ready. But even I wasn't dumb enough to go into the Strawberry Mansion area of North Philadelphia alone. After some nagging, Kenny finally relented. Now we drove down Lehigh Avenue in his battered pickup, doors locked and our white skin making us stand out in a decidedly bad way.

Strawberry Mansion reminded me of the images of developing countries that charity organizations use for fundraising. Drugs and violence ran the neighborhood, and it was nothing to see someone scrounging through overflowing trash for their next fix or meal, or both. The sidewalks flowed with garbage no one seemed to care about.

"This all started in 2003 with the murder of a teenager," Kenny said as we eased down the street. "Since then, gunfighting has hurt a bunch of bystanders. Witnesses are too scared to come forward, and the streets just get more and more dangerous. The young men living out here are from a generation of anger, and they've just made things worse."

I peered out the window. A young black woman bolted inside her house. "But the drug situation here is very real."

"Sure it is," Kenny agreed. "But it's not making the money it used to. All the shootings have sent customers away and brought in the cops. And it's the same old story with an impoverished area: image is everything. These boys gotta earn their place and the respect of the alpha group to survive. So they're doing what it takes. And they tell themselves this stuff is more important than money."

We crawled past a crumbling brick row house. "Number 2021." The numerals were barely visible on the cracked glass above the door. "This is part of the Philadelphia Housing Authority."

Kenny snorted. "They're doing a great job with the place, aren't they?"

I shrugged. "There's only so much money allocated to them, and the housing authority does the best they can. It's the nature of poverty that really amazes me."

"I don't follow," Kenny said.

"Kids from areas like this try to get out, and their family or peers resent them." I'd witnessed the same scenario time after time during my years with CPS. It was one of many harsh realities I learned to face. "They'll call them out for leaving their people, for turning their back, that sort of thing. The support of your immediate circle—or the lack of it—is a powerful thing. Most of the time, the achiever will give up and go back to his roots."

"Exactly why things will never change." Kenny made a U-turn and headed back down Lehigh Street. "Why are we here again?"

"Because I'm investigating a man who goes by the name of Preacher. He's involved in child sex trafficking, and I think he's Riley's pimp. Kelly traced the number he gave me back to this place." I stared at the building's grimy windows. "I honestly thought it wouldn't have an address. But maybe Preacher isn't as smart as I gave him credit for."

"He might live with family," Kenny said, "and figured it was safe enough to use the number."

"Probably." I didn't add that Preacher had to be making enough money from trafficking to afford a better place than this. But for whatever reason, he'd chosen to remain.

"What exactly are you hoping to find out?"

"Preferably, his real name. But somehow I doubt you or I will get that information."

"I expect not. So what else? Please tell me you're not going to knock on doors."

"I'm not stupid enough to do anything besides drive around. I'm hoping to see Riley or another girl her age who looks like she doesn't belong. Or even better, Preacher himself. That will at least confirm Kelly's information." I glanced at Kenny, who looked nervous. We'd stopped at a red light where three young men had taken up residence. The tallest one had his back to us, and another young man hung over his shoulder. But the shorter man—or more correctly, barely legal teenager—watched us with narrowed, suspicious eyes. "Have you heard anything from your sources?"

Not taking his eyes off the men, Kenny hit the gas. "No. But I'm still waiting on a couple of people."

"Hopefully something pans out." We drove around the block to the back of the building. It looked even worse from this angle.

"I heard on the news the owner of Exhale salon was found dead yesterday. The woman you were after." Kenny's tone had changed. His voice was tight, as if something were caught in his throat.

"I heard that too. I wondered when she didn't show up for our meeting." I filled Kenny in on my plan to milk Sarah for information. "But she didn't answer the door for Preacher, and I didn't try to get into the salon."

"Jesus," he snapped. Evidently whatever worry he'd had about my involvement in Sarah's murder had eased. "What if you'd been there when the killer showed up?"

"Then it would have been two against one," I said. I didn't add that I would have been prepared. I'd have brought something a lot more threatening than cyanide. That thought gave me the perfect topic diversion. "I'm learning how to shoot."

Kenny twisted to stare at me. "As in, a gun? I figured you already knew."

"Why?"

His cheeks reddened. "Well, you know how to take care of yourself. And you aren't afraid of much. So I just figured..." His voice trailed off and he looked sheepish.

"I've shot my stepfather's SIG Sauer a few times," I conceded. "And it wasn't pretty."

"So what brought this decision on?"

"Chris thought it was a good idea, given some of my more dangerous jobs."

"Chris Hale?" Kenny's red face turned the color of storm clouds. "The one whose mother turned out to be the real killer of those girls, and who got her other son labeled a sex offender and stuck in prison for most of his childhood?"

"The very same."

He drove down the street. I wondered when he would find a place to park. Parking probably wasn't a good idea, but the locals were going to get sick of us driving around gawking at them like tourists. "I don't know about that guy."

"Seems like a hard decision since you've never met him."

"He comes from a really dark place, Goose."

"So do you. So do I. So what?"

"I don't like how he just popped up in your life all of a sudden."

I almost told Kenny that Chris didn't just pop up, that he'd been watching me for a while, but caught myself. Instead, I gave Kenny a wry smile. "Yeah. He's kind of a pain in the ass. But he's a good friend. He helped me find Kailey. Helped me out of trouble with the police too."

"I guess." Kenny looked like he wanted to say more. "I just don't know if he's the sort you want to get mixed up with."

Something like shame crept into my head. If only Kenny knew what sort I was and that I'd used his information to kill people. He'd be devastated. I'd like to think he'd understand in the end, but deep down, I wasn't sure. "He's all right, Kenny G. You don't need to worry about me."

He didn't laugh at my silly, singsong rhyme. "Lucy, I'm serious. Since you've met this guy, you've changed. You're darker somehow. More jaded. Taking more risks, like coming into Strawberry Mansion on a goose chase. The Lucy I know wouldn't have done that."

But I had. I'd done so many more things than Kenny realized. Chris's presence in my life had only brought my true self into focus.

"I'm sorry," I said. "I think the last few months, seeing what happened to Kailey Richardson and realizing how big the network of filth out there really is, has brought me down."

Kenny's hunched shoulders eased down. "Well, that's fair. But don't let the world hurt you. There's still plenty of good out there even if we don't always see it."

I smiled my first genuine smile of the day. This was why I loved being around Kenny. He was a warm, fuzzy beacon of hope. "You're right. I promise I'll do better."

We stopped again at the red light. The three men had gone from curious to agitated. The shortest one, wearing a black jacket and a crisp white cap with gleaming white sneakers to match, strode toward us.

"Shit," Kenny hissed.

I didn't respond. My gaze was locked on the tallest of the three men. Attention on his phone, head down and his cropped hair hidden by a red, wool cap, but it was definitely Preacher. Dressed to fit in with his boys, not stand out.

I shrank back in the seat. I doubted he'd recognized me, but I wasn't taking any chances.

"That's Preacher," I said. "This is definitely his area."

The shortest man had crossed the street and was only a few feet away from the truck. He spread his arms wide as if to challenge us.

Next to Preacher was a younger boy, perhaps around eighteen. Now that the alleged leader had moved, I could see the boy hovered close to Preacher, mirroring his every move. Another protégé, perhaps?

I didn't have time to ask. The leader was too close, and Kenny hit the gas.

FOURTEEN

I didn't hear from Chris until his shift ended and then only a simple text asking if he could stop by. By that time my nerves were frayed, and I'd nearly worn a path across my hardwood floors. My fat tabby cat, Mousecop, watched from his perch in the windowsill. Although Chris had dropped me off numerous times over the past few months, he had never been inside my apartment. My place in Northern Liberties wasn't a dump, but it was lived in. The furniture, comfortable and generic, was unlike Chris's fancy place in Center City. I reminded myself it didn't matter. Chris had a trust fund to supplement his paramedic salary, and my chosen field wasn't exactly full of wealth. Material things weren't important to me, but the part of my brain that could never completely shed my mother's judgment fussed about my plain and embarrassing decor.

The buzzer announced his arrival; I let him in the building and answered the door on the first knock. I don't really know what I expected. Chris was normally dressed to the nines, wearing designer coats and jeans and sweaters. Appearance was important to him, most likely because he had so many self-esteem issues. After all, some part of him believed he was destined to be a sociopath. Looking good established another layer to hide behind.

But tonight Chris still wore his navy paramedic uniform, including a heavy fleece coat with the Philadelphia Fire Department's logo. His short blond hair was mussed, his cheeks pink from the cold. A Band-Aid covered his left middle finger. He'd just come off a twelve-hour shift, and heavy shadows ringed his normally bright eyes. My insides warmed at the sight of him until I saw the expression on his face. Beyond the exhaustion was barely concealed anger.

"Come in." I stood aside. He walked past me, bringing his usual scent of musky cologne. Something deep inside me stirred. I squashed the sensation. "I take it you got my message."

Still glaring at me, he stood in the middle of my living room and unzipped his department-issued jacket. Mousecop jumped down from the window, stretched, and then strolled over to sniff Chris's black boots. The cat's mouth hung open for a moment before he hissed and stalked off, tail in the air.

"Weird," I said. "He likes most people. Then again, I don't get a lot of visitors."

"I was inside a nasty house a couple of hours ago." Chris finally spoke. "God knows what's on my boots."

I hugged my chest. Feeling foolish and strangely intimidated, I hung back near the door and hoped he'd talk first.

Chris raised an eyebrow. "Really?"

I sighed. "All right, so you're pissed off at me for using you for an alibi. Sorry about that."

He gritted his teeth. "You also forgot my building has cameras. It won't take Todd Beckett long to realize your lie. Backing you up means I lie to the police too. That could cost me my job."

My shoulders drooped. I shuffled to the nearest chair and plopped down. "You're right. I realized my mistake as soon as I said it, but I couldn't take it back."

"That's unlike you."

"I know." I still had no idea why I'd been so stupid. *That's how good criminals get caught.* A shudder rippled down to my toes. Considering myself a criminal was new. In the eyes of the law, I was no doubt worthy of the death penalty. But my victims —if you could call them that—were the worst of the scum. Ask any average Joe on the street about killing child molesters, and he'd likely give me a pat on the back.

"I shouldn't have put you in that position," I said. "I can't blame you for telling Todd the truth."

Chris's sharp expression finally softened. "I never said I did."

Our eyes met, his full of blue and warmth and loyalty, and mine feeling strangely leaky. I actually moved to cross the room to throw my arms around him but stopped myself. "You lied for me?"

He nodded. "But we're on borrowed time until the security footage comes back. So we're going to have to figure out something."

"What are you thinking?"

Chris took off his jacket and folded it nicely across the end of my couch. His Philadelphia EMS shirt clung to his shoulder blades as he stretched. He quietly made his way into the kitchen, trailing his fingertips across the countertops. "Got anything to eat?" He opened the fridge as if he'd been in my apartment a hundred times before. As if he belonged.

Fuzziness spread through my already foggy brain. I connected with very few people. My sister, Kelly, Kenny. And now Chris, in a way I'd not thought possible. He was the only person on this earth who came close to knowing my true darkness. Even more frightening was that he stayed around in spite of it. "There's leftover sausage casserole. Put it in the microwave for a couple of minutes."

We sat in silence as the gentle whirring of the microwave

filled the air. I couldn't stop staring at Chris. His shoulders were broader than I realized. His hair darker in the back, almost brown. A small scratch peeked out from the collar of his shirt. Self-inflicted or left by a female conquest? My cheeks heated up just as he turned around, stuffing a forkful of steaming pasta in his mouth.

"What?" He spoke around the food.

I shook my head. "Nothing."

He sat down on a barstool and once again gazed around my small apartment. "I like your place. It's very homey."

I laughed. "Is that rich-people code for 'cheap'?"

"Not at all. It's a compliment. My place is sterile, and I don't have a clue how to fix it."

"Try color."

He smirked. "Good guess. And don't think I'm not still pissed off at you."

"I know. I shouldn't have used you as—"

"It's not that." He savored another bite. "This is really good. Did you make it?"

"Yep. Cooking is one of my little-known talents."

"I'll remember that." He licked the fork, finished his pasta and then washed the bowl out in the sink. He didn't speak again until he sat down on the couch and fixed his perceptive eyes on me. I hated the way he seemed to see through every protective layer I possessed. Resting his chin on his hand, he yawned. "So what are we going to do about this alibi thing?"

"I'm not sure what to do. Were you home that night and the next morning?"

He closed his eyes. "I didn't work that night. I went out with some guys from the department and then to my aunt and uncle's." An impish smile spread across his face. "Actually, I fell asleep there and didn't come home until around eight the next morning."

My heart leapt. "So... you won't be on the security tape?"

"Not until after the time frame Todd gave you."

"What did you tell him, then?"

"He asked if you were at my place. I said no, we'd gone out to dinner at Chatzky's, a restaurant by my aunt and uncle's. Then we went to their place and wound up too drunk to drive home. We crashed there, and then I took you home that morning. Dropped you off at 7:30." He leaned back, spreading his arms over the back of the couch.

My hopes crumbled. "Your uncle is the freaking ADA. He isn't going to lie."

"That's the beauty. They weren't home. I had to go over to feed the dog. But their security system logs will show that I used the code to enter the house and then reset the alarm several hours later. No camera set up. But as long as you were home and not seen anywhere else, they can't prove otherwise."

"What if they ask around the department?"

He shrugged. "I doubt Beckett will specifically ask about my going out with the guys that night. It's not something I do very often. They'll tell him I'm a good worker, never miss a shift. All around good guy." He wrapped his hands around the back of his head. "And one or two will probably tuck their heads, mumble and hem haw around, until they say it's amazing how adjusted I am, considering where I *came from*." His eyes dimmed into a hazy gleam. "If they only knew."

The hairs on the back of my neck rose as chills washed over me. "The papers pretty much covered most of it, didn't they?"

Chris's arm wobbled, making his head sway to the side. He sat up. "Most of what's common knowledge, yeah."

"Did you remember something else?"

"No." Chris rubbed the scruff on his face and stared blankly past me. I'd gotten used to this habit over the last few months. As if some kind of veil descended over him, Chris's attention slipped away from the present. I imagined his locked memories bludgeoning his head in their attempt to escape. He blinked and focused on me. "But there are things you don't know about me, Lucy."

"There's plenty you don't know about me too."

"Possibly. But this is"—he blew out a nervous breath— "worse than you might imagine."

"So why are you telling me?" Part of me wasn't comfortable with Chris's sudden need to share. It strengthened our bond, and I didn't like that.

"First call of my shift was to a house in Chestnut Hill. Nicest ten-year-old on the block had beaten the shit out of the neighbor boy. Guess the neighbor kid was a bully and had it coming, but this ten-year-old took it too far. He broke the kid's jaw."

If he expected me to be surprised, he'd be sorely disappointed. "Kids of all social status have anger issues. And often the middle and upper class are all kinds of screwed-up. Skeletons in those walk-in closets."

He leaned forward, elbows on his knees and hands clasped so tightly his knuckles were white. "Believe me, I know. This boy has one of my favorite diagnoses: ADHD. Everywhere you look doctors are slapping on that label and drugging up kids." He paused, looking straight at me. The air suddenly swelled with tension. Claustrophobia nagged at me. "He doesn't have an uncle who's an assistant district attorney to get him out of trouble."

Realization sank in. I was about to hear something very bad, and I couldn't say no. "What did you do?"

"I was about eight," Chris said. "No one in the area knew who I was—my uncle kept it secret. But this kid at school—his dad was a social worker—was an eavesdropper. He confronted me in front of all the other kids, and I lost it." Chris picked at his cuticles. "It was like a movie scene. Me and Kyle in a circle. He kept calling my dad a murderer, my mom a bad mother. I just started beating on him."

I wanted to close my eyes, but I kept contact. "How bad was it?"

"I broke his nose and gave him two black eyes. Broke his ribs, and he ended up with a punctured lung. Kid almost died because of me." He wiped moisture from his forehead. "He was in the hospital a long time. And my uncle made it all go away. We moved to another part of town and started over. And I got counseling."

"Did it help?"

He nodded. "Yeah. I was so afraid I'd end up like my dad." He laughed bitterly. "Turns out I should have been worried about dear old Mom."

"You didn't know." I repeated the same words I'd be saying for weeks. "I know it doesn't make you feel any better, but you were just a kid who'd been through a lot. We know now, and we *will* find her."

"I know." He relaxed into the couch. "Seeing those kids tonight was like being back in that schoolyard. And I just needed to tell you about it." Uncharacteristic pink dotted his cheekbones.

"I'm glad you did." I felt hot all over, down to the roots of my hair.

"So I'm not so innocent after all," he said.

"Believe me, I never thought you were." I attempted a grin, and he laughed.

"You know me better than I thought." He stretched out his legs. "So when Todd presses you on the alibi, we've got our story. Hopefully it sticks. In the meantime—Sarah. What's the story?"

I told Chris about my conversation with Todd. "Until I saw the crime-scene photos, my first instinct was Preacher. But this was an up close and personal killing. I'm not sure Preacher would be that involved."

"Unless he had something on the side with her. And when

she told him about you, he felt betrayed and lost it." Chris played with a loose string on the hem of his shirt. "He's a pimp, after all. I'm sure he gets violent. How bad were the pictures?"

"Bad. Blood everywhere. She was stabbed."

Wincing, Chris shuddered. "I don't know what kind of monster can kill a person like that. It's too..."

"Personal," I finished. I certainly couldn't do it. The act of slicing through skin and muscle to reach a vital organ was callous. Cold. Brutal. I couldn't allow myself to go there.

"What about Preacher?" he asked. "All you've got on him is that you followed him into North Philly. That's a big area."

It was my turn to grin. "Kelly got a lead, and Kenny and I followed it today. Preacher hangs out in Strawberry Mansion."

He jerked to a sitting position. "You went to the ghetto with only the wonderful Kenny G for protection?"

"You've never met Kenny. How do you know he's not good protection?"

"Because all you talk about is how fun and happy Kenny is. What is it you call him? Your light in the dark?" He rolled his eyes. "Not exactly a bodyguard."

"We were surrounded by people." I shrugged, pretending I hadn't been every bit as scared as Kenny. "Nothing was going to happen. He knows the streets."

Chris scowled. "I'm sure. Once again, I can't believe you'd be so stupid. And so much for Kenny having a brain in his head."

"Enough," I snapped. "You can insult me all you want. Leave Kenny out of it."

The sheer coldness in his glare caused a rash of gooseflesh on my arms. "So you know Preacher's home base is in the worst area of Philadelphia," he said. "But Sarah's dead, and she was your best shot at bringing this ring down. Isn't it time to move on?"

"Are you kidding me?" I nearly slid out of the chair. "I've

got a lead to Preacher. He's the one who can get us closer to the big boss. That's who we need to find."

Chris's head jerked back and forth. "You understand you're walking into something bigger than you imagined, right? Preacher and his boss and who knows who else are willing to kill to keep their secret."

"I don't care. I've got to make someone pay for this." I couldn't take the words back. After witnessing Brian Harrison dying at my own hands, I thought I'd never take another life. But the knowledge of children being trafficked for sex right under my own nose brought out the vengeance monster. And how many other kids had been forced to pose naked for the camera just like Aron?

Chris regarded me in silence. Sometimes his face was so easy to read. Other times, like now, he wore a silent mask. I could continue my investigation without him, but I didn't want to.

He sighed. "I wish I could make you forget that video."

"Aron wasn't the only one we saw." A lump swelled in my throat, followed by the crest of guilt. "He was the only one I could get to."

Chris reached for my hand. I stilled at his touch, unsure of how to react. "I'm sorry you can't let this go, but I don't think you should keep looking into Preacher. I'm afraid you're going to get hurt."

"I promise I'll be careful."

"Right." He released my hand and relaxed back into the couch again. He didn't believe me any more than I believed myself. "So what's your next move?"

"I need to talk with Preacher about his offer of employment."

FIFTEEN

I lied to Chris. Being careful hadn't helped me track these guys down, and I wasn't about to start now.

I left a message for Preacher, and Chris thought I was still waiting for his call back. He'd find out the truth eventually, and he'd be upset, and I'd apologize. Then we'd dance again. Sometimes I wondered if I lied to play the game—to see what the consequences would be. There's no fun if I can't stay one step ahead and in control.

Shaking in the dark cold, I pulled my scarf tighter around my face and stuffed my hands in my pockets in an effort not to scratch my head. The blond wig and glasses were back, and I stood in front of Ward 8, an honest-to-goodness speakeasy in West Philadelphia. Preacher insisted on buying me dinner, and this place was his suggestion, instantly putting the owners of Ward 8 on my radar.

Decidedly plain, the only sign of popularity surrounding the old, brick building was the line waiting outside of it. I checked my watch. Preacher was unsurprisingly late. A show of authority to which I'd have to make sure I deferred.

A yellow cab stopped. Preacher exited, clad in the same

trench coat. His dress shoes tonight looked to be name brand, and the suit pants peeking out from beneath the coat were high-quality fabric. He smiled in greeting, and I saw a flash of the boy he still was.

Intellectually, I knew my reaction should be fear. Or at least caution. But my breathing increased as if I were on the tread-mill. I suddenly tasted the basil and oregano smell of authentic Italian wafting from Ward 8. Preacher's trench coat almost glowed against the snow. I steadied myself against the adren-aline, channeling it into the part it was time to play. Twirling a lock of my wig, I shyly smiled back. Preacher approached with confidence, jerking his head at the doorman.

"It'll be just a minute, sir." The doorman spoke directly to Preacher. "It's good to see you again."

"Thank you." Preacher stood at my elbow. "You look very nice, Lily. That blue scarf is pretty with your skin."

The shock of being addressed as my sister was brief and I mentally composed myself quickly. "Thank you." I flitted my eyes at him. "You too."

He seemed to enjoy my apparent shyness. "I bet you didn't even know this place was here." He spoke slowly, making sure his words were polished and without any trace of today's youth.

"I didn't." I played up my shock and his ego. "It must take connections to get a reservation."

Preacher adjusted his purple tie. "It does."

The doorman motioned for us to follow him. Preacher took my elbow and led me through the door. A hostess wearing an emerald flapper dress with intricate beadwork observed us with what I assumed was faux suspicion. The mix of beads and sequins were a darker green, and they glittered in the soft light. A layer of fringe outlined her collarbone, and I wanted to reach out and touch the material to see if it was as silky as it looked. Her wide, black headband matched her dark, bobbed hair, and she'd mastered the art of smoky eyes, with black eyeliner setting off the bright blue. "Do you have a password?"

"White horse," Preacher said. I raised my eyebrows. She nodded, and another staff member dressed in plus fours and a matching vest with a tie led us through a corridor with only vintage gas lamps. The narrow, dark corridor made me feel trapped, and I wished Preacher hadn't pretended to be a gentleman and ushered me in front of him. I focused instead on the slim shoulders of the host as we descended down a felt wall-paper-covered stairwell. We emerged into a tiny, dimly lit bar with mostly full tables. The staff was dressed in 1920s-era clothing, the women's sequins and beads shining, with the men wearing suspenders and newsboy hats. A gilded chandelier hovered over red leather booths, a golden arch proudly showed off the bar, and the entire room was bathed in vintage wallpaper that was loud enough to warrant an aspirin.

We sat down in a booth, the leather pliable and warm. A candle burned in the center of the table, the candlelight making Preacher resemble a hungry jackal as he watched me take off my coat. To play the part of poor working girl, I'd worn a nice, fitted blue dress that wasn't especially expensive but still looked good.

"Order whatever you like," Preacher said as I sat down. "It's all on me."

My wig tickled. I ignored it and smiled. "I suppose it's all a tax write-off for you."

He burst into a deep chortling, covering his mouth and glancing through the restaurant as if he and the walls shared a private joke. "Sure is."

I imagined what it would be like to stab him in the eye with my fork and then focused on the menu. "Do you recommend anything?"

"The filet mignon is excellent," he said.

"And really expensive." I played with the thin gold chain

around my neck, the only jewelry I'd worn tonight.

"Don't worry about it." He folded his menu and leaned across the table. "You look like you could use a good meal, anyway."

This time, my flush was natural. After hearing my mother hint I'd been gaining weight, Preacher's compliment, whether sincere or not, felt good. We ordered steaks and salads, and I made a show of being afraid to drink wine but finally agreeing to a nice red. After our Jay Gatsby-styled waiter left our wine, I took a careful sip.

The red slid down like velvet, warming my stomach. Instead of praising the taste, I wrinkled my nose and shuddered. "Strong. I'm not used to that."

"It's an acquired taste." Preacher's grin widened. He clearly enjoyed showing this older, culturally challenged woman a fancy time. Like most, his transparency made him easier to manipulate.

I adjusted my awkward glasses, put my elbow on the table, and then giggled before removing it. "Oops. I'm not used to eating in places like this, either."

"No worries." Preacher laid a long arm across the back of the leather. The speakeasy's dim lighting hit his face at just the right angle, exposing the youth in his brown skin. His hazel eyes were very enticing. It was easy to imagine him as the gallant knight saving the mistreated and vulnerable girl from the street and then methodically warping her brain until she belonged to him.

"So, tell me more about this new position that might be opening up."

"Hold on." He raised his hand, needing to direct the conversation just as I'd expected. "I want to hear about you first. It's Lily Smith, right?"

Kelly chose one of the most generic surnames in the country for a reason. It made creating a scant identity much easier.

According to public record, Lily Smith resided with Mr. and Mrs. Warren Smith of Kensington. I'd chosen another lower-income area of the city, but far enough away Preacher shouldn't know any middle-aged, blue-collar workers. The cheap prepaid phone I'd purchased yesterday was easily explained: I was too damned poor to afford a smartphone, and I didn't want to borrow from Mom and Dad. Living with them was enough.

"Well..." I fidgeted with the napkin before laying it across my lap as Preacher had done. "I live in Kensington with my parents. But you knew that."

"Right. How old are you?"

He was the only man who'd had the guts to ask me that in recent years, and I nearly laughed. "Twenty-five," I said, thankful for being blessed with good skin.

"Where'd you go to high school?" The shift in his tone was slight, but I caught it easily.

"Home schooled." I looked down at my lap and then peeked back up at him. "Paranoid parents."

Resting his chin on his hands, he nodded. A cagey smile played on his lips. "Guess that means you didn't get out much?"

"Nope. After high school, I went to Ohio to stay with my aunt and uncle. I thought the change of pace would be good, but they lived on a farm, and I hated it. Nothing but animals and Amish."

Preacher laughed. "So you came back to Mom and Dad?"

"After a couple of years, yeah. Started dating a guy, but it didn't work out."

He ran a manicured fingernail across his bottom lip, looking even more like the starving jackal. "How serious were you?"

"Well..." I chewed the inside of my cheek and thought of one of my more embarrassing moments, hoping for a natural blush. "I thought we would get married. I mean, he was... my parents are religious... so..."

To his credit, Preacher played it mostly cool. Just the quick lick of his lips gave him away. "So you and him—he the only one?"

I knitted my eyebrows together. "Are you asking what I think you're asking?"

"Well now"—he made a dissatisfied face—"if you can't talk about this, I'm not sure you're right for the job."

Sliding forward in the booth, I put both elbows on the table. "I really need to get out of my parents' house. They're suffocating me."

"Maybe they just care about you," he said. "You shouldn't take that for granted."

I continued to pout. "They care too much. I'm twenty-five years old, and I've only dated one guy. We broke up because I was too timid." I brushed some wig wisps off my cheeks. Hoping the emotion carried through, I started waving my hands as I spoke. "I just feel... caged, you know? Like I've got this pressure building, and if I don't change something, I'm going to snap. I need to do something different. Something no one will expect."

He didn't respond right away. Hands hiding his face, he stared over his knuckles with curious eyes. I broke eye contact first and looked away. "Sorry. I didn't mean to get all crazy. I've just been feeling especially trapped lately."

"I get that." He continued to size me up. My need to control a situation surged through me. I forced it back with a painful swallow of velvety wine and made a show of studying the busboy cleaning up a nearby table. His slicked-back hair and thin suspenders over a crisp white shirt perfectly fit with Ward 8's theme. He caught me staring and winked and then gave a nod of recognition to Preacher.

"You must come here often," I said. "If the busboy knows you. He looks like a baby."

"He's old enough," Preacher said. "He does good work."

The dual meaning in his tone slithered through me. I

committed the busboy's face to memory before turning my attention back to Preacher. "Good. Seems like kids his age don't want to work very hard."

"Oh, he works," Preacher said. "Always willing to do what it takes."

His knowing grin, meant as his own private joke, made my stomach sick. Just in time for our steaks to arrive. I took another large gulp of wine to calm myself. "This looks delicious."

"Eat up. We'll talk business after the meal."

The steak was tender and the salad divine, but I barely made it through without running for the bathroom. The act was taking a toll. The bloody juice oozing from Preacher's barely cooked steak and the innocent face of the busboy battled for attention until they bled together, making me half dizzy. I pushed my unfinished salad aside. "I'm so full."

Preacher slowly chewed the final bite of his rare steak. He dabbed his mouth with his napkin and then set it aside and motioned for the waiter to refill our wine glasses.

"I hope you enjoyed it," Preacher said as the server left.

"Absolutely. Thank you."

I shifted in my seat, hoping he'd take the hint that Lily was anxious. I also needed some fresh air.

"On to business." Preacher's soft voice strengthened with authority. "I have an established network of gentlemen looking for quality female companionship. And right now I'm looking for quality females to fill that need."

Quality females. As if our gender were no better than produce at the market. Keeping my expression neutral was excruciating. "Exactly what kind of companionship?"

"Whatever the client needs. These are professionals looking for a distraction—a release—from high-pressure lives. Some may just want good conversation. Others may expect more. Our ladies will need to be willing to comply."

His word choice sent another wave of fury through me. I

inhaled slowly. "Well, what if one man wants to talk and the other wants"—I rubbed the side of my neck—"more? Do they pay the same rate?"

"I like the way you think. Yes, they do. That way if they change their minds during the course of the meeting, the fee is covered."

"And what if the lady isn't comfortable with certain requests?"

Preacher shrugged. "She's always able to say no. But unsatisfied clients would likely result in no more bookings."

He spoke so smoothly, without any struggle for the right words. I wondered how many times he'd had this conversation, or if he changed it when he convinced young kids to allow men to violate them for a fee.

I chewed on my lip. "How would I get paid?"

"The clients pay our fee directly, through a private online system. They'll pay you in cash. We set the fee."

Of course they did. "What if they don't pay or try to cheat me?"

"Then you let me know immediately, and I'll handle it. We're running a fair trade."

"Women who do this sort of thing sometimes get physically hurt." As if he cared. His concern would be limited to the quality of the merchandise. Men looking for high-end call girls didn't appreciate bruised-up women.

"It's a risk, but I don't believe it's a very large one. My boss has many connections and screens the clients himself." He preened, stretching his arm over the back of the booth.

Now we were getting somewhere. If I could just get a first name, it would be a start. "It's not your company? What sort of connections could ensure my—the ladies'—safety?"

"I'm essentially the operations manager," Preacher said. "As for connections, I can't say. Just know that he has them. And we've got a good track record."

Good track record meaning you have your street prostitutes and trafficked kids under control, and now you're confident in branching out to a more socially acceptable form of prostitution.

I cocked my head to the side. "But I thought you were just now expanding into this form of human relations?" I forced a giggle at the pathetic innuendo.

Preacher didn't laugh. Instead his expression turned stony. "You'll have to trust me. Either you want to get out of your parents' house and make some real money, or you don't."

It was evident he wasn't used to answering a lot of questions. If he was telling the truth and actually looking for higher-end girls, he'd have to show a lot more patience than he did with his street girls.

Lifting the glass of wine to my mouth, I twitched my fingers, making the liquid slosh against the glass. "Exactly how much money?"

"For you? As a beginner-in-training? Eight hundred dollars an hour. You'll get more as you gain repeat clients."

I widened my eyes until they hurt. "That's a lot of money."

His snake-charmer smile might have scared another woman, but its appearance had the effect of tossing fuel on a burning fire. I counted to three before voicing my next question.

"How does your boss find the clients?"

"I'm not allowed to answer that. Just know they are rich men with no violence in their pasts."

I twirled my fake hair again. So not regular street johns. Preacher and his boy were going after a fresh market. "Okay, I know I'm pushing, but this is all so new to me. How are you paid? Like, would you be considered a"—I glanced around and lowered my voice—"a pimp?"

His upper lip curled, and he sat back with a sharp huff. "That's really offensive, girl." His silky-smooth veneer slipped on the last word. "You think I beat my women and keep them on dope and barely give them enough of a cut to eat? 'Cause that's what a pimp is. You think that because I'm black?"

"Oh no, no." I started waving my hands again. "I just thought that's what the men who found the clients were called. I didn't know!"

"Well." He adjusted the lapels of his shiny suit jacket. "You did grow up sheltered." The polished Preacher had returned, and I had little doubt he believed the lies he spewed. He'd convinced himself he was different than the rest of his kind so he didn't have to face the consequences of a shattered conscience.

Just like me.

My confidence faltered; I felt my expression sink to my shoulders. Preacher rattled on.

"So now you know. Pimps are pigs. I'm not forcing anyone to do anything, and I want the girls to be paid a fair wage. So we're all happy. No drugs involved." He scowled again. "Anyone on drugs is out, period."

Mind spinning, I nearly forgot I was playing a part. I stared at Preacher, trying to figure out what he wanted to hear. The trucker's face snapped into my memory, his froggish voice pleading for mercy. My reasoning why he didn't deserve it, why I was justified. What was his name? Had I already forgotten?

"Don't freak out now." Preacher peered across the table at me. "You look like you're about to faint. I'm just saying, I don't like to be called a pimp."

A pimp. That's what we were talking about. Somehow I sucked myself out of the void I'd been swinging over. "I'm really sorry. I didn't mean to offend you."

"Apology accepted." Another wide smile revealed nicely capped teeth. "You've got an innocent thing going on. I like that. And so will my clients."

Still foggy, I pretended to think about it. Preacher waited patiently, arrogant grin firmly in place. He liked being in this position, I realized. When Kenny and I saw him on the street in Strawberry Hill, he was clearly a follower, just a link in the chain of command. Now he was the boss, for all intents and purposes. The only person he answered to was an unknown phantom. Maybe Preacher was the real boss.

My mind reeled. I needed fresh air and the privacy of my apartment to digest everything I'd learned.

And to get away from Preacher and every fragment of myself I saw in him.

But first things first. I'd finish this job. "So what do I need to do to get started? Do you have a client in mind already?"

He licked his lips again, loosened his tie. Leaned toward me. The jackal again. "Well, first, to be blunt, you have to pass inspection. I need to make sure you're really the right fit. Like a trial run."

Sweat trickled down my spine. "What sort of trial run?"

"With me, of course."

"I... what? How do I know you're not just trying to hook up with me?"

"Because..." His voice dropped, and his eyes were hooded. "I could do that without offering to pay you, now couldn't I?"

Revulsion consumed me. Then rage. Preacher continued to leer, and I had to admit, if I didn't know what he was and I was really as naïve as the Lily I claimed to be, I would have been flattered. And maybe suckered right in. *That's who I have to be right now.* "Yes," I whispered.

"Good." His smugness made me want to slap him. "You can take a few days to think about it. If you decide you want to go through with it, call me. I'll tell you where to meet."

"And that's it? I'll be hired?"

"As long as you don't freak out or change your mind during the act. See, I can't have you doing that with a client. That's why it's better to go a round with me first." Another piggish grin, tongue stroking his lips. "And I promise you'll enjoy it."

I looked down to keep from launching myself across the table at him. "All right. Give me a few days."

It was time to go. To think. Decompress and figure out exactly where to take this. Take a shower.

Preacher caught my mood. "I'll head to the bar and pay the bill. Then you can get out of here."

I nodded. "I'm just going to use the restroom."

My knees were weak as I weaved through the tables, my palms and back sweaty. I'd almost made it to the ladies' room when I ran straight into a solid mass. Startled, I stumbled back and found myself eye to eye with the busboy. "Sorry. I need to watch where I'm going."

"It's okay." The boy shrugged. "I do it all the time."

I laughed, feeling marginally like myself again. And this was serendipitous timing. "Can I ask you a question?"

"Sure."

"Well, this is going to sound strange, but when you were clearing tables back there, it seemed like you knew Ryan."

The boy stiffened, stepping back. "From the restaurant."

His defensive tone was answer enough.

"Okay. I just, this is our first date, and I'm not quite sure what to think of him. I thought you might have some insight." I rolled my eyes. "Stupid, I know, asking a kid for dating advice."

Another bristle. "I'm sixteen."

"Oh gosh. I'm sorry. I keep putting my foot in my mouth. Of course you're not a kid. It's just I'm older and should have some kind of radar for this sort of thing, and I'm just hopeless." I slumped against the wall, peering up at him through my glasses.

The busboy finally smiled. "It's okay. Ryan's not bad. He's honest, even if it's something you don't want to hear. That's got to count for something, right?"

I perked up. "Yes, it really does. Does he come in much?"

"He has business meetings here," the boy said. He flushed

and looked away. "Is that all? I'm working a private party in the back room."

I widened my eyes. "A private party? Must be someone really special."

He rubbed the back of his neck, shrugging his shoulders. "Senator Coleman. He always requests me."

I worked to keep my expression neutral even as my insides twisted into a burning knot of energy. "The senator, really? What's he like?"

"Like any other person with power." The boy shrugged. "But he leaves good tips."

"Does he come here a lot?" Did the senator know about Preacher, or was it just a coincidence?

"Why do you care?"

"Because he's a senator, and he's all over TV with his task-force stuff." I pushed out a fake laugh. "Guess I'm a little starstruck."

He snorted and then leaned in closer. "Don't be. Senator Coleman's no different from any politician. Two-faced. You just gotta know which one you're dealing with."

My instincts flared. "What do you mean?"

His gaze flashed over my shoulder, and he stepped quickly away. "I've got to get back to work."

"You have to give me your name, at least." I stuck out my hand. "I'm Lily."

He regarded my hand like I'd offered him poison. Before he could shake it, a hand closed over my shoulder. "His name's Eric." Preacher's voice trembled with the authority he'd hinted at earlier. "And I'm sure he needs to get back to work. I know the senator doesn't like to be kept waiting."

Eric nodded and then hurried down the hallway, disappearing into a side door.

"You ask a lot of questions." Preacher's fingertips pressed into my shoulder. I gently ducked away from him.

"I slammed into the poor kid and nearly knocked him down," I said. "Figured the least I could do was flirt a little. Did you see him blush?"

Preacher seemed to consider this, staring at me with hardened eyes. I flashed him my sweetest smile. "Are you going to tell me your real name now?"

"Preacher's all you need to know."

"Come on." I tapped my finger on the knot in his tie and licked my lips. "At least tell me how you got the nickname."

"Next time," he said. "If you decide to accept my offer, I'll tell you everything you need to know."

He wasn't going to give me any more information, and my nerves were frayed to the point of disintegration. If I had to flirt with this piece of trash any more, I'd end up stabbing him with a steak knife. Or something sharper if I could get my hands on it.

Preacher motioned for me to lead the way, and I followed him through the darkened restaurant and into the even darker and frigid night. For the first time all winter, I welcomed the cold blast of air.

He zipped up his jacket, giving me a final once-over. "I'll be waiting for your call." He strutted away, hailing a cab at the end of the block.

Rooted to the spot, I watched the cherry taillights until they blended into rushing traffic. My head spun, and I inhaled the winter air until my lungs burned. It blew away the confusion and reprimed my senses. I was me again. Back to the agenda, leave the rest behind.

The senator's presence wasn't altogether shocking. It stood to reason he'd know about a place like this. Were they both frequent customers? I couldn't imagine the senator coming into contact with Preacher unless the younger man's involvement in the speakeasy was more than as just a patron.

More pieces to a very complicated jigsaw. The question was, how far would I have to go to fit them all together?

SIXTEEN

My body trembled with every pull of the trigger. Empty cartridges littered the floor around me. Sheer power rippled through my body. Envisioning the blue and white target as a living, breathing monster—the devil who'd ruined my sister and made her take her own life—helped ensure most of my shots landed center mass.

Gold cartridges littered the cement floor around me. I reached for more bullets, but I'd already gone through the pack in less than twenty minutes.

"You out already?" Chris stepped out from the next partition. His safety goggles had a singe mark from a stray brass. "Want to buy another box?"

I rolled my neck and shoulders back, realizing how much tension had mounted since I'd started target practice, the opposite of the way it was supposed to work. I shook my head, putting my gun back in its safety box. "I'll wait for you outside."

I hadn't reached the door of the shooting range before he caught up with me. "I'm good for today. You want to get some lunch?"

He held the door open, and we went back out into the gallery, returning our rented guns and earmuffs. I'd called Chris this morning because I thought going to the range would eliminate some of the stress last night caused, but I felt no better. Without the gun in my hands, I felt as confused and powerless as ever.

The cloud of apprehension and dishonesty hovering over me didn't help matters. I'd have to tell Chris everything sooner rather than later.

"No," I finally answered. I struggled with my coat, and Chris helped slip the bulky wool over my shoulders. Still holding on to the collar, he held my gaze until I felt bare and had to look away.

"You going to tell me what's wrong? Did you hear any more from Todd?"

"No. I just ... I need to tell you something."

My confession came out in a carefully practiced rush: why I'd chosen to go alone, how safe I was, Preacher's offer, and finally what I'd found out. "I should have told you, I know. But, he called, and it was a last-minute thing." I couldn't tell the entire truth. He'd be disappointed in me, probably hurt. I didn't want to see that. "So please don't be too mad. Or be mad, but can you just wait a few minutes so I can talk about everything else?"

Chris's unmoving gaze heated my skin. It was as if I were suddenly back in the girls' locker room after gym, forced to strip and shower with the other girls who didn't seem to mind being naked. Fixating on how my breasts didn't look as nice as theirs, how my thighs were more round than the cheerleaders'. I always hunched my shoulders forward, as if that somehow protected them from seeing me.

I was doing the same thing now. I pushed them back.

"Are you going to have sex with Preacher?" He was suddenly a blustering storm cloud, the big, black kind that sweep in out of nowhere and lie in wait until the perfect moment to unleash torrential energy.

Feeling wobbly on my feet, I tried to gather myself. Consumed with everything else that happened last night, Preacher's "test run" was the last thing on my mind. "I hadn't really thought about it."

"You can't do that." He continued to stare at me as though he could somehow project his fierce will into my consciousness. I pictured it wrapping around the synapses of my brain and embedding itself into my cellular makeup.

Shivering, I wrapped my hands around my chest. "Why? I've done worse."

"No," he said. "You haven't. Lowering yourself to that level for information, that would be the absolute worst thing you could do to yourself."

I didn't know what to say. So I kept quiet and waited for his lecture. When it didn't come, I finally cleared my throat. "I'm not sure what you want to hear from me."

He kept staring, almost blankly, as if he'd stepped out of himself and his body was just a shell. Just as startling, he suddenly snapped back to himself. "I want to hear you say you won't have sex with Preacher."

"Fine, I won't." I didn't plan to. But if it came down to being the only way to get information, I'd be forced to reconsider it. But saying that aloud to Chris was not a smart idea. Or a necessity.

He shook his head. "How am I supposed to believe you? You lied to me once. You said you wouldn't meet with Preacher alone."

"That wasn't a lie. I told you, it happened quickly. I couldn't risk turning him down."

"You didn't want me there." He raised an eyebrow, his glare hollow and cold, daring me to challenge him.

I felt meek—my own out-of-body experience. "No, I didn't. It was too risky."

"Right."

We stood at a standoff, invading each other's personal space as only the most intimate of partners do.

I stepped back. "I can take care of myself. See you around." Slinging my bag over my shoulder, I rushed into the blistering cold before he could stop me. Icy air stole my breath, and I blinked at the crushing wind. Chris had just enough time to catch up to me and block my path.

"How can you even consider this?"

I blinked against the bitter air. "I can handle it."

"You think so. But once he's got you alone, who knows what will happen? How far you'll allow yourself to go to get what you want?"

I brushed past him in search of my car. "That's none of your business."

"You're my business." He grabbed my arm, his strength throwing me off guard. "I'm your alibi, remember? Willing to lie for you. That makes you indebted to me."

I yanked my arm away. "Which I intend on paying back as soon as I take care of this problem."

"What? This trafficking thing? You think you're going to bring that down?" He was on the verge of laughter. I wanted to dig my nails into his cheek.

"Kelly's doing her best, digging around in the online depths. She'll find something that points to this operation eventually. But until then, I've got Sarah's death and Preacher to deal with. I'll find out who's in charge. Maybe Riley and some of those kids will have a way out."

"Sure. As if it will all work out happily ever after."

"What are you saying?"

"I'm saying that this isn't just a few people, Lucy. This is a network that's bigger than you, and you're never going to find them all. Banging some worker bee for information isn't the answer."

My teeth were clenched against cold and rage. "Good thing that's not for you to decide." I turned again to walk away.

"You can't keep doing this." Chris kept the pace. I wished he would slip on the ice-covered parking lot. My eyes teared from the wind. Where the hell was my car?

"You're running in circles with this, and you know it."

"We've had this discussion."

"And we're having it again."

I stopped again, searching. Finally I spotted the Prius in the opposite direction. I turned on my heel and started marching forward.

"Look, I appreciate your concern. But I don't need you to be my moral center, okay?"

He held up his hands in a sign of defeat. "Fine. It's all about what you need, anyway. So what it is you want from me? What am I supposed to tell you?"

"I wanted to know what you thought of the information I had," I said. "About the senator being at Ward 8 and the busboy knowing both him and Preacher. I think I'm missing something, and it can't be just the senator's involvement."

"Why not?" he asked. "People lead double lives all the time. Look at you. You lie to friends and enemies alike."

His guilt trip crawled onto my skin like a filthy mite and made a nest. I didn't have time for that sort of thing. *Guilt is for the weak.* "That's not fair."

"Probably not, but I'm not taking it back. Not right now."

"Whatever." I unlocked my car, fumbling with the ignition. I'd figure things out on my own. Easier than being held accountable to someone for my every thought and decision.

Chris rapped his knuckles on my window. I shook my head. He rapped again.

"Asshole." I dug my fingertip into the button to roll the window down. "What?"

"You want to know what I think?" he asked.

I shrugged. Damned if I'd admit that his opinion mattered now.

"I think there are no coincidences, and you need to walk away from this before it gets a lot worse."

If I were an alcoholic, I'd head for the bar right now. Shame coated my skin; resentment filled my head. I needed Chris in my life. And yet sometimes I wished he'd never approached me. No matter what he'd said earlier, his allegiance was unconditional. The thought warmed me, yet also brought a needling despair. With Kelly safely hidden behind her computer, I never answered to anyone. Now I'd somehow put myself in the position of both needing Chris's help and having to ask for his moral permission. As if I needed his consent. I didn't want to operate that way, but the fault was my own. Using him as my alibi had been selfish and stupid. But he'd come through as I knew he would, moral baggage and all. But did that give him the right to be the voice of my conscience?

My hand cramped from shooting. I eased my grip on the steering wheel and took the exit to Northern Liberties. Sleep was what I needed. My brain could reset and approach the problem rationally. I'd find a solution, just as I always did.

SEVENTEEN

Parking in Northern Liberties was brutal in the winter, and my cheeks were chapped and frozen by the time I reached the door to my building. Inside the lobby, trying to shake off the cold and fatigue, I didn't see Detective Todd Beckett until he stepped out from behind the row of mailboxes.

"Nastiest day yet."

I stumbled back into the wall. "Good God. You nearly gave me a heart attack."

"Sorry about that. It's too cold to wait outside. I needed to speak with you in person."

Suspicion roiled through me. "About what?"

He didn't waste time. Our relationship had long progressed past the bullshitting stage. "Several green fibers were found with Sarah's body. Our lab believes them to be cashmere."

An icy sensation spiderwebbed down my back as Todd continued. "Witnesses at Exhale and at Maisy's stated you were wearing a green dress, and more than one believed it to be cashmere. The girl at Exhale specifically remembered it because you normally dressed very... drab. That was the word she used."

So my vanity had royally screwed me over. "All right."

"So I need the dress. For fiber analysis." He showed me the signed warrant.

"You know we interacted, and her body was found near my desk. The fibers being a match aren't a stretch."

Todd fluffed his hair, the roots damp. "But these were found mixed in with her blood. Unless they migrated from her dress to the gaping wound in the back of the head, it doesn't look good for you."

Confusion and panic mixed together for a heady cocktail. I hadn't killed Sarah. The green fibers might not match. But what if they did? It was enough to arrest me, maybe even take me to trial. Circumstantial evidence had done plenty of people in.

Images of my apartment made me dizzy. Everything was hidden. They'd never find my stash of poison and other supplies. My head cleared. "Let me see it, please."

I read the orders carefully. "You're allowed to recover the dress only."

"Of course. What else would I look for?"

I said nothing. I didn't need to. The implication hung between us, impairing my ability to think straight. Todd finally jerked a nod. "I'll follow you."

The air inside the elevator steamed with tension. My chest felt as if it would crack from the imaginary weight bearing down on it. "There's more to this."

Todd leaned against the opposite wall of the elevator. "Excuse me?"

"Something you're not telling me."

He smiled grimly. "There's lots I don't tell you."

"I'm talking about Sarah's murder. Downstairs, when you said your boss wanted it solved yesterday, you weren't looking me in the eyes. You always look me in the eyes."

He sighed, leaning toward me, his fingers outstretched. I froze as he moved a lock of hair off my face. "You give me too much credit."

Neither one of us spoke again until we reached my door.

"It's not the cleanest." I turned the key, hoping my hand wasn't shaking. "I left in a hurry this morning."

Todd slipped on a pair of blue, latex gloves. "I'm not inspecting your hygiene. By the way, the senator was happy to hand over the phone you stole from Sarah once he found out it was part of a murder investigation. He also gave me a copy of all the legwork you've done. Interesting. You really believe she was involved."

I refused to play his game. "I'll just get the dress. It's in the laundry."

"Perfect."

"I'm sorry to say, it doesn't have any blood stains." I headed for the bedroom, thinking about the compartment in my bedroom closet. My neck muscles felt tight as rope, my insides a maze of painful knots. The compartment was in the closet, behind a shoe rack, and barely visible even to me. Todd wouldn't see it. He had no right to search as long as I gave him the dress. Everything would be fine.

Mousecop started up from the bed when Todd entered the room. He ambled to the corner and eyed the detective with suspicion. At least someone was on my side.

"Fat cat," Todd said.

"He's healthy." I moved to the bathroom, but Todd caught my arm.

"I'd like to get it myself."

My jaw tightened. I pointed to the door. "It's in the wicker hamper. Halfway down. Please keep your hands off my delicates."

He had the decency to look embarrassed.

My mind wandered to every criminal case I'd ever read. Most of the prolific ones who believed they were smarter than the police were all caught by silly mistakes or blind luck.

Would my story end with blind luck?

Not that I was like any of those criminals. I didn't stalk the innocent. My killing had a purpose. I made society safer. And I certainly wasn't drawn in by the thrill of the hunt. No, it was a duty. A necessary evil.

I grew short of breath. My legs jerked with the urge to defend myself. I sat down on the bed, refusing to look at the bathroom.

"How's Justin?" I had to say something, distract myself somehow. "Still seeing that girl?"

A muffled shuffling came from behind the bathroom door. "Fine. And yes, as far as I know. What about you?"

"What?"

"You and Chris? Since you were with him the night Sarah Jones was murdered."

I blew out a hard breath, trying to think of the right response. All I could see was my little storage cache. Insulin and cyanide and needles and the ketamine I'd bought just a few weeks ago. Todd was too close. "I don't discuss my personal life with someone trying to pin a murder on me."

"That's not what I'm doing," Todd called back. "I'm trying to solve a murder."

"You might want to look in the right place, then."

His footsteps made my heart pound. Why was he walking so fast?

He reappeared with the wrinkled dress in an evidence bag. I wanted to remind him how much it cost, but I refrained.

"Get everything you needed?"

"I think so." He made a show of sealing the bag, his gaze flickering to the bed and then back to me, sitting rigid. Pink dotted his cheeks.

And then I knew. Knew how to regain control, how to bring him over to my side. It was as easy as doing what came naturally.

I made myself relax, leaning back on my hands. My hair

dangled toward the mattress, a wispy lock grazing my jaw. "Do you really believe I killed Sarah Jones?"

His Adam's apple bobbed. Shifting his weight from foot to foot, he looked steadily out the window. "I think you had a motive."

"Please, enlighten me."

"You believed she was trafficking kids. Then she allegedly admitted it to you, makes a deal." He played with the corner of the bag. "You show up, and she's been lying. Maybe she's going to take care of you herself. Then it was self-defense."

I shook my head. "Then wouldn't there be blood on the dress?"

"Maybe it's on your coat."

"But you don't have a warrant for that." I smiled, cocking my head and twisting so that my V-neck collar inched toward my cleavage. "Of course, it's the same one I was wearing earlier. And no, it hasn't been dry cleaned."

Uncertainty flashed across his face. We both knew the fibers, no matter where they were located, weren't enough. "Why didn't you tell me you were researching more cases than just Sarah's?" He changed the subject.

"You didn't ask. I told you everything I knew about Sarah Jones. And what have you done with it?" With my secrets safe, my anger mounted. This is why I no longer believe in the system: Todd refused to listen, focusing on what society deemed the more important issue. "You know, with everything your brother went through at the hands of Mother Mary, I expected you to be more compassionate toward these kids."

His nostrils flared, his thin upper lip nearly disappearing. "Do not question my devotion to this city. I handed all of your information to the Special Victims Unit, which is what you should have done instead of taking it to the senator. You chose him because of some kind of agenda."

"You're right. He's got the power to get things done. You

guys have to work around red tape and make sure you give these monsters their due process."

"I don't like the way our legal system works, either. But I'm a documenter of facts—that's my job. To find out the truth and then give it to the district attorney's office. I can't control what they do with it, and believe me, sometimes that's a hard pill to swallow. But we're all bound to obey the law. Even you."

I slid off the bed, my shoes clacking against the wood floors. We faced off, Todd looking ready to run. I stepped closer. He tensed. The knowledge of the power I held over him spurred me on.

"I know you're doing your job." I lowered my voice. "And I don't make it easy. But I've been honest with you."

"You haven't given me the kid's name, the one you intercepted. I can't confirm any part of your story without it. It's all hearsay against a dead woman."

"You have the phone now."

He flushed deep red. "It's useless. Some kind of protection program had been installed. Whoever the senator had working on it screwed up, and the entire thing erased its data. We're trying to recover something off the SIM card, but it's a fifty-fifty shot."

Screwed up? Coleman had assured me he had some of the best technical people around. How could they screw up something so basic?

Todd looked down at his feet. His loafers were scuffed, and the brown leather looked worn thin. It's a wonder he didn't fall on the ice. "Tell me the kid's name. Give me something to work with."

"How is that going to help? I only have a first name, and I don't know where to find her."

"Maybe I can. If you're right, and Sarah was killed because of this sex trade thing, this kid might know something. Something that could get you off the hook." He failed to hide the pleading note in his voice.

"I thought you wanted to bring me down, Detective Beckett."

"I want to find out the truth. I want to be *trusted* with the truth."

But you're an honorable man. A good cop. Even if you believed I'd done the right thing in killing the Harrisons and all the others, you'd still have to follow the law. You couldn't live with yourself if you didn't.

Still, Todd was right. Withholding Riley's name meant I could be setting myself up for big trouble. But betraying her meant risking the chance at earning her trust.

Self-preservation, my dead sister's voice whispered in my head.

This would be on my terms. Stepping closely enough to Todd so that our personal spaces disappeared, I gazed up at him with wide and hopefully frightened eyes. "Promise me you won't arrest her. Think about Justin and what a wrongful arrest did to him."

The emotional impact was obvious. Todd sucked in a breath and briefly closed his eyes. He bore the same guilt over his younger brother as I did.

"I promise."

"Her name is Riley, and she lives somewhere in North Philly. This guy Preacher seems to oversee them all, and I'm pretty sure he lives a double life."

Just like me.

"What do you mean?"

I told Todd about Strawberry Mansion.

"Jesus," he snapped. "You shouldn't have gone there."

"I'm trying to find answers. Sometimes that means big risks."

He shook his head, half reaching for me, then fisted his hand and shoved it into his pocket. "Thanks for trusting me."

"Don't make me regret it."

"I'll do my best." He started for the door, pausing to lean against the frame. "Listen, it's not just me, all right? Exhale had a lot of powerful clients, and they're upset. Which means they're leaning on the boss. Get it?"

My smile was brittle. I'd known Todd was omitting something crucial downstairs. "Of course. And that, Detective, is our justice system in a nutshell." I debated and then figured throwing more chips on the table couldn't hurt me. "Sarah told me a lot of her salon clients were indirectly involved in the sex trade. She uses the salon to essentially launder the money. And half of these guys send their wives to the salon to help it look legitimate."

With his back to me, all I saw was the rigid set of his shoulders. "Got it."

I locked the door behind him. Now that the threat was over, necessity fueled my thoughts. I needed to get to Riley before Todd did and warn her about him. And what the hell did the senator's people do to the phone? Even worse, did he know Preacher as it had seemed last night? Had I sent Sarah into a trap?

The only way to find out was to ask Senator Coleman himself.

EIGHTEEN

About thirty minutes away from the city, the town of King of Prussia was close enough for the politicians to still call themselves Philadelphians but far enough away from the grit and grime to live the quiet life. The drive gave me time to get my raging thoughts straight and form a plan. I needed to stay on the senator's good side if I wanted his help. Going at him with anger and threats wasn't the right approach. He'd want his power to be validated, respected. Sugar gets a person a lot more than spice.

His office was on the second floor. The elevator ride seemed suspended in time, mocking me. Finally, the gray doors opened with a ding, and I stepped into the senator's lobby.

"Ms. Kendall."

Seconds passed before I remembered the aide's name. I gave him the smile I knew men loved. "Jake. How are you?"

He ran his hand through his hair, his embarrassed gaze flickering to his desk and back to me. "You remembered my name."

"Of course. Why wouldn't I?"

"A lot of people don't," he said. "Aides come and go. There are so many of us, we blend into the scenery."

Another bright smile and a lean on the side of his desk. "Sometimes that's a good thing."

He looked as nervous as an alley cat. "So, uh, how can I help you, Ms. Kendall?"

"Please, call me Lucy. Is the senator in?"

Jake's cherub lips hinted at a frown. "Well, yes, but you don't have an appointment."

"I know." I leaned forward as though we shared a secret, letting my hair fall around my shoulders. Jake blushed. "But he and I are working on something very important, and it's vital I speak to him in person."

Jake glanced at his boss's closed door. "I can ask if he'll see you."

"Please."

He picked up the phone, still blushing to the roots of his hair. "Yes, sir. Lucy Kendall is here. Do you have time to speak with her?"

I leaned closely again, resting my hands on the desk. My hair brushed against Jake. Even his arms turned scarlet. "You were? All right. I'll send her in."

He hung up the phone, smiling weakly. Poor kid probably spent his life feeling invisible. "He's been expecting you. Go on in."

The door closed behind me with a loud click. Senator Coleman remained seated behind his impeccable desk. We eyed each other, the silence brewing tension until my chest felt like bursting.

"What happened to the phone?" My calm tone did nothing to ease the intensity steaming the room.

Senator Coleman sighed, reaching for a large, stainless-steel coffee mug. Circles smudged the skin beneath his eyes. "Good question. Have a seat."

I wanted to remain standing, but doing so was a direct challenge that would force this man to look up to me as we spoke, a position he wouldn't like.

I sat.

"I sent the phone to a former forensic computer specialist. He still consults for the state police, so he's up on the latest technology." Coleman took a drink of coffee and then glanced around the room. "I'm sorry, I haven't offered you any. Would you like Jake to get you some coffee? It's strong."

"No thank you. The phone?"

"Yes," he said. "I don't understand all the technical details, but evidently a program was set to wipe the phone clean after too many login attempts. He was going to try to recover data from the SIM card, but then I received the phone call from Detective Beckett. I handed the phone over to them."

I tried not to let my anger bleed into my words. "I knew about the program, and we were able to get around that. I would think any computer specialist would be able to as well."

The senator's smile was wry. "You'd think so. At any rate, I did tell the detective you'd been to see me. Of course I couldn't withhold any information from him."

"I wouldn't expect you to. But because the phone is now worthless, I had to give him the name of the girl I intercepted at the Rattner. Without the phone, my story looks like bunk. But I really need to get to the girl first. I don't want her to think I sold her out, and I'd like to prepare her for Detective Beckett."

I hoped staying on the senator's good side was worth the risk of sharing information. It was my best chance at getting inside information from his task force.

"Her name is Riley, correct?"

My mind turned into a white sheet.

"Don't worry, I'm not following you." His attempt at humor fell flat. "My task force received a tip about underage prostitution at the Rattner Hotel, and one of the members was following up when he saw you speaking with the girl. He caught her first name and gathered she was part of a larger group. He also heard you give her your name. That's the reason I took your original meeting."

"You told me you weren't looking into prostitution." Now the idea of Senator Coleman and Preacher choosing Ward 8 as a favorite place seemed even less coincidental. He'd known about me in advance. What else did he know?

"We're not. But like you, the informant thought there was more going on. You know how it works—a lot of these girls think they're in love with this guy, he's all wonderful. And then he either manipulates or forces them into sex for money, and after that he's got them where he wants them. And the legal line between prostitution and trafficking can be pretty gray. But my guy's been canvassing the area around the Rattner, and he's got some leads."

"Why didn't you give Riley's name to Detective Beckett?"

Coleman tapped his fingers on the steel mug. "I felt our task force could handle things better. You know the situation is delicate with these girls. Depending on the Vice officer, at the very least, a threat of arrest will be made. She probably won't give up the pimp, and going to jail won't help her." His oily smile returned.

"That's why I need to find her before Detective Beckett does. He's a good guy, and he'll try to do right by her, but it will only make the situation worse."

"That's why I planned on contacting you," Coleman said. "We've got a lead on where she's at, and I think you can help us get close to her. The police might push her farther away, and that's the last thing we want. This ring, however big it is, needs to be handled with absolute care."

I suddenly had the very unsettling feeling of pulling the string of Pandora's box. "Why are you suddenly convinced this is actual trafficking and not prostitution? You said it can be a gray area when it comes to the law. Something changed, and I'd really like to know what. If we're going to be working together, I think I deserve access to all your information." The hypocrisy of my request almost made me smile.

Coleman seemed to be deciding how much he wanted to share. "A tip came in. I was just informed about it yesterday, but a couple of days before you came to see me, a young boy no older than thirteen was seen arguing with Sarah Jones and an unidentified black male behind Exhale salon. It was past midnight, the boy seemed very scared, and kept saying he wanted to go home. He was ushered into an SUV with the man and left. Sarah went back inside."

My heart hammered against my ribs. "Why didn't the person call the police? Why didn't you?"

"At first the tipster thought she was making a big deal out of nothing. But when she couldn't let it go, she decided to call us. She's had some sour dealings with the police and decided the task force's tip line was the better option."

I didn't know if I was mad or understanding. As many issues as I had with our legal system, I knew most cops did their best to do the right thing. But their hands were just as tied by the system as everyone else's.

"The bottom line is that my task force and its officers have more outreach and more power than the police do," Coleman continued, echoing my own excuses to Todd. Hearing them from him sounded far less convincing. "The FBI is slammed with more kinds of trafficking cases than they can count. The best thing for Riley and any other children involved is for my people to find them. Bring whoever is behind this to public justice."

Bells clanged in my head. "You want the glory. This is a multi-state thing, probably the biggest uncovered yet. And you want to be the one who brings them down."

He shrugged. "Wouldn't you? And it's an election year."

No matter the good intentions, men like Coleman were politicians through and through. Not to mention his presence at the speakeasy and the ridiculous incident with the phone. I didn't know if Senator Coleman was involved with the ring or operating with an agenda I'd yet to uncover, but I knew he wasn't a man I could trust. "What about justice for Sarah?"

"I've given the police everything pertinent to Sarah's involvement, including your notes. And now they have Riley's name." A clang of disappointment in his voice.

"I had no choice now that your people screwed up the phone."

"I've been told you have a rock-solid alibi."

"You checked my alibi when you heard I was a suspect."

"I like to my sure my associates have clean records."

I let the information sink in. Exhale had a lot of powerful clients, one of which was clearly leaning on the Philadelphia Police Department. Senator Coleman's name never appeared in the appointment book, but what about his wife? She was a highly successful commercial real estate broker, operating under her own name. I just couldn't remember what it was. I'd have to get Kelly on it, but I doubted she could get into Exhale's system now.

Good thing I still have a copy of the key to the back door. I turned my attention back to the senator.

"Fine. But I need to find Riley and fast. Can you help me?"

Ten minutes later, I walked out of Coleman's office in a daze. The informant—a man the senator assured me was a highly experienced member of his task force—would call me soon. Together we'd approach Riley. Apparently the informant hadn't been able to get close to Riley, but he and the senator believed that with my help, they could.

"Are you all right?" Jake asked shyly. He reminded me of

the geeky kid with the heart of gold who was always picked last for gym class.

"Yes," I managed. "Just processing some information."

Jake laughed. "Senator Coleman's good that way. He likes to spring things on you. Like being thrown in with the wolves."

I tried to smile at the cliché, but it felt wrong. "That's about how I feel." I pushed the button for the elevator and willed it to hurry. I couldn't make idle conversation.

My feet couldn't move fast enough when it finally arrived. "Take care, Jake."

"You too, Lucy." He stood up from his desk, his expression tight with worry. "Remember the wolf likes to hide in sheep's clothing."

As the elevator doors clanged shut, I acknowledged the shiver trickling down my spine, filing Jake's words into my growing concern about the senator's motives. I'd waded far too deeply into the web of suspicion to change course now.

NINETEEN

I brought my gun to meet the informant. Senator Coleman had assured me this man, John, was a retired law enforcement officer who knew his way around the streets and was very observant and careful. None of those things made me feel any better about sitting in a car for hours with a cop.

John looked the part too. He didn't give me his last name, his expression was permanently grim, and the stress creases in his forehead looked like craters. He kept the heater on and his knit cap pulled low over his ears, his coat zipped. Ready to jump out at a moment's notice.

After nearly an hour of silence with the exception of the occasional idle bit of chit-chat, I was still trying to figure out who I was more leery of: the senator with his agenda, the surly investigator sitting beside me, or Todd Beckett and whoever was breathing down his neck.

"So you saw the exchange with Riley and the client at the hotel?" I broke the silence before my head burst.

John gave me a cursory glance. "Yep."

"Why didn't you say anything?"

He expanded to an incredulous stare. "Really? Aren't you a PI?"

"Right." Even my neck flamed. "You didn't want them to see you."

"Smart girl."

Boiling with embarrassment, I tried again. "But Riley left when my friend showed up. Surely by then you knew I was on your side."

"I never count on anyone being on my side."

"Nice attitude to have."

"Keeps me alive."

I rested my head against the back of the seat and tightly crossed my arms, jamming my fists under my armpits. "Were you an undercover officer, then?"

He jerked a nod. "During the nineties, yeah. Vice and Narcotics."

"Police don't rely on undercovers as much anymore," I said. "Too expensive."

"Informants are better. A rat is a rat is a rat." This time he attempted a grin.

"After years of being on the good guys' side, you don't mind trolling with the rats?"

"Not if it's for a good cause."

We fell silent once more. I watched the street hoping for a sign of Riley. Parked in a strategic lot that gave us a nice view of both sides of the street, we were just a few blocks down from the Rattner and a two-minute walk to the subway station where she'd met up with Preacher. John had spent days following first Preacher's and then Riley's movements, resulting in our supposed prime position.

"So how did you guys find out about Preacher?" I asked the question that had bothered me since meeting with the senator. I had no intention of telling either man about my private conversation with Preacher or my invitation for a call-girl tryout. The senator informed me they believed him to be close to the head of the organization, and I admitted Sarah had told me as much. But that's where I left it.

"We got a lead on him a while ago."

He'd bite off his own tongue before he'd reveal his source, so I tried a different track. "What exactly do you know about the guy?"

John's mouth twitched, his eyes shooting to my side of the car before focusing back on the street. "His real name is Roderick Reed. Lives in a shitty place in Strawberry Mansion with his mother and another woman believed to be his sister. No priors, which is shocking. Attended CCP for a semester and then dropped out and came back to the ghetto."

"Roderick, huh? No wonder he goes by Preacher." Community College of Philadelphia had multiple locations and tuition was relatively affordable, but I wasn't surprised Preacher had gone back into the Strawberry Mansion fold. It's hard to escape when family is left behind. "Any idea where the nickname came from?"

"Nope. Probably gave it to himself for some asshole reason." John leaned forward and peered at the busy sidewalk. "That's one of the kids I see with Riley a lot. He's older and got a real attitude problem. The one in the blue cap."

Immediately I spotted the boy in the blue cap. "I saw him with Preacher in Strawberry Mansion," I blurted out.

"What were you doing in Strawberry Mansion?"

My turn to smile. "I've got my sources too. He and Preacher and another kid were hanging out on a corner. Preacher wasn't dressed in his business suit and tie. He was dressed like this kid, and he wasn't the leader. The short kid was."

"Interesting."

"You have any idea who this boy is?" I asked as blue cap passed us.

"No details. But I'm guessing he's a PIT."

"A what?"

"Pimp in training."

Two lives. Preacher was lower on the totem pole in his neighborhood, likely dragged back by family pressure or duties. He hadn't been able to rise to a leadership position with the boys he likely grew up with, so instead he took one with the man selling kids for sex. Instead of being another wannabe tough guy waiting on a rap sheet, Preacher was a bona fide businessman in a four-hundred-dollar suit and all the power he'd been denied by his socioeconomic group.

Two lives, two different roles. One very good actor. A spark of admiration dredged its way up for Preacher. *He knows how to play the game.*

"When I first talked to the senator, he didn't seem as interested in what was going on at Exhale because it looked more like clear-cut prostitution. What changed?"

John pushed his hat back, revealing a large forehead and thinned hair. "Your intel was good. Matched up with a couple of other tips I'd received but hadn't been able to act on."

"So what's your take on this operation?"

"Hard to say. Some of these kids, like this Riley, are probably runaways from bad lives. Preacher does what every pimp does: makes himself the hero and latches on to her. Maybe she says no to selling herself for sex, maybe not. But"—he glanced at me—"after the tip about the young boy behind Exhale, it's looking like a lot more than local prostitutes."

"As if that's a minor thing we should all ignore."

"I know it sounds shitty," John said. "But we have to pick our battles, and after decades of watching these girls go back to their pimps no matter what I say or what a counselor tries to tell them, no matter what kind of shelter or safety we offer them, you get pretty jaded."

I craned my neck to see the boy disappear around the corner. "Where do they live?"

"Isn't that the big question?" John said. "I'd hope they were all together in some sort of subsidized place or maybe a hotel, but that doesn't appear to be the case. I think they're carefully parsed out. Finding a nest is looking like a small miracle."

"A nest? You sound like they're parasites." The term was better suited for the pedophiles paying to have sex with them.

"Bad word choice. But it sure would make the job easier."

"How do you raid without going through the proper legal channels?"

This time his smile was full, revealing dimples that took ten years off his age. "Come on now. If we had the time, sure, we'd go through the system. But it moves slow and these people are paranoid. Preacher or one of his lieutenants get a whiff we're coming, they're gone."

"His lieutenants?"

"Like I said. The older boys."

My fake laugh made my throat sting. "What does that make Preacher? The admiral?"

"That's navy," he said. "Preacher's the captain. His boss is the general."

"You were army?" I knew the answer already, but asking made the conversation keep flowing.

"That's right. Served in Desert Storm."

I thought about all the images of the Iraqi wars we'd been bombarded with over the past decades. "Which is worse? Being a Philadelphia cop or war?"

"Being a cop is war."

I saw Riley before John did. She came from the same direction as blue cap kid, her chin tucked against her chest and her hands jammed in her pockets. She wore the same faded knit hat, and wisps of her dark hair fluttered in the freezing wind. A young, dark-skinned boy walked with her, clutching her hand. Every limb tensed. Was the boy a victim too?

"There." I pointed.

"You're up," John said. "If she runs, don't follow her too far. I can't give my position away to cover you."

"Right." I stepped out into the frigid air. At least the wind had slowed down today. But the still, cold air embedded its way through clothes within seconds. Even my eyelashes were cold.

Dodging equally freezing passersby, I stepped into Riley's path. "Hi, Riley. Do you remember me?"

She stopped as if someone had yanked her from behind. Her wool hat was worn through in places and her coat much too thin. Surely she made enough money to buy something warmer at the Salvation Army. Riley took a step back. The boy mirrored her stance. On closer inspection, he was even younger than I thought, perhaps eight. He didn't have anything on his head in this miserable weather. Riley glared at me. "What do you want?"

"Just to talk to you." I cocked my head toward the end of the block. "There's a tiny coffee shop. Let me buy you something hot to eat."

Riley glanced around, eyes wide and face chapped with cold. "You trying to set me up with the cops?"

"Absolutely not."

The little boy stared up at her with wide brown eyes. With his long lashes and plump lips, he was too pretty to be a boy. My heart ached at the idea of the life he might be leading.

"I'm babysitting," Riley said. "He's too little to be hearing this."

"That's no problem. This place is kid-friendly. He can hang out in the little toy area while we talk."

"How am I supposed to trust you?"

I took a chance. "Because I knew Sarah too. And I'd like to find out who killed her."

. . .

Riley didn't tell me the boy's name. After making sure he was settled with some worn plastic toys and dog-eared books at the shop's kid zone, she sat across from me, suspicion rolling off her.

"What do you want to eat?"

She shrugged. I ordered us both black coffees and warm, gooey banana nut muffins, plus one for the little guy.

She raised her eyebrow. "Coffee for a kid? Nice."

"Somehow I figured you for a coffee drinker."

Her answer was a noncommittal shrug. She ripped off a piece of the muffin and stuffed it into her mouth with an appreciative moan. "So good."

It was good and worth every carb. I let her eat and thought about how best to approach her. "Who's the little guy belong to?"

"A friend," she said. "Can't get out of the life, but that doesn't mean her kid needs to see it."

I nodded. "I'm glad you're trying to shield him."

She didn't seem impressed with my compliment, instead staring me down with dark eyes that had seen enough bad things for two lifetimes. "I don't think you were Sarah's friend."

"Why?"

"Because you tried to catch me. You wouldn't have done that if you were Sarah's friend."

"First off"—I leaned forward—"I never said I was Sarah's friend. I said I knew her. And I wasn't trying to catch you. I was trying to help you. Believe me, if I wanted you caught, I'd have done it."

She laughed. "Right. Because your pretty boyfriend had to save you."

"Sometimes things aren't what they seem." I let the words sink in. What would she think if she knew she sat across from a woman who'd killed several men? Would it matter that I'd saved countless children? Or would she see only in black and white?

"So why do you want to find out who killed Sarah?"

Because I'm a suspect, and I'd like to clear my name.
"Because she didn't deserve to die." The lie came smoothly, as so many others did. "And because I think she was killed by the people you work for."

She stiffened. "You don't know who I work for."

"Preacher."

Her dark eyes gazed at me over her still-full cup of coffee. Steam swarmed her young face, creating an off-putting picture of a half devil, half lost child. "You know Preacher?"

"I know of him. So do other people."

"Your mistake."

"You don't like him."

She finally took a drink of coffee. "Tastes better with cream and sugar. You don't know what I think, lady. Unless you're a mind reader, and if you are, you're in the wrong business."

"Nope. I'm just observant. I saw the way you looked when I said his name. Voice got a little harder." I pushed my cup aside and leaned across the table. "You don't like him at all. But do you think he killed Sarah?"

Riley jerked back. "How the hell would I know? And I wouldn't tell you if I did."

"You're scared of him. But you're also loyal, because he saved you in some way. He takes care of you. But I bet he also takes care of your ID and your money, right? Keeps your clothes and whatever personal belongings close in case you decide you've had enough?"

She glared at her coffee. The muscles in her narrow cheeks flexed.

"I don't blame you. He seems like an intimidating guy."

"He likes being boss." She unconsciously rubbed her arm and winced.

Preacher was a nobody on his home streets, but here, he was a captain, second only to the general. Watching Riley rub her arm and brood into her coffee, I wondered how far Preacher liked to take his much-relished authority.

"What happens if you guys want out?"

"Why would we want out? We get easy money."

I couldn't play the social worker here. Riley didn't want to listen to me tell her she was worth more than this, that I could help her if she would only allow it. And I certainly couldn't threaten bringing her to the police. She needed to be considered an equal with something important to say. And she needed someone to listen.

"Okay," I agreed. "But what if you do change your mind? Decide you want to move on to something else?"

"Not a lot of options out there for kids like me."

I bit back the lecture. "But if you thought there were, and you told Preacher you were done, would he let you go?"

Riley took another bite of her muffin. And then another. Bite, chew. Bite, chew. I waited.

Finished, she folded the crumb-covered wrapper into a neat triangle, smooshing it flat. "I swear you seem familiar."

I made a show of raising a single eyebrow. "That's because we met the other night at the Rattner."

"No, before that. Something about your voice."

My stomach twisted in knots. "Honestly, I don't know how you remember any details given the amount of people you deal with. Can you stop avoiding my question? Would Preacher let you go?"

She ripped the triangular-shaped paper in half. "He says so, but most of the girls don't try to leave. They're all like me. But there was one kid..."

She chewed a nicely manicured fingernail. Did Preacher do that himself or did he allow her to go to Exhale under supervision? Riley rubbed her arm again. "She came from Western Pennsylvania, and she did well enough for a while. Then her mom got sick, and she wanted to go home. Preacher said she could go. Even helped her get a ride."

"Really?"

Riley nodded. "He knew a guy from Ohio passing close enough to her place and got her a ride. Some long-haul semi driver in a truck the color of a nasty booger. Pulled up at the motel we were staying at and took up half the parking lot."

I kept my face still as stone.

"And some of the boys"—she glanced at me, watching for my reaction—"they're from other places around the country. He doesn't let us talk to them much. We don't really see them. But I heard about one boy who wanted out and was going to go to a safe house for troubled boys. Knew a lady there that would help him, no questions asked. He disappeared."

"You don't think he's at the safe house?"

"I know he's not. A few weeks after he left, I went and checked. Wanted to say hi." She squashed the mashed paper with her knuckles. "Maybe I was thinking about starting over too. Lady who wanted to help him said he never showed up. I left. When I got back to my place, Preacher showed up a few minutes later with Sam, one of the older boys. Total asskisser and wannabe. They kept asking me questions about my day, like they were suddenly concerned I was running loose in the city. Preacher looked pissed, and I just got this feeling. Bad feeling. He hasn't hit me in a long time, but I thought he was going to."

So Riley was already a career girl, as I'd thought. Preacher probably watched her from a distance for a while, making sure she was worth the approach. He was good enough to know he had to snag her at her most vulnerable. "Where do you live now?"

"Not telling you that."

"Does it at least have four walls and a roof?"

"Yeah. We all do. Preacher makes sure of that, even if they aren't worth a shit. Got hot water too."

"Does Preacher know about your little friend back there?" I watched the boy crawl on his hands and knees, pushing a tiny, yellow dump truck.

"No." Her voice was hard. "He don't like girls with kids. And he's not getting to this one."

"So you think he forces kids into this life?"

She shrugged. "Probably. They all do it. You know how many sickos out there would be interested in him?" She jerked her head toward her busy charge. "I know he's got stuff online, a big website full of kids I've never seen."

I leaned forward. "How do you get to the site? Do you know the name?"

"I only saw it once," she said. "He shut it down and yelled at me for spying on him. I think you need a password."

I had at least a portion of her trust. Sarah must have treated her kindly, or Preacher had given her one too many beatings. Or maybe she just wanted out and was feeling around for a solution. I decided to keep pushing. "I don't know how old you were when you got into this life, but the little kids you're talking about, they're not being coerced or convinced to believe they're doing what they want to do. They're being taken and flat out forced. Just like what you're afraid Preacher will do to your friend's son if he finds out about him."

White-faced, she shrugged her shoulders helplessly.

"If you wanted to help them, you could get Preacher's laptop and bring it to me," I said. "I could take it to people who could—"

Her eyes went wide. "Are you kidding me? He's all I got, and there's a lot worse people I could end up with." She snapped her head back and forth. "I shouldn't even be talking to you. No freaking way am I going to steal from him."

Now wasn't the time to waste energy and convince her. He'd had her long enough, she probably couldn't be set straight.

"So back to Sarah and Preacher. What do you think happened?"

Riley started tearing the wrapper into tiny pieces, scattering crumbs all over the table. She mashed those down with her fingers.

"I promise you can trust me," I said.

She made a disgusted noise. "Everyone says that. But they're liars."

"You're right. People lie. I lie. All the time. I know how to get what I want from just about anybody. I learned from a young age how to manipulate people, and it's getting easier and easier."

She looked as if she didn't know whether to believe me. "This isn't helping me trust you."

I smiled. "But you know what? Kids are the only people I've ever been really devoted to. That's why I was a social worker for ten years, and that's why I left."

"If you left, then you're not devoted."

"Wrong. I'm more devoted than ever. I'm out here with no one to answer to, doing whatever it takes to protect you guys."

She considered this. "I don't think you'll turn me in. But I don't think you can protect me, either. If Preacher found out I talked to you, he'd kill me."

If only she knew the truth. Would she feel safe then? My ego chattered in my ear, at war with my common sense. But who would Riley tell, really? Who would believe her?

"Did you know," I started, "that a few weeks ago, a young boy was dropped off at a fire station in Maryland. He'd been the victim of a national sex trafficking ring. And he was brought from Ohio. Some people think he was sold to a man driving a semi. You know, a long-haul driver."

Riley stared. The fear and apprehension on her face thrilled me on some deep level I didn't want to acknowledge. As if feeding the beast would give it so much power, I'd lose myself.

"What's even more interesting," I continued, "is that a few days later, a truck driver was found dead not twenty miles away, in a green semi. He was half dressed, and at first police thought he'd had a heart attack and frozen to death. But drug tests are showing something wasn't right. Some people think that man was killed because he was helping sell kids."

She swallowed hard, looking as terrified as the elementary school kid hearing about Bloody Mary for the first time. "Who are some people?"

"The ones who are willing to help you."

That was all she was going to get. I'd risked enough already.

She looked over at her small charge, still playing happily with the truck. Sensing her attention, he waved and gave her a gap-toothed grin.

"I don't know if Preacher killed Sarah," Riley finally said. "He didn't like her paying special attention to me. He threatened her about spending alone time with me. She was better than you think, you know."

I didn't argue the point. "And Preacher?"

"He hasn't acted sad over her dying. Pissed he's lost a location. But that's not what bothers me." She took a deep breath. "Sarah had this locket. Always wore it. Some kind of special meaning."

I had no idea if the necklace was found with her body, but I had the feeling I was about to find out.

"The thing is," Riley said. "Preacher's wearing it now."

Riley was long gone by the time I re-joined John, the informant, in the car. I slammed the door shut and shivered in the cold. I'd given the little guy my hat, and my forehead was freezing.

"Well?" John sounded impatient.

My mind warred. Telling John meant more muscle to use against Preacher and a witness to help sell the truth to the police. But did I trust him and the senator? The nagging feeling I hadn't been able to pin down since talking with the senator finally clarified itself. Why did he need me? John might not have any connection with Riley, but he had enough experience he would have figured out a way. My involvement felt more like a distraction. A way to keep my nose out of whatever was really going on.

"It sounds like it's business as usual since Sarah's murder, but I may have a lead on a trafficking case." I gave John the information about Riley's friend. "I've got a name and description, but I don't know if that will help. At any rate, maybe that will make the senator realize there is more than just prostitution going on."

John grunted. "Maybe. I'll drop you off at your car."

TWENTY

Some time before dawn, the piercing ring of my cellphone drummed me out of a deep sleep.

Bleary and still semi-trapped in sleep, I hit the green button and forgot to speak.

"Hello?" Todd Beckett said. "Lucy?"

"What? Yeah, it's me. What time is it?"

"Four a.m. I shouldn't be calling you. But for some damn reason, I'm risking my job."

The cobwebs cleared even as my limbs turned to heavy weights. "What is it?"

"As a former social worker, your DNA is in the system."

"That's correct."

"The skin under Sarah Jones's fingernails has been positively identified as yours."

Sweat trickled down from my hairline and into my ear. "Are you still at home?"

"As a matter of fact, I'm outside your building. I think it's better if we speak in person."

All my fears balled into a knot in the middle of my shoulder blades. I couldn't let him know how scared I was. That would cause mistakes. "Give me five minutes."

Todd refused to take off his coat, standing in the middle of my living room in his trench coat, his ears pink from the cold. I should have offered him coffee, but I didn't want to take the time to make it. "You know she and I had physical contact at Maisy's."

"The problem is, we've got two different witnesses at Maisy's who confirm your altercation and also confirm the dress you wore. Green on a redhead stands out." His eyes flickered to mine and then just as quickly to the wall behind me. "They're still testing those fibers. But if they match, I'll have to bring you in on a hold."

"I wore that dress in the salon that day. The fibers being in her blood only means my dress shed, and she bled onto them. That's not conclusive evidence."

"It's enough to make life really miserable for you."

"Why?" My voice began to rise. I snatched back the fear and composed myself. "Why am I the only one you're looking at? You know Sarah was into bad things, and there are any number of suspects. You are too good of a cop to be so narrow-minded, and it's more than just your boss wanting to get the case closed. Who's leaning on you?"

He sighed. Looked down at the floor and then finally back up at me. Pity and frustration darkened his face. "You know things aren't always black and white. Sometimes people get involved in these investigations when they have no business."

"Who is it?"

"I can't tell you."

I rubbed my aching jaw muscles. I'd been grinding my teeth, and the headache crept up my temples. "Can you give me the less detailed version?"

"A high-end client is claiming Sarah called, distraught about a thief in her salon. She told the client there was valuable personal information in her phone that could lead to her investment accounts. The client offered her husband's help in recovering the phone. He's got a lot of pull, and now he's using it."

It all began to make sense. "You ever stop to think why he might care? Were they personal friends of Sarah's?"

"Business only."

"Business." I spit the word. "I bet he was involved in the business. Probably the sex business without his wife knowing. Or hell, maybe she does. Either way, he's trying to protect himself. He thinks I have the phone and if I expose Sarah, I could expose him. Have you told him I don't have it, and that all the information from it was lost?"

"It doesn't matter." Todd paced my small living room. "He believes our personal history is enough to make me skew the truth for you, and he's got enough pull to put the seed of doubt in my superiors' heads. This guy is in the mayor's camp. Who's my chief's boss. You get the picture."

"So what am I supposed to do? Allow myself to be railroaded? And I've got an alibi."

"Do you?"

I hesitated a fraction of a second. "Yes."

He stared at me for what seemed like far too long. I should have taken advantage, tried to wheedle the string-puller's name out of him, but I was struck numb with fear and anger and whatever conscience I actually still possessed.

"For what it's worth, I'm on your side with this one," he said. "But this whole thing is slipping right through my hands. I'm already being accused of not running the investigation properly because of our prior relationship. I'm telling you, get yourself in order because shit is coming down whether I like it or not."

"Thank you." It almost hurt to say the words. I wanted

Todd to be the enemy, even if having him as an ally saved my ass. His friendship made my decisions complicated, and I didn't like it. "Have you looked into Roderick Reed?"

"Who?"

"Preacher. The guy I told you Sarah was working for. That's his real name. He's wearing the pendant Sarah always wore. Strange, isn't it?"

A flicker of agitation in Todd's eyes. "And you found this out how?"

"I can't reveal my source."

"And yet you expect me to believe you, as always."

"I know you believe me," I countered. "That's why you're here. That's why I gave you Riley's name. You have evidence Sarah was part of an active child prostitution and human trafficking ring. Preacher was her immediate superior, and he's Riley's pimp. Either he killed Sarah for talking to me or had someone else do it."

"Except there's no solid evidence Sarah was involved in anything. Just a lot of notes and accusations on your part. The phone's worthless. If this is for real, our—*your*—best shot is getting this Riley to come in and tell us what she knows."

"You haven't found her."

He shook his head. "But I'm sure you have. So go back and get her to talk. She's not going to get arrested. I'll meet her anywhere."

"She won't do it." I wanted to scream. All the kids I'd helped, and the one I really needed to back me refused to stick her neck out. "She cared about Sarah, I think. But she's afraid of Preacher." I told Todd about the kids who disappeared. I didn't dare mention the truck driver because the suspicious death of a pedophile would get Todd's instincts up.

"You better figure out a way to get her to," Todd said. "Because without her corroborating statement, here's what it looks like: you're tracking down sex rings, you've admitted that.

You found one—or you think you've found one. You're still traumatized from seeing what Kailey went through, maybe even blaming yourself because we all know that's a favorite thing of yours. You confront Sarah, steal her phone. You have some kind of public conversation, and she winds up dead. Witnesses claim you argued, even got physical. The DNA under her fingernails, the fibers. See how easy it looks?"

"I'm not a big woman." I was grasping. "Sarah and I were the same size. How did I kill her?"

"It was a blitz attack from behind with some kind of blunt object. Maybe a hammer. There's no sign Sarah fought back, so her attacker wouldn't have injuries. You know how to pick a lock."

"I have an alibi." I felt like I was clinging to the edge of a sharp cliff, with just my fingernails to anchor me to the rocky earth.

"Lucy." Todd closed his eyes. They flickered behind his lids, back and forth, making his thoughts easy to read. Should he tell me more? What good would it do? Was I worth risking his career? He opened his eyes. "ADA Hale isn't going to lie for you. His housekeeper claims she stopped by that night and neither you nor Chris were there. Her information gives enough time for you to have gone to the salon and killed Sarah."

"But you're on my side." The desperation in my voice was humiliating. My hands shook, and stupidly, shockingly, I reached for Todd's arm. "You believe me."

"I'm not the only one working the case. Two more detectives brought it, thanks to Mr. Big Shot client. He found out I had a personal connection to you."

I dropped his arm and stepped back. "Personal connection? I thought your little brother was the scum of the earth and tried to put him back in prison."

"But you ultimately did right by him, and I admired you for that." He flushed and looked down. "Publicly."

Shame slid over me like rotting slime. Any plans I might have had to manipulate Todd into doing my bidding evaporated. "I didn't know that."

"Lots of things you don't know about me."

"And yet you think I did something to the Harrisons."

He nodded. "I do. I think you believe you had good intentions, but you still did it."

"So why try to help me now?"

He dragged his fingernails across the side of his neck, leaving red marks on his fair skin. His fingers went to the lonely spot above his lip where his mustache used to be. "Because there's a lot of good in you."

A strange sting settled in behind my eyes. I blinked and hoped the tears wouldn't fall. "What do I do?"

"Get Riley to talk. Soon. I'll check out this Roderick, but don't count on it going anywhere unless he's got a nasty record."

Throat bound and aching, I stepped away. Todd walked to the door. Before he could close it, I swallowed the fear blocking my throat. "I like you without the mustache."

TWENTY-ONE

I called Chris as soon as Todd left. Sitting at the kitchen table with my legs curled up in the kitchen chair and Mousecop snoring in the window, I didn't bother with a greeting. "Your uncle knows you lied. His housekeeper said she was there, and we weren't."

"What?" Chris's voice was thick with sleep. "How did you find this out?"

I told him about Todd's visit, including Mr. Big Shot client and probably pedophile pushing me for suspect number one. "But you said the security system would show—"

"I forgot to set it when I ran out for food." He groaned. "She stopped by and the system was off. No wonder she remembers. Shit, my uncle is going to be mad as hell."

I dropped my head to the table. "I'm sorry. That's my fault."

"You're right."

I couldn't be angry at his honesty. Chris and his uncle were close, and I'd put him in a lousy position. "I honestly don't know what to do now."

"Todd's right. You need to find Riley. Put the pressure on her."

"It's not that easy."

"You know how to do this," Chris said. "You manipulate, wheedle, extract what you need. You know what kids like her need to hear. Make her understand."

"It feels wrong."

Chris started laughing. "After all the things you've done, this feels wrong?"

I didn't see any humor in the situation. Chris hadn't seen the real effects of a pimp like Preacher. Riley represented all the girls I saw in CPS who'd been manipulated into believing her pimp loved her, only to be turned out when the moment was right. Girls like her didn't know how to believe in themselves, and people like Preacher knew how to turn that weakness into a festering sore. "She's a kid who's been beat down emotionally and physically most of her life. Low self-esteem and scared. And I'm supposed to take advantage of that?" I dragged my empty coffee cup in circles around the table, leaving an ugly trail of liquid.

"It's rotten," Chris admitted. "But if you don't, you're on the hook for this."

He was right. A horrifying sense of desperation wracked my body. How did I get here? Up against the wall when I'd really done nothing illegal? I could hide my own crimes. I knew their nuances as well as I knew my own brain. But this? When someone else was pulling the strings and I couldn't even see the end of them? I had no idea what to do.

"Like I said." Chris's voice softened. "I know it sucks to have to work the girl over. It's not right. And she might end up more screwed-up. But if you don't, you're in big trouble. And no one is going to help her or any other kid involved in this mess."

He knew that would get to me. Knew the helpless kids were my weakness. "I don't like how well you know me."

"I told you, we're cut from the same cloth. Even if yours is dirtier."

. . .

Chris drove me to North Philly, insisting I was too keyed-up to drive. Besides, if Preacher or another pimp showed up, I'd have backup. Any other day I'd be insulted, but today I was grateful.

"I have no idea how long this will take," I said. "We might not even see her."

"Kelly has no other information?" he asked.

"None. Riley doesn't have a record, and she's not listed as a missing person, which means either her family didn't care or that's not her real name."

"I guess I'm naïve," he said. "Which is kind of ridiculous considering what I came from. How does an organization like this not get brought down?"

"They're criminals, and they're good at it," I said. "With the girls, even though the pimps have classed up and sometimes the girls too, it's the same story. These men are the ultimate players. Voyeurs, you know? I knew a girl, back in CPS, who'd been at her boyfriend's in Kensington. Not the best area, not the worst. They got into it, right? She took off walking, planning to go to the bus stop. Boyfriend called her, they had a big argument over the phone. Before long a nice car rolled up with a harmless-looking guy. She told him what happened, played right into his hands. He started in about how she deserved better than that, no man should make her cry." I rolled my eyes. "He convinced her to come hang out with him and some friends at a place nearby."

"And she said yes," Chris says.

"Yep. Because she already had the home issues and the self-esteem problem. She went and partied for a couple of days and then decided it was time to go home. That's when the guy said she wasn't going anywhere unless she made him some money, maybe slapped her around." I had seen this happen more times than I could count when I worked for CPS. The girls' faces changed, but the circumstances remained mostly the same. "He told her he gave her weed and booze and she owed him. So she gave in. But after a day or two, she begged to get out while he dragged her from hotel to hotel, holding her ID and her cell. And when she finally got away, an older girl showed up to defend the pimp. He'd snowed her just like Preacher has Riley."

Chris stared out the window. Fresh snowflakes were falling, making the evening commute even more dangerous. A man carrying a bag of groceries lost his footing, skating along the icy sidewalk and clinging to the bag. Chris started to laugh and then caught himself. "Sorry, I know it's not funny. But I'm nervous because I know you're not going to like what I have to say."

I braced myself.

"Even though you're operating on two sides of the spectrum, you really aren't that different from the pimp."

I whipped my entire body around to glare at him. He held up his hand. "Just wait. Obviously you're not a pimp, but look what you can do." The note of awe in his voice eased a fraction of my tension. "You can read people and know what to say to get what you want. I've seen you do it over and over again."

"It's different."

"Because you're doing it for a greater good. Not for selfish reasons."

"Yes."

"And you really believe that?"

"What?"

He smiled, tugging on my winter hat. "I love this white hat against your hair, by the way."

Warmth rushed through me, but I refused to acknowledge the compliment. "Back to my question."

"Right. You think your choices are all about helping people. Saving kids."

"We've been through this. I know part of it's to cover my

own guilt over Justin and all the others I couldn't save. I get it. It's about finding control. And I should stop. Maybe I can't stop. I don't know, and I don't want to think about it right now."

"Do you want to stop?"

My throat went dry.

"See, that's the real question. The one that will tell you how far gone you really are."

The softness of his voice and the Audi's blasting heater made me dizzy. Chris's sharp gaze made me feel like I was about to jump in with man-eating sharks. "I don't want to discuss it."

"Okay." His razor-like eyes found me in the window, his reflection doing little to dampen the effect. "But just so you know, whatever the answer is, I'm sticking around."

For the second time that day, I felt like crying. "Why? Because there's good in me too?" I thought about Todd Beckett and how disappointed he would be if he knew the real truth, even if he already thought I was a killer. Some part of him had to think he was wrong. If he knew the answer, knew the true horror of what I'd done, would he still see good? I slunk down in the seat.

"Something like that." Chris patted my knee.

I laid my head against the glass and watched for Riley.

Three inches of snow had fallen before I saw her. A gray scarf covered most of her face, but I recognized the hunched shoulders and the quick gait. "I've got my phone. You stay here." Chris stopped the car, and I was out of it before he could respond.

Dodging the few people still brave enough to deal with the miserable weather on a Saturday morning, I cut across the street and jogged up the sidewalk. The snow was slippery under my boots, and more than once I thought I'd end up on my butt. I wondered if Chris was laughing now.

"Riley." The wind picked up my voice and carried it away from her. She walked fast, scurrying around people like a timid mouse. I quickened my pace. She hit the corner and yielded to the "don't walk" sign. I caught the cuff of her coat sleeve just as she started to step off the sidewalk.

She jerked away, nearly falling into the street. Her left eye was badly bruised, her nose swollen. "What the hell?"

"What happened to you?"

She jammed her hands into her pockets and crossed the street. I followed.

"Get away from me."

"Tell me what happened."

"Got my ass put in line."

"By who?" For a small girl, she took long strides. I worked hard to keep up.

"None of your business."

Anger warmed me. "Preacher? Did Preacher do this?"

Safely across the street, she ducked into an alley. "*You* did this! So leave me alone."

She didn't need to tell me any more. Preacher had busted her up for talking to me.

"I'm sorry."

"Whatever. I knew better." She glared at the brick of the old pharmacy. It looked as ancient as the city, paint peeling off so the lettering was barely legible. "What do you want?"

This wasn't going to go over well. "Your help."

The eyebrow of her good eye shot up. "For real?"

"Listen, the police think I killed Sarah."

She stilled, her narrowed eyes suddenly looking at me in a new light. "Why?"

"Because I was investigating her involvement in the sex trade, and I took her phone. She and I talked; she ends up dead.

All they've got is circumstantial evidence, but there's pressure from the boss to make this whole thing my doing."

"Why?"

I debated, but if I wanted her help I needed to be honest. "I think one of her clients—and I'm not talking Exhale clients—has a lot of pull and is afraid I've got information on him."

"He wants you to go away."

I nodded.

She pinched her lips together, and I noticed the small cut on the corner of her mouth. I catalogued each and every mark Preacher left. "What can I do?"

"Talk to the police. Tell them what you know."

Riley started laughing. "You're crazy. They don't want to hear what I have to say."

"They do. I've got a friend, Detective Beckett. He believes me, and he wants to talk to you."

"So he can get to Preacher." She caught on. "But here's what'll happen. I come in and talk, they offer me a deal. I take it and go to some safe place or shelter so I can get back on my feet. Even if Preacher does get arrested, his boys come for me. I get the ass-beating of my life if I'm lucky. And I'm out of a job 'cause no pimp will ever trust me again."

Now was the time. I could leach into her subconscious just like Preacher had, tell her I understood. I could even talk about my sister, about how I was damaged because of her. Bring up the dead trucker. I would read her expressions and know exactly what the next thing to say was. If she wanted money, I had it. Power, I had it. I could make her do what I wanted.

Instead, I could only manage, "I trust you. And you can trust me."

"Sarah trusted you. Look where that got her."

Her words sliced me as sharp as a switchblade. "Sarah talked about me? When? It had to be just before her murder." I stepped too close, taking away her personal space, forgetting about anything but my own desperation. "What do you know?"

Riley must have seen something in my eyes, or maybe a sixth sense warned her she was up against someone much more dangerous than Preacher. Maybe I'd hinted just enough for her to be legitimately scared. And maybe she should be. I didn't know what I'd do to protect my freedom.

"Sarah called me, freaked out, after she talked to you," Riley said. "She didn't really believe you were a con artist, but she thought you might be her way out."

"Then why was she scared?"

Riley tugged at the ends of her scarf. "She'd been drinking. She did that too much. And she kept talking about how he was watching her, that he always knew what she was doing. She was afraid he'd ruin everything before she could fix it."

I grabbed her shoulders. Riley flinched. I let go, but not before I gave them a hard squeeze. "Who? Who is 'he'?"

"She never said. I assumed she meant Preacher. Especially when I heard she was dead, and he showed up with her locket." Fat tears welled in Riley's eyes. "Sarah was trying, okay? She didn't want to be involved, but Preacher had something on her. But she still tried to help us."

"Help you how?"

She clamped her mouth shut, backing away. "I can't say any more. Sarah was right. He's always watching. If he's not, then one of his boys is."

"Riley, you can't walk away from me. I need you to talk to Detective Beckett. Tell him everything you know."

Her head snapped back and forth. "Can't do it. Won't."

"You have to!"

"I ain't got anyone else," she burst out. "No one's going to take me in off the street, give me a meal or two. Preacher's the only one who ever said nice things to me."

"Because he knew what you wanted to hear," I shouted

back. "You're an easy mark for people like him. You sop up the compliments like a drug. He knows exactly what he's doing every time he gives you anything. And so do you."

"What are you getting at?"

"At some point"—I jabbed a shaking finger at her—"it's not coercion anymore. It's not trafficking. It's your decision. At some point, the police are going to say, 'You know what, you've had all the opportunity in the world to get out,' and when you need them to believe you, they're going to charge you and put you in jail. And Preacher will still be out here pimping and selling little kids. Let me tell you something. Your friend who got a ride on the green semi? You think she's free and clear now? She's not. She dared to find a way out, and Preacher sold her to someone else. That truck took her to Ohio, and she's probably way worse off now than she was then." If she was even alive. She might have been used and then tossed away.

Riley swallowed hard.

"And what about the little boy I told you about the other day? He wasn't even ten. Taken away from his family, stuck in that semi with that nasty man. You know what he made him do. He was destined for Philadelphia, and probably for Preacher. If not Preacher, then someone just like him."

"Why are you telling me this?" Her lips twisted, her hands digging into her hair.

"Because I want you to know what you're protecting. Whatever Sarah was doing that got her in trouble, if it was talking to me or something worse, you need to man up and tell the truth."

"You have no idea—"

"I don't care!" The ugly burst out of me. "I don't care what your consequences are, because I know I can protect you. I will stop Preacher. Detective Beckett will do right by you. So I don't care about whatever fears you have. I am giving you an out your friends didn't have. One that Sarah didn't have."

Tears dripped off Riley's nose and into the blowing snow.

As if I'd been dropped into a christening tub, I realized my hands and face were tight with numbing cold. Still, anger coursed through me at a frightening speed. The empathy I'd felt for the girl—that I still felt, somewhere deep—was buried beneath the intense desire to save myself and to regain control. I hated her for making me feel so shattered.

She cowered away from me, arms raised to cover her face. There were scratches on her hands to match the one on her cheek. Behind her splayed fingers were dull, frightened eyes. Her entire body trembled.

Without realizing it, my fingers had walked into my pocket, searching for the vial they wanted to be there. I saw myself throwing it on her, watching her fight for air and collapse, just like Brian Harrison. Would I feel remorse?

Chunks of broken bricks were scattered around the foundation. I could smash her head in before she knew what hit her. The darkness would give me cover. Who would miss her?

I stepped back.

"I shouldn't have yelled at you." I barely opened my mouth in the effort to hold it together. "I'm freaked out, and I'm desperate."

She sucked back a sob and wiped her dripping nose.

"You still have my card?"

She nodded.

"When you decide you want justice for Sarah, call me. Or call Detective Todd Beckett. I swear to you he'll be fair."

I left her in the alley before it was too late.

My breath came in hard gasps. Blindly, I made it back to Chris's car. I fell into the seat.

"Christ." He took my arm and twisted me to face him. "You're white as a sheet. What the hell? Did Preacher show up?"

I shook my head and then pulled my knees to my chest without thinking of Chris's expensive leather seats. Burying my face against my jeans, I curled into a ball.

"You're freaking me out." Chris nudged my shoulder and then tugged at my hair. I refused to budge, pinching my eyes closed and breathing in the smell of cold that still clung to my clothes.

Finally, his hand came to rest on my back. "What happened?"

I didn't want to talk about it. I couldn't voice it out loud. "Nothing. I'm just... stressed out. Please, take me home."

He didn't want to. He argued. Pleaded. Offered to buy me a carb-loaded and extremely unhealthy breakfast, the kind he knew I usually couldn't resist.

"Just take me home."

He finally obeyed. The second he stopped in front of my building, I raced out of the car, shouting a promise to call him later. I wouldn't keep it.

Inside my apartment, I locked the door and stumbled to the couch.

I'd truly wanted to kill her. Not for duty or justice, but because she'd pissed me off and I'd had enough. That truth absolutely terrified me.

TWENTY-TWO

Chris called on and off all day. I ignored him. Hours ticked by, and I sank further into the couch. Any moment Todd and the other detectives would show up to arrest me. And maybe I wouldn't put up a fight. What would be the point? Someone wanted me to take the fall, and I was certainly guilty of murder. The rest was just semantics.

Midnight came and went. Sleep tormented me along with the infomercials that seem to dominate the television. And then my buzzer rang. Glued to the couch with my own damp sweat, I felt as if I'd just stepped off the Flying Turns ride at Knoebels: swishy and sweaty and shaking with adrenaline, but this time it wasn't driven by joyriding. Mac took me there during the summer of my freshman year of college. We'd spent the day riding the thrill rides at the park and eating all the food my mother said would kill us. Mac was going to be so disappointed in me.

Was the lethal injection table cold?

The buzzer wouldn't stop. I stood up and nearly toppled onto my coffee table. Stumbling for a center of gravity, I shuffled to the door and hit the button.

"Who is it?"

"Justin Beckett. I've got to talk to you."

Immense relief nearly made me sink to the floor, and then déjà vu rolled through me. Last time this kid showed up unannounced, he dropped an atomic bomb on my life. "It's the middle of the night."

"It's an emergency. My brother sent me."

Since Chris still refused to see his newly discovered sibling, Justin was referring to Todd. A flicker of hope or a warning signal? Either way, I had to know. I pressed the button on the intercom so hard my finger turned white. "Come on."

Justin moved quickly, softly knocking just a few minutes later. I didn't hesitate. "Get in here."

Still lanky, with the characteristic gait of today's lost youth, Justin hurried into my apartment. His hair was a bit shaggier, but his eyes were brighter. He stood straighter than he used to, a new confidence coloring his once dark aura.

"You look good," I told him.

He blushed. "Thanks. I'm seeing somebody."

"I heard. Looks like she does you good."

"Yeah." He brushed his bangs off his forehead. "Listen, Todd sent me. He can't contact you directly."

Fear singed the hairs on the back of my neck. "What is it?" I knew the answer, heard it in the frantic tone of Justin's voice.

"Tomorrow morning, the district attorney is going to charge you with Sarah Jones's murder. They're still waiting on the fibers, but he's been convinced they've got a strong enough case without them. They broke your alibi."

I expected to feel a resurgence of panic, for my legs to go weak and my stomach to revolt. But all I could do was stand and stare at Justin. My brain was aware of the irony of my being arrested for a murder I didn't commit but probably would have eventually, and the unstable part of me wanted to laugh, but I could do nothing but stand in shock.

Finally, I spoke over sickly cottonmouth. "ADA Hale is charging me?"

"No," Justin said. "The district attorney is handling this himself."

So the client pushing the buttons had serious power. Senator Coleman's greasy smile flashed through my mind, and I swayed. I grabbed the arm of the couch.

"Todd knows you're innocent. He got into it with the chief, and he was kicked off the case."

"And he sent you?"

Justin nodded.

"He's going to get in trouble." Why was he helping me? He thought I'd killed others, so what did the technicalities matter? I didn't want to owe him anything. And I didn't want the shame of knowing he'd helped me at great risk to his job and his own ethics.

"He didn't use his phone. Used a pre-paid one like I have."

I looked around my apartment, wishing Chris were here. "What do I do now?"

"We think you should hide."

"What?"

Justin spoke so fast, my addled mind barely kept up. "We thought about putting you on a plane, but they'll track that. They might even catch you before you leave for the airport. Right now they think they can spring you out of sleep, but if your credit card is used, they'll track you."

I finally sat down. He'd lost me several sentences ago. "Hide?"

Justin sat next to me. He smelled like Aqua Velva. "I don't know the details, but the guy behind this and his wife are willing to testify that you and Sarah had a bad relationship."

"That's not exactly true."

"They're willing to lie."

"To hide his crime." I couldn't even feel disgust at the wife's choosing to aid her husband's sickness. She wasn't the first, and she wouldn't be the last.

"Plus other witnesses, and the phone thing and a bunch of other stuff Todd mentioned. He said if you get arrested, they'll find a way to take it to trial. And then you're screwed."

"Not if I get a good attorney!" I lied to myself again. "Chris will help me."

Justin winced at the name of the man who refused to acknowledge him, but he shook his head. "Todd said other people in the department know his theories about the Harrisons, whatever that means. They'll start digging. He said you'd know what he meant. And that he's sorry he didn't keep that theory to himself."

My head dropped against the back of the couch. That's why the district attorney felt so strongly. If he couldn't get me on one charge, he had more to go after, and whoever was pulling the strings would be happy, because I'd be silent.

"I don't have anywhere to go," I said. "My parents"—an involuntary shudder tore through me at the idea—"can easily be found. They know about my friendship with Chris. I've got some cash, so I can try checking into a low-rent motel, but that's the first place police will look, and I don't have enough cash to stay long." And I didn't want to face my mother's smug attitude or see her revel in the glory of yet another child embarrassing her.

"No. The best place to go is the shelter I volunteer at."

"Are you serious?" It wasn't a bad idea. If I played the part, I could blend in. And I was good at playing a part.

"It's crowded with this cold, but I can get you a bed. No one's going to think of checking there, at least not for a day or two."

"But what's the point? I can't run forever, and they'll charge me when they find me." Helplessness seeped into my system.

"It gives you more time with this Riley girl, gives my brother a chance to keep investigating. I'll help too. And Chris, if he'll answer my call." He grimaced. "You've got to listen to Todd."

Mousecop meandered in from the bedroom to check out the visitor. He jumped onto the couch and settled into my lap, gazing up at me with accusing eyes, as if he knew I was thinking about abandoning him.

"My cat," I choked out, rubbing the top of his head. "I can't leave him."

"You won't be gone forever, and I'll take care of him. I promise."

"You'll be seen coming and going. They'll watch my apartment. If they see you..."

"Then Chris will. You know he will."

I wanted to call him and ask what I should do, but he was working, and he wouldn't want me to go to a shelter. He'd try to hide me in some fancy hotel, implicating himself. My attention shot back to Justin.

"You can't do this," I said. "You're working on getting your name off the registry. If you get in trouble, they'll find a way to use that against you."

"I don't care," he said. "I won't let you go to jail."

"Why? I tried to ruin your life." These Beckett men had their priorities seriously messed up. What about revenge? Vengeance? The bitterness the rest of us lesser beings dragged around?

"But you didn't. And you helped give it back to me." He set his jaw, and I knew he wasn't giving in.

My fingers wove through Mousecop's long, silky fur. "You'll make sure Chris takes care of him?"

"I swear."

I didn't want to go to the shelter. But it was a good idea, a solid plan. Better than the alternative. I wasn't quite ready to give up. "I need to pack a few things."

"Light," Justin reminded me. "No weapons, and nothing

that looks like it's worth anything. Hide your cash in your shoe. If you've got a backpack, use it. If not, I have one."

"I have one." Valuable items were the least of my concern. If the police were planning on arresting me, they'd search my apartment. I couldn't leave the cyanide and the insulin in the hidden compartment in case they found it.

And I had a feeling I was going to need them.

TWENTY-THREE

Wearing my scratchy blond wig and the oldest coat I owned, I followed Justin onto the subway. We sat shoulder to shoulder, saying nothing. This time of night meant the train was mostly empty, save for the insomniac or night worker. Talking would have been safe. I just didn't feel like it.

How had my life derailed so fantastically in such a short amount of time? And why did all the people who should despise me want to help me? I wasn't sure which question made me feel worse.

Disappointed faces flashed through my thoughts, as real as the streaking lights on the other side of the train windows. My mother's, laced with a smug satisfaction because she'd have something new to be a victim about; Mac's, his skin gray and his heart weaker; Todd, because he'd really been hoping to be wrong about me; and Chris, because I'd made a stupid mistake and gotten caught.

Except I hadn't made a mistake this time. Had I? I slogged through my murky memory, knowing the answer waited. I just didn't want to see it.

I'd taken Sarah personally. Let my ego run the show. I'd

wanted to embarrass her, to make her feel guilt. To make her understand I was the one in charge. And I'd gotten careless. I shouldn't have allowed the confrontation. Shouldn't have been so vain about the cashmere dress that shed so easily.

I should have listened to Chris and not tried to bring down the ring. It was too big for one person, especially someone like me who wasn't looking for legal justice. I'd just as soon kill them all. My mistake was not walking away from Exhale. If I'd listened to Chris, he and I would be together, searching for Mother Mary. We might be slamming into dead-end walls, but I wouldn't be riding the subway in the middle of the night on my way to hide at a homeless shelter.

We exited at Spring Garden station and walked the remaining blocks to the same shelter I'd found Justin at months ago when I was determined to pin Kailey Richardson's kidnapping on him. My eyes teared up against the blistering cold, and my face felt like it was splitting in two. Finally the shelter loomed, its plain brick walls and dimly lit windows a glorious sight.

"Follow my lead," Justin said.

"Whatever you say." I didn't have the energy or the right frame of mind to argue. My brain was more numb than my feet.

Justin pushed open the heavy wood door. Meager warmth greeted us. The furnace in this old, poorly insulated building likely wasn't big enough to keep up with the cold, but it was a hell of a lot better than standing out on the street. I shivered, and without thinking, tucked my hand in the crook of Justin's elbow. He patted my gloved hand, and unexplainable tears singed my eyes.

I'd nearly destroyed his second chance at life, and he was helping me. Not because I'd skillfully manipulated him or backed him into a corner, but because he wanted to. Like his brother, who no doubt risked his job tipping me off, Justin saw some kind of good inside me. I wished I could.

Surely Todd had never shared his theories of Lucy Kendall's double life with his little brother.

"Frank," Justin called softly through the dark foyer. "It's Justin Beckett. I've got a lady here who really needs a bed for a few nights."

When I'd been here a few months ago, I'd barely taken notice of the interior. As my eyes adjusted, I searched for my bearings. Once a single-family home, the shelter had been converted into a duplex before it had been turned into the space it was now. The front entrance was a narrow hall with an office to the side, and the stairs were directly in front of me. The men were to the left, I remembered. That's where I'd found Justin, in a room to himself, painting.

The office door opened and a man exited. He was the same man I'd spoken to in the fall. I shrank against Justin and hoped the wig was a good enough disguise.

"Hey there, Jay." Frank shook Justin's hand. He smiled at me. "And you are?"

"Meg," Justin answered. "I met her a few nights ago. Down on her luck. Can we spare some room?"

Frank scratched his chin. "We're pretty full with this cold snap." His watery blue eyes searched mine. What did he see in my face? Desperation? Resignation? The cold eyes of a killer?

I shivered again.

"I've got some extra blankets," Frank said. "But I'd have to put you on the floor. Still warmer than being out in that wind."

"Thank you." The voice that creaked out of my mouth sounded nothing like my own. It sounded like the helpless girl who'd lost her sister and spent years wandering trying to figure out the meaning of everything terrible that had happened in her life.

I thought I'd left that girl behind a long time ago.

"Women and children are upstairs," Frank said. "Jay'll show

you the way. Of course, he'll have to stay in the hall. We like all of our ladies to feel safe."

Justin took my hand. "Come on."

My too-small boots—I'd chosen them because they were old and tattered—scraped against the wooden stairs. My footsteps were robotic, the timed thud sounding like a prison march.

Upstairs, four large bedrooms housed countless women and children. Lights were out, but the whispering and occasional shuffling showed not everyone slept.

"Which room should I go in?" I whispered.

"I'd try this first one on the right," Justin said. "Hank usually fills them up from the back of the house first. The bathroom is down the hall to the left."

I didn't want to go into that room. I'd been in others like it. Cramped and humid with body odor and clothes that needed laundering, accompanied by the soundtrack of snores, coughing, and the occasional fussy baby. But those times, I'd been there to help.

I knew I was being stupid. I still had an apartment and a fat cat waiting on me. This was just a disguise.

But the sinking feeling refused to believe that.

Justin squeezed my hand. "I'll come back in the morning. We'll go to breakfast. And hopefully I'll have some more news from Todd."

"Chris?" A knot formed in my throat, and I couldn't say any more. Never in my life had I wanted to see someone so badly.

"I'll get him here, I promise."

I nodded my thanks, patting his cheek because if I hugged him, I wouldn't be able to let go. Then I headed inside the room.

Cots were set up in an orderly pattern, with a couple of night lights on either side of the room. Feeling like an intruder, my palms sweating and my shoulder blades damp, I crept silently between the sleeping women. I tried not to look down, but I saw their faces. All ages, all colors. Too many little ones snuggled up to their mothers.

Senator Coleman needed a task force for this tragedy too.

I went to the farthest corner, quietly depositing the blankets Hank had given me. My old college backpack was still strapped to my back, and I wasn't ready to take it off. I reached in my pocket for my phone before I remembered I'd left it. Justin was bringing me a pay-as-you-go phone in the morning. My spot was far away from the nightlights, and I fumbled in the darkness, making a thin bed for myself. At first I tried to lie down with the backpack on, but my movement was too encumbered. Jumping up quickly wasn't an option. I slipped it off and clutched it to my chest, tucking my face into the polyester.

I wouldn't sleep. Too much at stake, too much danger in my hands. One of the last things my sister said to me before she killed herself was to remember to put myself first. Self-preservation, she'd called it. At eleven years old, I didn't really understand what she meant, but it didn't take long for me to learn.

When I'd decided to take justice into my own hands barely more than a year ago, I'd believed I was doing it for the kids who couldn't defend themselves. My freedom—my own life—was worth risking if I could make a difference. And for a while, I thought I had. Then I'd watched Brian Harrison die and realized I was no better than any other killer out there.

I didn't have the urge to kill just to kill someone. My urges were about making things right, about showing the world the truth. I didn't lie in bed at night, visualizing new and better ways to end a person's life. But I did spend hours thinking about my methods and how to get away with it.

Self-preservation above all else.

And look where I'd ended up. One foot in a jail cell despite my innocence in this particular case.

I didn't think any of it mattered anymore. Not my grand

plans, or my pathetic justifications, or the lies I'd told myself about stopping and leading a normal life. I'd always known I would be caught and have to pay the price, but I'd never imagined it would be for a crime I didn't commit. But that didn't matter either. I would have killed Sarah. I daydreamed about it while I dealt with her whining customers. So perhaps I was getting what I deserved.

The same didn't go for the women and kids sleeping around me. Shame kept me overheated. What if some other woman who truly was down on her luck came in, and I had the last available spot, even if it was on the floor? All because I was too much of a coward to face the song I'd composed.

My legs jerked, making my boots scrape across the floor. I shifted, bunching up the blanket so my shoulder wasn't in so much pain. The idea of lying here the rest of the night, fighting to stay awake on the damned hard floor, threatened fresh tears.

I'd get up and find Hank. Ask to use his phone and call Todd. Tell him I appreciated everything he was doing, but I wasn't going to hide from the police. They could come arrest me at my place, and I'd fight. If my real murders were discovered, then I'd accept the consequences. After all, I'd always said I would.

If I was convicted for my murders, I'd die in prison.

The creeping fear of death came without warning. It seized my chest and my throat with a spidery fingers, squeezing away my sanity. My breathing turned to gasps, my heart rate skyrocketed, and I saw only blackness. *Would I know anything in the void? Is there a fade to black or simply an off switch? And what if there is an after-life?*

Where would I go? Who would be waiting for me on the other side? Certainly not my sister. But there were others, the men I'd killed. What if their spirits circled me, waiting for the moment I entered their dimension?

I am going to die.

I sat up too fast, my backpack skidding away from me. I lunged for it, snatching the straps like they were liquid gold.

"Knock it off," an angry voiced hissed out of the darkness. "We need to sleep."

Someone else grumbled agreement.

Still breathing too hard and clutching the backpack, I lay back down.

I wouldn't sleep. Doing so would allow the familiar nightmare to take over. Me, dead. Cold and stiff and no longer existing.

I don't want to die.

If I was convicted, I'd die in prison.

Running made me look guilty. *Go in with shoulders high, make them do their jobs.*

I thought of Riley. Her terror and my joy. I wanted to kill her, at least hurt her. And my plans for Preacher. Big plans for whoever pulled his strings.

Either path I chose held nothing but certain death. The only difference was who administered it.

A familiar scent surrounded me. Warm, summery. Sandalwood, maybe. Or the beach. My grandmother used to take us to the Jersey Shore before Lily died. Even my mother made the trip without too many complaints about her looks or the people or whatever else she could find to gripe about. My memories of those days are fuzzy, but I do remember walking hand in hand with my sister, eating cotton candy and hearing the delighted screams of the older kids on the rides. My mother usually walked behind us, chattering a mile a minute to my grandmother, who would cluck sympathetically from time to time. Grandma had taken the brunt of my mother's criticisms on those days so my sister and I could enjoy ourselves in peace.

My body jerked, shoulders thumping against the floor.

"Luce." Someone tapped my shoulder.

Wasn't I awake?

"Lucy, it's me." A tug at my backpack.

My eyes fought their way open. Sticky sleep blurred my vision for a second. Early morning light streamed in one of the windows. Unwavering blue eyes held my gaze.

For a brief moment, I thought I'd fallen asleep on Chris's couch. But the agonizing creak in my back quickly brought me back to reality.

I licked my dry lips. "You're here."

"Of course I am."

"You were mad at me."

"I'm usually mad at you. Doesn't mean I'm not going to help." He grabbed my hand and pulled me to a sitting position. My arms were still locked around the bag. He tugged one of the straps. "I take it you don't have your best jewelry in here?"

"No."

"Good thinking." He glanced behind him. I saw Justin for the first time. "Which is the only smart decision you made last night."

My senses were coming back to me. "This is the women's room. How come you guys are in here?"

"They're all down eating," Justin said. "Hank told us we could wake you. Although your boyfriend didn't give him much choice." He scowled at the older brother he'd been trying to get to know.

"He's not my boyfriend," I answered. "And he likes to get his way."

Chris glared at Justin. "You and Detective Dumbfuck brought her here instead of calling me. Why should I come in here like I'm on a Sunday visit?"

"Don't talk about Todd that way," Justin snapped back. "He's the only reason she's not in jail. And I told you all of this earlier. Anything associated with you is the first place the cops are going to look."

"Good thing I've got places no one knows about." He pulled me to my feet. I swayed, trying to catch up to their conversation.

"You do?"

Chris ignored me. "And surely you could have gotten some cash and put her up—"

"Stop," I said. "Justin and Todd were right. Police are going to be looking at hotels. This was a safe place." I smiled at Justin, although it probably looked more like a grimace the way my head pounded. "And I can't thank you enough. Tell Todd I said thank you as well."

"You can tell him yourself," Justin said. "I've got the phone."

I shook my head. "No. He's not going to lose his job for me. And you aren't going to get in trouble." I nudged Chris. "Either of you."

"What are you getting at?" he asked.

I looked up at him, for once not feeling put off by his scrutiny. "I knew this day would come. And being here, this isn't right. What is right is accepting I've done some good things, even if they were bad. Maybe I'll walk away from this, maybe not. But running isn't who I am."

"Lucy," Chris started.

"I've thought about this a lot. You know what my plans were for Sarah." I didn't bother to worry about Justin. He'd stay loyal to the end. "I would have carried them out. And then moved on to the next. I've lived in denial, convinced myself I had some calling. It's all a lie."

"You're exhausted," Chris said. "Let me take you somewhere safe while we work this out. You can sleep, get your head on straight."

"My head is on straight." I tugged at his collar, bringing his face close to mine. My whisper was only for him. "If I don't go, I won't stop doing bad things. That girl, Riley. What I nearly did to her... that's not who I want to be."

He grabbed my shoulders. "I won't let you do this."

"Isn't it the right thing, though? I always said I'd accept it when the time came. Not run around taking up space where I don't belong." I waved my hand toward the empty room. "Using these people. I'd rather sit in a cell."

"This isn't the time." Chris held me too tightly. His eyes were harder than I'd ever seen them. Pleasant chills shot through me. "This isn't the plan. You know it. We've discussed it. And I won't let you throw your life away for something you didn't do."

"Me neither." Justin spoke again. He cleared his throat. "Listen, my brother—Todd, you know, the one who actually accepts that I exist?" Chris rolled his eyes. "He told me what he thinks you do. He's not sure how you do it yet, but he thinks he can find out."

Chris and I stared at each other. The air stilled; my heart slowed to a painful thud.

"The thing is, I'm not sure he really wants to do anything about it," Justin continued. "When he talks about you, about the men he thinks you... he sounds like he admires you. He wishes he would have killed my mother. *Our* mother," he added for Chris's benefit. "He thought about it, you know. Couldn't go through with it. He blamed himself for what happened to me, and that's why he became a cop."

I tried to look around Chris's broad shoulders to see Justin's face, but Chris held me firm.

"Todd wants to know what you did. He wants to figure it out. But in the end, I don't think he'll arrest you. He just wants to know, for himself."

"Why on earth would you say that?" I choked out.

"Because this business of being all honorable and not wanting you arrested for the wrong crime is a bunch of shit. He brings people in on holds or suspicion of crimes they didn't commit all the time, and it's no more than a ploy to get to the truth. And yet he's doing just the opposite with you."

"What's your point?" Chris finally released me and turned to face his younger brother.

"That she needs to stop comparing what she's accused of to what she's actually done." He stepped past Chris, brushing the older man's shoulder. They glared at each other, so different and so much alike. Justin stopped in front of me, ignoring Chris's fuming. "Todd doesn't want you in trouble for anything, and the people who are trying to bring you down are the same kind of monsters you hunt. His hands are tied. If you throw in the towel now, everything you've done—every dark decision you've made—is for nothing. Because this trafficking thing just gets bigger. And the leaders get more powerful. And more kids get hurt."

Maybe his words got to me. Or maybe my coward side won out. I'd probably never know the answer. I rolled my neck and shoulders and then slipped on the backpack.

"I've got two conditions." I poked Chris hard in the shoulder. He turned to glare at me. "Thanks for coming for me, in spite of everything. I'll go with you, but I've got a stop to make first. If we're careful, we should be safe. That's the first one."

He raised an eyebrow. "And the second?"

I felt the blood pulsing through me now as my old self returned. I gave him my most charming smile. "You start spending time with Justin. No arguments. You guys need each other. Or you might, one day. And you're lucky to have one another."

Chris's mouth twitched. Justin hid a smirk.

"Whatever," Chris finally said. "Let's go."

TWENTY-FOUR

When I first started down my chosen path, Kelly and I hashed out all the possibilities. She had the foresight to think of a code in case I wasn't able to use my own phone. I texted her from the pre-paid cell Justin brought me, and we made arrangements for me to stay with her. I'd kept my relationship with her secret from everyone except Chris, and neither one of them would allow me to spend another night in the shelter.

Kelly locked the door behind me, her eyes wide and scared. "You're crazy. You're running from the cops on information from Todd? The same guy who wants to arrest you for multiple murders?"

"Technically"—I dumped the bag on her countertop, feeling safe with it for the first time since I left home—"I'm not on the run. I left before they showed up. I'm just hiding."

"How'd you dump your heroes?"

"Justin was easy enough. He still listens. Chris, on the other hand, I had to threaten, but he's getting some cash from his uncle's place. He didn't want to use his ATM."

"He keeps cash at his uncle's?"

I shrugged. "He's got a history of forgetting his bank card, I guess. Safety measures. You sure it's all right for me to stay here? You need your space."

"It's fine," she said. "You'll have to sleep on the couch, but it's better than the shelter. I can't stand the idea of you out there alone." She took my hand and squeezed it. I squeezed back, wishing I'd never brought this sweet girl into my web of lies and death.

Forty minutes later, I emerged from her tiny shower with clean hair and in the only change of clothes I'd brought. The hot water stripped away the physical and mental grime, and I'd been able to bury whatever feelings of doubt and fear I'd dredged up during the night. "You said you had something you wanted to show me?"

She motioned for me to sit down in her makeshift office. "I've spent way more time than I wanted to going through these dark net sites. Some of the things people post... what they request, for kids... I can't even describe them." She was pale, I realized. And her face was thinner. Scouring these sites took a horrible toll on her.

"Stop looking," I said. "I'm not sure you'll ever find what we're looking for, and it's not good for you. Didn't you say all the double blinds and overseas server routing makes it nearly impossible to prove where a site's really coming from?"

"That's why I've been digging deep," she said. "Because if you go through enough pictures and posts"—she shuddered—"you get an idea of where the owners might be operating from. The problem for law enforcement is they need more technical information to get a warrant, which is where the trouble with the overseas servers come in. Plus there are so many thousands of sites they can't really dig into them without some kind of tip. I, on the other hand, can spend countless hours obsessively surfing and looking for specific locations and requirements."

"You found something related to Philadelphia?" I couldn't believe we'd be that lucky. "Surely the operators weren't so dumb as to make their location obvious."

"They aren't." Kelly pulled up a browser window. She bit the inside of her lip. "Listen, we're dug into the cesspool of life right now. I shouldn't need to click on any of the graphic images, but you've been warned."

"Got it." Although I'd heard countless depraved stories of abuse, one thing I'd learned is that there is always something worse out there.

"So this one site, the Candy Market"—she winced at the name—"has a whole bunch of pages with kids being horribly victimized. I don't need to show you those, but they have an actual market page, where interested parties can shop."

"By shop you mean looking at pictures of the available kids."

She nodded.

"Christ. And it's local? How could you possibly find that out?"

"I wasn't sure at first, because everything is so damned buried, but then I started looking at the names of the kids." She started talking too fast, and I knew she'd found something good. "A lot them are old-fashioned. They just didn't seem like something parents would name their kids nowadays. And they were weirdly familiar. As soon as I started Googling the names, I hit on the connection. They're all Philadelphia historical figures."

That was the last thing I'd expected to hear. My mouth actually dropped open. "Are you kidding me?"

"It's kind of ballsy, but these guys are so sneaky they figure they're deeply hidden, and unless someone is specifically looking for this area, who's going to notice? Look." She clicked on the Market page. At least thirty small pictures of children popped up. Likely taken with a cellphone, most of the kids sat on a bed or a couch looking tense and frightened for the camera. Some were teens, others much younger.

"Agnes Radcliffe," I read.

"Agnes Irwin, first dean of Radcliffe," Kelly supplied.

"Cornelius Tiller."

"Cornelius Van Til, theologian."

"Cecilia Beaux."

"A painter way back in the old days," Kelly said. "You get the point. All of these are carefully chosen historical figures, nothing recent. Names run the gamut from historians to teachers to musicians. Carefully selected so as not to stand out, but the theme is there. And every one can be tied to a historical figure from this city. I'm absolutely positive we've found the right site."

I scanned the pictures, trying not to look at their eyes. Even with the forced, tight smiles, most of these children had dead eyes. Likely sexually abused before they were selected, and now suffering horrific things.

"There's a new arrivals link," I said. "Have you looked at those?"

"Nope. That's recent as of today." Kelly clicked the red link.

Two more boys came up, both younger than ten. For a moment I thought I was seeing things, and then dizziness washed over me, followed by acute nausea. "William Allen."

Kelly did a quick search. "Mayor of Philly from 1735 to 1736."

"It's the little guy." I tasted vomit.

"What?"

"The little boy with Riley the other day, the one she was babysitting. He's wearing the knit hat I gave him. Preacher must have found out she talked to me," I said. "She was attached to the little boy, said Preacher would never get him. He's punishing her."

Now I'd had it. Any thought of giving up my plan and

turning myself in evaporated just like that little boy's innocence had. I was going to kill Preacher. But first, he'd give me the information I needed. "Give me that pre-paid phone."

"What are you going to do?" Kelly handed me the phone, looking scared.

"It's time I had my test run with Preacher. He'll talk, and then I'll take care of him."

Kelly stood up and began to pace. "Are you sure you want to do this?"

"Absolutely."

"Are you going to have backup?"

"I'll talk to Chris." I didn't want to pull him into my vendetta. But I needed him, and if he wanted to help go after his mother, this experience would be good practice. "I'll probably need help pulling it off since I'll have to be on Preacher's turf. But we'll manage."

She steepled her hands against her lips. "Think about where this is going. It will change everything, including who you are. Are you prepared for that?"

"I don't know." It was the truth. "All I know is that I can't go down without a fight, and this bastard deserves to pay. And if that means doing something I never thought I would, then I'll accept that. If the time comes."

"Preacher isn't going to just share his life story with you."

"I'll get the information I need." I'd accepted my decision the minute I decided to leave the shelter with Chris and Justin. "I need to find out if he killed Sarah and who's behind this ring. And then I'll take care of him once and for all."

TWENTY-FIVE

Preacher was very happy to hear from me. Within minutes, he'd made arrangements at the Capri Motel, nestled conveniently between Strawberry Mansion and the dangerous area around Temple University. Chris nearly refused to drop me off when he saw the place, but I managed to convince him this was my best shot at clearing my name and moving on to bigger targets, namely his mother.

A large two-story motel with a parking lot that backed up to an industrial area, Capri advertised its hourly rates with a bright, neon sign. Working girls, many of them wrecked from drug use, loitered along the sidewalks. Either the police had forgotten about this area or the girls were too far gone to care; one even had a crack pipe sticking out of her purse.

I arrived at the motel first as requested. Preacher had provided fake names for both of us, and the room was already paid for. I didn't even have to show identification. The manager looked equal parts bored and smarmy. He smirked at me as I took the elevator to the second floor. The fire escape was at the end of the hall. Preacher had chosen well for reasons he'd never know.

The room was like every other one-star room: barely clean with the faint scent of the previous bodies, the walls stained with dried splashes and crusty streaks of unknown liquids. I set my bag down and did a bed bug check, yanking out poorly tucked-in sheets. All clear for bed bugs. A small television with a crack in the screen sat on a scratched chest of three drawers. The blinds were closed.

Our room faced the street. The woman with the crack pipe got into a junker of a car that quickly disappeared. An old man ambled out of the lobby of the hotel with a can of cat food. He rattled a fork against the tin, and soon a stray cat came to greedily gobble the stinking feast. The man went back inside, and I closed the blinds.

Inside the square and dirty bathroom, I regarded myself in the mirror. Someone had written a number in the corner, and the maid hadn't bothered to clean it off. If a maid had been through the room at all. I brushed the brand new blond wig, figuring Preacher wouldn't notice the difference, tucking a strand behind my ear. Applied a bit more powder to cover the sprinkling of freckles across the bridge of my nose. Put on some mascara. Brushed my teeth and then applied lip gloss.

My backpack contained the more essential items. Preacher was too smart for me to slip him the ketamine in a glass of wine, but that was fine. Ketamine could be injected into the muscle, and if I choreographed the dance right, he would be singing in a matter of minutes.

I slipped on my latex gloves, checked the already prepared syringe, and then surveyed the used bed. How would Preacher want me?

He liked to be the boss, so domination was likely. But this was an audition. He'd want to see if I could take control, make a man salivate for more. Wasn't that every man's fantasy? A woman who operated with complete confidence in the bedroom? Minutes ticked by as I envisioned the night playing out. I'd have to let him touch me, make him relax. I couldn't seem too eager, but he'd have to believe I was into him. Maximum ego boost.

Blocking out the cheapness of the act was easy. This was simply another role on a foreign stage. My skills were good enough to pull it off.

I chose the hiding spot for the syringe, hid the gloves in the trash underneath a wad of tissues, and sat down to wait.

Preacher arrived ten minutes late. I admired his effort at controlling the situation. He wasn't an amateur. But I was better.

I'd chosen a form-fitting white sweater top over skinny jeans. I opened the door after his second knock.

He'd dressed casual too, looking more like the kid from the street than the businessman he pretended to be. All swagger, his eyes swept over me, lingering at my chest. He made a circling motion with his index finger. I obeyed, turning a slow circle.

"Very nice. My clients like a girl with some ass."

I giggled. "Thanks." I stepped aside to let him in, twirling a lock of hair and popping my spearmint gum.

"You nervous?"

I ducked my chin. "A little."

He used his index finger to tug my head up. "That's part of your charm. I like that. So will the boys. But you got to loosen up too."

He set his hat down on the desk, draped his jacket over the chair. Pulled off his bright red hoodie and tossed it over the jacket. Down to a white T-shirt and jeans, he looked younger and even lankier than before. His jeans were loose, but they didn't hide his enjoyment.

The ketamine would take away Preacher's ability to fight, and his reflexes would be greatly slowed. Still, he'd have a moment, a single moment when he felt the needle go in and realized he was no longer in control.

My skin heated. I pulled at the collar of my top. He smiled, showing white, wolfish teeth. Taking my cue, I stepped forward until the space between us evaporated. He was shorter than Chris, the top of my head touching his cheek. His fingers trailed up my covered arms. I shivered.

"Take this off."

I obeyed, tossing the garment onto the bed. In only the lacy, beige bra and my tight jeans, I waited for his next order. I felt the skin on my chest burning, the sensation sliding up my throat. Even the roots of my hair tingled. Whether the cause was embarrassment or anticipation, the results served their purpose.

"Damn, I love you fair-skinned girls." Preacher's voice turned husky. He ran his hands from my collarbones down to my breasts and roughly squeezed.

I let him touch me, his hands wandering from my breasts, over my stomach, down to my behind. He moved to the front of my pants. I gritted my teeth to keep from jerking away.

"Yeah," he said. His voice was rough now, his breathing growing heavy. "You want it. They always do. Good girls are the best kind of whores." He grabbed my neck, angling my face to his, and roughly kissed me. Firm lips, benign breath, altogether not a bad kisser. His other arm snaked around me and brought me flush against him.

He was hard against my stomach, his movements faster and with purpose. He wanted me, and he was at his weakest point.

I returned the kiss with as much passion as I could dig up, my hands flush against his chest, and then pushed him down on the bed. My aim was perfect. He landed on the right side, near the edge. Too turned on to notice, he hit the mattress with a satisfied moan, his mouth moving down my neck and his hands slipping inside the back of my jeans.

Arching my back, I shifted to my left, gasping as if I enjoyed his touch. He didn't notice my hand slipping over the side of the bed, where my fingers dug underneath the mattress. His only response to my change of position was to yank down the bra cup of my right breast and latch his mouth on to the nipple.

Shame and shock froze me for a brief second. And then I retrieved the syringe, gracefully pulled myself up and away from his mouth, before planting my lips firmly against his. Grinding my hips over his erection gave me the distraction I needed.

I opened my eyes first. His were closed, his face sweating. He had long lashes. A dribble of acne on his nose. A tiny scar on his forehead.

Completely clueless.

I jammed the needle into his bicep and waited.

His eyes shot open. "The fuck?"

"I just want you to have extra fun," I whispered against his mouth. "This will make it so good."

Ketamine acts very quickly, and the dose I gave him was strong. It would hit in two minutes or less, and I'd have at least thirty minutes with him at my command. Letting the syringe fall to the floor, I rocked my hips against his. He stared at me, fear and lust dueling in his eyes. His erection grew and then began to fade. His body stopped writhing; his breathing slowed. He went slack, his eyes still wide and staring.

"What'd you do to me, girl?"

"Showing you who's really in control, Roderick."

TWENTY-SIX

With Preacher lying motionless, I took the time to discard the wig and put my shirt back on. My hair was pulled back in a tight knot, and I resisted the urge to torment him by letting it fall around my shoulders. Just more evidence to clean up.

"Liar." Preacher spoke slowly. After a few minutes, he was probably already experiencing the floating feeling the drug brings. Users claim it's as if the mind and body have been pulled apart, with some likening the sensation to a near-death experience. Entering the K-Hole, as recreational users call it, makes a person compliant, but the longer the trip, the more likely he was to start having hallucinations.

"No more than you." I took out the scalpel. I'd prefer not to use it, but tonight had to be a success.

"I feel big," he slurred. "As big as the universe."

"You're just an invisible speck in the mass of darkness." Let him chew on that for a while. Sitting down next to his head, I shoved one of his heavy arms out of my way. "Tell me who you work for."

"Myself."

"No. Sarah explained this all to me. You're the captain. Who's really in charge?"

"I don't know his name."

He might be lying. But the drug should make him compliant. Was the big boss really that secretive? I tried another track.

"Why did you kill Sarah Jones?"

"I didn't kill that bitch. Glad someone did, though."

"Why?"

With his body effectively paralyzed, only Preacher's eyes moved. They flickered rapidly around the room, staring at the water-stained ceiling, the walls, and finally, my face. "You're that red-headed bitch who figured out our business."

I smiled. "Good job."

His eyes rolled back in his head before focusing on me again. "Why you doing this to me? I thought we were going to have a good time."

"Because someone is telling the police I killed Sarah. I don't know his name, but I know he's got a lot of pull over the police and the district attorney. His wife was a client at the salon. He, on the other hand, likes the little kids you guys provided. He knows I took the phone Sarah stored her information in, and he's trying to protect himself by making sure I get the hook for murder."

His mouth fell open, revealing two dull silver fillings. A huffing sound rolled out of him. For a second I worried he was having a bad reaction, and then I realized he was trying to laugh. "None of our clients got balls enough to do that. They're all scared men who want to hide behind..." He trailed off, eyes popping wider. "I think the ceiling is changing colors. What did you give me?"

"It doesn't matter. While you enjoy your trip, you can give me some more information. You said none of your clients would do this? Someone is, and I'm going to clear my name."

A moment of clarity brightened his dull gaze. "You're going to kill me."

"Not if you tell me what I want to know." Did he believe me? I hoped so. It would make later all the more satisfying. "Sarah had one hell of a coding system in that phone. I didn't find anything else. So you tell me who you think would be trying to hide information."

"Easy." Drool rolled down his chin. His arm jerked with the effort to wipe it up but remained in place. "Dietz. The boyfriend."

"Dietz?" I racked my memory. There were a lot of Ds in the phone, but her email had been protected.

"Big country attorney."

My turn to still. United States Attorney Cameron Dietz, operating out of Philadelphia for the Eastern District of Pennsylvania. A newsmaker, Dietz looked like a retired model and had the whitest teeth of any man I'd ever seen. He'd just won a big case against an organized crime family, and he'd reveled in giving interviews on the courthouse steps. The distinguished attorney always wore a tie bright enough to match his teeth. "What's his wife's name?"

"Feet." Preacher's eyes rolled back in his head.

I smacked his cheek, and slowly, like spoiled milk that's curdled, the whites of his eyes rolled back down, and he focused on me. "No, US Attorney Dietz. What's his wife's name?" I'd seen her in the salon more than once, but Sarah always made sure no one else but her helped Mrs. Dietz.

"She does feet." His words were slurred. "Fat bitch too, with that ugly ass mole on her cheek and irritating voice."

Then I remembered. Amanda Rollins, Sarah's client the night I stole the phone. Of course. Sarah must have freaked out and told her it was missing. "So what's Attorney Dietz's preference? Little girls or boys?"

"Sarah," Preacher said. "Him and Sarah."

"An affair?" So Sarah was making money off the wife and doing her husband at the same time, plus dealing little kids. Why did Sarah Jones deserve justice again?

Preacher closed his eyes, pursed his lips. His head jerked up and down. I took that for a nod. "Long time. His wife's a bitch and has all the money. Big prenup."

Anger coursed through me. I pressed the scalpel against the soft skin beneath his eye. "You're lying. Sarah wouldn't share this information with you."

"Riley. She and Sarah buds. Riley told me, 'cause she my girl and she know her place."

The scalpel trembled. A tiny droplet of blood oozed out of Preacher's skin. I caught it before it hit the mattress.

"Is that why you took her friend's little boy for your sick site?"

His mouth opened and closed, making me think of the trout that flopped against the bottom of the boat when Mac and I went fishing. I never could kill them. He had to take care of that messy deed. "That's right. I found the Candy Market. Quite smart using obscure Philadelphia historical figures. A nice middle finger to the authorities unable to bring you down. And too smart for you to think of. Boss's idea?"

"Yeah."

"Did you take the little guy from Riley to punish her?"

"She felt bad. Wasn't hard to do."

I could probably slice through his carotid with this scalpel and let him bleed out. But that left evidence that was impossible to clean up, and I still needed information. Fighting for control, I pushed on. "So Dietz stood to lose money and his reputation. He thinks I know about his affair and figures this is the easiest way to get rid of me. But what if the charges don't stick?"

"How should I know?" Preacher snapped. His shoulder jerked. "And I'm glad that bitch is dead. You know what she did? That night you tried to blackmail her, you naughty girl?

She came to me at Ward 8 and said she wanted out. I had to take her back to the salon and show her I was boss."

"You did kill her."

He grimaced. I tightened my grip on the scalpel and checked my watch. Twenty minutes had passed. Ketamine trips could last anywhere from a half hour to hours, depending on the person. Preacher might be having a short ride.

"Nope. Just smacked her around until she understood how things was." The corner of his mouth twitched up as he tried to smile. "Took that gold locket she loved. Begged my ass to give it back, said her mama gave it to her, and I said I would if she proved her loyalty to me. See, I knew she'd been visiting that senator's office. Told my boss that too. Just waiting to hear from him on how to handle her. But I put her in line, thought maybe she'd be good. But someone else didn't."

Sarah met with the senator? That meant he recognized the name and hadn't said a damned word. I didn't have time to think about it right now—Preacher's fingers were moving.

"She alive when I left her."

"You think your boss killed her?"

This time, his laugh actually produced some noise. "Never gets his hands dirty."

I straddled him, pressing the scalpel between his eyes. "What's his name?"

"I told you I don't know. We only communicate online, and he's smart. Got himself protected. He's the one who runs the website too. I don't handle that shit. I'm a people guy."

"You're just a stupid street pimp who didn't think to investigate," I corrected him. "Don't you know anything about manipulating people? Or are your skills limited to vulnerable girls?"

"What'd you mean?"

"You could have found out who he was, turned the tables, took control. Made my life easier." He disappointed me. We weren't as equal as I'd thought. He probably hadn't even figured out I was really going to kill him yet. What a fool. "Riley. Where can I find her?"

"This week got her in a place not too far away. Motel North. She working right out of there. But she won't betray me. Got that girl right where I want her."

"If you were so mad at Sarah, why'd you go back the next day to pay her?"

"Because money talks, don't it?" This time, his entire body twitched. I didn't have any more time to waste.

I slid off him and grabbed the other syringe out of my bag.

"No more." Both shoulders moved, his face looking strained.

"I have to take care of you. And you'll never know what happened. Painless. That's more than I can say for some."

Understanding ricocheted across his face. My pulse kicked up at the fear brimming in his eyes. "You're really going to kill me?"

"You're a bad person. How many kids have you pimped out over the last few years?"

"They're willing!"

I had to drop the scalpel, or I would have stabbed him. "Really? The ones you bring in from other states? The boys? That sweet little boy Riley was babysitting? Is he willing? What about his mother? Did you dope her up until she didn't care if you took him or not? And the girls you prey on and beat down until they're broken? They're willing?"

"You're too pretty to be a killer; you won't do this." Even facing death, the pimp tried to worm his way into my good graces. Sad thing was, he probably believed he could do it.

I started laughing. "Oh honey, if you only knew. This isn't my first time."

Sheer terror, his body dumbly thrashing, trying to get his arms and legs to move and defend himself. "I'll tell you anything you want to know."

"Your boss? That's the only thing that will keep you alive."

"Don't know his name, but I know how he works. He knew I had girls. He contacted me, said he had access to people who wanted more than just street hookers, and how'd I like to make some real money? So we set up our business. All on the Internet—you saw it! We got people who bring in boys and girls from Ohio and New York, mostly. Sarah's phone had all them clients."

"Do you keep records?"

Tears sprang into his eyes. "Only of who I pay."

"I want the boss. And the johns. How did Sarah get involved?" What a waste of space this guy was. All bluster and no brawn at the end. How could he get involved in this whole mess with no inside information in case he needed it? He wasn't even worthy of being a captain. Preacher was just a grunt.

"The boss found her. Said she was perfect for what we were doing. Needed a lot of money, and she couldn't turn us down. He sent me to her."

"It was more than just money he had on her, wasn't it? What was it?"

"He didn't tell me much. But it wasn't hard to push her into dealing. She wanted the money. Boss told me to mention Sam, and she fell right in line."

"So." I climbed back on top of him, unbuckling his belt. I grazed his flaccid penis, and his choking breaths eased. As if he thought I was going to reward him. I worked his pants down to his knees. He'd dribbled urine on his red underwear. "We've got Sarah having an affair with US Attorney Dietz. Dietz has a lot to lose if that's found out. Did he know about Sarah's involvement with you?"

"No. I don't know; Riley might know."

"And it was just your partner, you, and Sarah?"

"Yeah. No one else."

"So small staff, wide operation. How many working kids you have?"

He tried to grind his hips into my hands, as if that would suddenly change his fate. Disgusting. "About thirty right now, not counting my girls. They mine. Boss don't care about them. Don't make enough money to keep him happy."

"Where are the kids I saw on your website?"

"Lots of places. Motels in North Philly. Couple at a project. I'll show you."

"No, you won't. As soon as you get full function back, you'll try to beat me like your other girls. But you see..." I leaned forward, letting the tip of the needle graze the big muscle of his thigh. "I'm not like the other girls. I'm the one who will fight back. Who's smarter than you. And the last face you'll ever see." I stuck the needle into the muscle, pushed down the plunger.

"Please..." The begging trailed off as the next dose took over. With the other shot still in his system, Preacher was so far gone he could no longer speak. For a moment I thought he'd lost consciousness, but his bloodshot eyes darted from side to side.

I could leave him like this. Ketamine destroys the memory, and chances are he would have little recollection of the episode. But I couldn't take the risk.

And he was an enabling piece of trash.

I reached for the pillow. His eyes followed my movement. He knew.

My lips brushed his immobile mouth. "This is for Riley. And the little boy you stole from her friend. And every child whose life you helped steal away."

I pressed the pillow over his face and lay on top of it. He couldn't struggle. His chest was the only thing that moved, gasping and sucking for air. I pressed harder. My heart pounded and sweat beaded on my temples. My cheeks hurt. I realized I was smiling. Gripping the pillow more tightly, I folded it over the sides of his head, clamping the material over his ears.

It took him seventy-two seconds to die.

I set the pillow aside and called Chris.

TWENTY-SEVEN

"You said you might not kill him." Chris stood at the foot of the bed, staring at Preacher's body. He fiddled with the latex gloves I'd made him put on before he touched anything.

"It didn't work out that way," I said.

"Was it the ketamine?"

I nodded. Easier for him to believe the lie.

He rubbed the back of his hair and then stopped. "Jesus, I probably just left evidence."

"No one is going to come looking for him," I said. "He set himself up. Used a fake name. Who knows if he told anyone. But this hotel doesn't keep records—they didn't even take my identification. And they definitely don't want the cops around. We just have to get rid of him before he makes a mess."

The hardness in my voice surprised me. I'd never disposed of a body before. Until today, Brian Harrison was the only victim whose death I'd witnessed. I'd made my escape before the others could die. But I saw Brian take his last breath, and I thought the reality of my actions scarred me. Instead, the wound had healed incorrectly, leaving an infectious tissue that seemed hell-bent on making me a mindless predator.

"How'd you luck out and get the room closest to the fire escape?"

I couldn't help the smile. "Preacher saved me the trouble of requesting it. My guess is for an easy escape if he needed it. Like I said, he set himself up."

"The rig is around the corner."

"You didn't have any trouble getting it?"

Chris shook his head. "It's an old one no one will miss. But just enough not to draw attention."

His offer to provide the ambulance had surprised me. "You're awfully calm. I expected you to be running around the room."

"Yeah, well"—he turned to me with an imperceptible gaze— "I learned from the best, didn't I?"

He rolled out his sleeping bag, revealing the black body bag.

"Something else you stole?"

"You can buy these online. Seriously."

"Gross. Okay, so you've dealt with bodies as a paramedic. I'll let you take the lead."

Chris laid out the body bag next to Preacher. The sound of the zipper made me shiver. He arranged the plastic bag so that it was open and then motioned for me to take Preacher's ankles. "He'll be heaviest at the top."

"Wait." I'd nearly forgotten. "We need to check his pockets, make sure we take his wallet. I'll get rid of it somewhere, but it will make him a lot harder to identify if he's found."

"Fine. You do it."

Preacher's left pocket was empty. In his right was a fine gold locket I recognized. "Sarah's. Just what I need to have on me." I tossed it in my bag. Chris rolled him over, and I wrestled his wallet out of his back pocket. Whatever hope I had of finding all the answers quickly faded. Nothing but cash and IDs. One of them was Riley's. At least I'd have that to bargain with when I went to find her.

"You ready?"

I nodded.

"On three, we'll lift him." Chris crawled on top of the bed and positioned himself at the front of Preacher's body. He stared down at the dead man's open eyes. "I can't believe I'm doing this."

"Me neither, but we need to get it done. And I'll owe you my life."

"My mother?"

"Yes. The second I'm not a wanted fugitive, we'll go after her with everything I have." I grabbed Preacher's ankles while Chris shoved his hands under Preacher's shoulders.

"One, two, three." We lifted, my back straining to maintain his heavy weight. The bed shifted with our efforts, and the bag dropped to the floor. "Put him down," Chris said.

I let Preacher's heavy legs fall. "What now?"

"I'll lift him up at the waist, you slide the bag under. Then we'll do the feet." His tone was all businesslike now. He pushed at Preacher's shoulders until the dead man was sitting up. I glanced back at the mirror hanging directly across from the bed. Preacher's dead eyes stared back. Behind him, Chris's blue ones were nearly as vacant.

I slipped the bag in place. Then we worked at his feet. In five minutes we had him zipped up and we were both panting.

"Now," I said. "There's only one guy on duty downstairs and one elevator. You bring the ambulance around and park at the fire escape. We know there are no security cameras, but you don't want to be seen. Keep your hood up. I'll stand watch at the elevator while you get him into the ambulance."

Chris's head bobbed up and down as I spoke. Bouncing on the balls of his feet, he looked ready to bolt.

"You don't have to do this," I said. "You walk away now and the harm is minimal. I'll get rid of him myself."

"I can handle it. You're going to need my help with Mary,

and this is a good test run. Besides, he wanted to put his hands on you and treat you like trash. That's enough for me to compartmentalize."

"Right," I said. "You see death on the job. You know how to block it out. Compartmentalize like you just said."

"Something like that." He looked at his watch. "It's nearly 3 a.m. Let's get out of here before people start waking up."

Preacher was loaded into the ambulance twenty minutes later. I wiped the room down with a strong disinfectant before we left, stripping the sheets and bringing the covers with me to burn.

"You're right, this sucker is old." I climbed into the passenger seat and glanced behind me. Preacher was strapped to a gurney. In the darkness, I couldn't see if the ambulance was fully loaded, but we wouldn't need medical supplies. "Where are we going?"

"Northwest. Lots of forests up there. We can dispose of his body, cover him with snow. The bears will find him in the spring before the park rangers."

"Good idea."

We drove silently for a while, lost in our own thoughts. Chris seemed resigned to becoming an accomplice to murder. I guess he'd accepted that's what being the closest part of my life meant.

"Why are you doing this for me?"

"I already told you." We got out of the city just as the sun began to peek over the horizon. Maybe the temperature would climb above zero today.

"You already had my promise to help with Mother Mary, so it's more than that."

"I can't handle you going away," he said.

"To prison?"

He nodded. "That means doing whatever it takes to keep you out."

"How'd I become so important to you? I'm not special. I'm dangerous. Unstable."

"You're the only person who understands me. Or at least comes close to having some real comprehension of what I've been through. I trust you." His voice softened, his face flushed. His eyes remained fixed on the road.

The serenity from killing Preacher began to wear off, and my emotions started to roll out of their prison. "I'm not sure I'm worthy of that trust."

"Too late." He gave me a weak grin. "You're stuck with me now."

I rubbed my stinging eyes. "Guess so."

By the time we reached the national forest, I'd recounted all of Preacher's confessions to Chris.

"Ketamine." He whistled. "Who knew it was basically like a truth serum?"

"Forget about that. What do you think about Dietz going to all this trouble to have me arrested instead of just pulling a good old-fashioned power play and threatening me?"

"Maybe it's not his style. Or maybe he's planning on swooping in once you're incarcerated and offering to save the day if you comply."

"That fits with a man like him."

We drove through a back entrance with so many trees the ambulance barely fit through. I could only hope there were no rangers around to ask what we were doing. I wasn't sure how we'd explain a morning drive in the state forest with a dead body. Chris finally stopped at the top of a hill where the brush was thick and the decline steep.

Preacher rolled down easily. I stood watch while Chris slid down the hill and pried the body bag off him. He covered Preacher with snow and icicles and fallen dead branches. He worked efficiently, moving with ease among the cold, dead things. I admired his ability to cope and wished I'd handled Brian Harrison's death as well as Chris had Preacher's.

Then again, he hadn't administered it. And just two weeks ago at an accident call, he'd pulled a dead teenager out of a pickup truck. Surely this had to be easier.

He returned sooner than I expected, and we used more fallen branches to maneuver the heavy snow over our messy tracks.

"That's the best we can do." Chris's fair skin was pink. His lips looked like he'd applied gloss. "With any luck, he'll be under until spring."

"The bears will do their jobs."

"You did clean him off before I zipped up the bag, right?"

"Wiped him down completely."

He led the way back to the ambulance. We rode in silence once again until Chris turned in to the county landfill. I dumped the body bag and everything that had touched Preacher's body into a black bag, and we paid in cash to have it tossed into the burning pile at the landfill.

"Good idea," I said. "Getting rid of that in the city would have been a pain in the ass."

"Thanks." He drove several miles before speaking again. "So you know what I'd like to know? Where's Sarah's mother?"

"What?"

"Preacher said her mother gave Sarah that locket. But both Kelly and Todd say there's no next of kin for her. Nothing anywhere. No one to even claim the body. So where's Mom? Is she dead?"

I hadn't even thought about the implication. I retrieved the locket from my bag. Small and delicate, it was a simple square shape with an "S" engraved in the fourteen-karat gold. It opened easily, but the inside was bare except for the serial number.

"What does that tell you?"

Chris glanced at the locket. "There's more to her past than anyone's digging up. What now?"

"Riley," I said. "She knows everything we need to."

"What about Todd? You going to tell him about Dietz? If he had the guy's name, maybe he could start looking for proof of this affair. Something to play ball with at least."

My biggest dilemma of the day. I didn't want to leave Todd out of the loop, not after what he'd done for me. But I was afraid he would simply be steamrolled by Dietz. "Not yet. I think I need to go to the senator first. He's the only person who might have more pull than the US attorney. But first, to Riley."

Chris's phone vibrated on the plastic dash, startling us both. He snatched it up. "Hello?"

My eyelids began to droop, and I yawned wide enough to make my jaw hurt.

"I see." Chris's voice sounded guarded. "I'm not sure I can help you."

I forced my eyes open. "What?"

The ambulance swerved as he mouthed, "Do you know a John with Senator Coleman's office?"

Nodding, I snatched the phone from him before he wrecked us. "Hello?"

"Lucy." John didn't sound any more enthused than he had the last time we spoke. "The senator would like to speak with you right away. I'll give you directions to his private retreat outside of King of Prussia. And don't worry, the police aren't involved."

TWENTY-EIGHT

Chris wanted to go with me, and since John had his phone number, I figured he was already involved. We traded the ambulance for the shiny Audi, and I brushed my teeth in the ladies' room of a gas station just north of King of Prussia. Senator Coleman's place was about ten miles north of that, and John waited for us at the top of the winding drive.

Shuttered from the cold by an impressive thatch of evergreen trees, the Cape Cod-style house looked cozy and warm, the perfect place for a mild-mannered politician with a noble crusade.

Who just might be the big bad general I'm after.

We followed John into the bright foyer. Signs of a woman's touch were everywhere: flowers and soft pastels, strategically placed candles, delicate lace tablecloths. Coleman waited in his office, a large room that overlooked the frozen lake.

"Lucy." He shook my hand and then turned to Chris. "You must be Mr. Hale. I know your uncle. He speaks highly of you."

"That must be how you got my cell number." Chris grudgingly returned the shake.

"Oh no," Coleman said. "I have other resources." He sat

down, switching off the droning National Public Radio station emitting from the computer's weak speakers. Chris and I took the other two chairs in the room, while John lingered near the door. I suddenly felt like we'd entered the mob's lair.

"So what's going on?" Exhaustion robbed my patience.

"I hear the police are looking for you regarding Sarah Jones's murder."

"'Looking for' is a nice way to put it," I said. "They want to charge me. And I'm trusting you by coming here. Did I make a mistake?"

"No," Coleman said. "Quite the opposite. I believe I can help clear your name."

I recognized the tone of an exchange. Coleman certainly had interesting timing. "What's the catch?"

"You leave the human trafficking investigation to us," he said. "Go back to your normal cases. My office is more equipped, we can operate within legal parameters, and we've got a lot more reach."

"I thought you wanted my help."

"You've got a bit of a tainted history," he said. "It's come to my attention that in recent months, Detective Beckett posed the theory you murdered two brothers, both convicted child molesters, after their release. He doesn't have the evidence to prove it, I gather. But it's not something I want associated with our task force."

There was more to it than that, but I kept my mouth shut. Let the senator believe he had the upper hand.

"Did you get this information from the same US attorney who wants me convicted of Sarah's murder? A murder I didn't commit?"

If the senator noticed I didn't deny the Harrisons' murders, he didn't show it. "Mr. Dietz. Yes, he's a very imposing man with quite an influence on the investigation."

Showing any part of my hand was dangerous, but the

senator liked his information. He wasn't going to help unless he was sure I'd given him everything I knew. He'd get about ninety percent. "Dietz and Sarah were having an affair," I said. "He's got money and a reputation to lose, and because I took the phone, he thinks I've got proof. What I can't figure out is why he hasn't just confronted me. Why go to all these lengths?"

"Because Dietz is dirty in more ways than the marital bed." The senator was about to spill his secret. I recognized his tone, the way he sort of hunched down in his big chair—all signs of a man preparing to divulge something he really doesn't want to.

"Sarah and Attorney Dietz were having an affair," he confirmed. "And yes, his wife is very rich and there is a prenup. But Sarah was smart. She collected information like other people collect change. In this life, she never knew what might keep her alive."

"You knew her." I hadn't expected this. Why was he telling me this part? So I'd back off and he could soak up all the glory of bringing down the traffickers, or because he was the man I was really after?

"She's my wife's cousin by marriage."

"So you knew she was running kids?" Chris spoke up. I'd nearly forgotten he was there.

Coleman held up his hand. "Let me explain. Sarah had a boyfriend that was, quite frankly, crazy. After they broke up, he stalked her for months. Slashed her tires, broke windows. Nothing the police did helped, and they couldn't get hard proof it was him. But she was terrified when the threatening messages came in, and she asked my wife for help. I brought her to Philadelphia from Ohio, helped arrange for a new identity. She used all her savings to start the salon under an assumed surname."

"His name was Sam," I said. Preacher's ramblings about Sarah falling in line made sense.

"Yes." The senator raised an eyebrow. "Sam Townsend. How did you know?"

"I have my resources." I smirked. "But I didn't know what the name meant until now."

"Well," he continued, "somehow, whoever Preacher works for found her. Knew she was vulnerable, and you know the rest."

"Blackmailed her with the threat of telling Sam where she was," Chris said. That's the piece I'd been missing. It had been about much more than money.

"Right." Coleman sounded tired. "But as I said, Sarah was smart, and her experience with Sam taught her to write down everything. So she did, and her information-collecting became almost obsessive. She knew I had the task force, and as soon as she felt it was safe, she came to me."

"You guys were working together to bring down Preacher and his boss."

He nodded. "Whoever employs Preacher is very good. Sarah hoped she could get close enough to him to find out a name, but in the end, she didn't believe Preacher knew who he worked for."

I didn't tell him he was correct. I could tell him about the Candy Market site, give him all the information his task force would need. But something held me back. Perhaps I just wanted to kill all the sick bastards myself. Or I didn't think the task force could move fast enough. And then there was the matter that while she was giving the senator the information, Sarah was still actively sex trafficking and collecting a paycheck from it.

But what really bothered me was Sam Townsend. How did Preacher's boss get the name if the senator was the only person in the area who knew? More importantly, what had turned the boss onto Sarah in the first place? How had he known she was vulnerable?

I stared at the senator with fresh eyes. If he really were the boss, his task force was the perfect cover. And he'd kept Sarah running in circles until she became too much of a liability. "So if she trusted you, why didn't Sarah call you after I threatened her with the phone, before we met at Maisy's?"

"She did." He sounded torn. "She left me a message saying she had an urgent problem. I was in committee meetings all day and didn't return the call until very late. She never answered."

"Did she ever wonder how Preacher and his boss found out about Sam in the first place?" Chris asked.

"Of course she did. We've had many conversations on it. She told no one the name, but she did attend a support group for stalking victims. I can only assume she was spotted there and marked as a potential target."

Maybe. Men were stalked too. "I think there are other lieutenants." I used John's labeling system. "Maybe one of them picked her out."

"That was our theory as well," Coleman said.

"So what about this Dietz?" Chris asked.

"As I said, Sarah was sleeping with him. But she had her reasons. She believed he or someone in his office might be Preacher's employer, or at the very least, funding part of the operation."

"Why?" I asked.

"Because she followed Preacher and saw him having dinner with US Attorney Dietz at a restaurant called Ward 8. She waited around outside and saw money exchange hands."

And you were there too, I wanted to say. *I could just as easily substitute your name for the US attorney's.*

"Preacher was—is—a pimp," Chris corrected himself. "Dietz could have been ordering a high-class escort."

"And Sarah suspected that," Coleman said. "But there was a lot of cash, and she wanted to know more. When she came to me, I told her Dietz was known for running around on his wife, and we devised the plan."

"You used her," Chris said.

"She agreed to it."

So the senator was a pimp himself, except he didn't acquire money. His profit was information he could use to further his cause. I admired him.

"So back to the phone and why Dietz—"

"Because Sarah told him," Coleman interrupted me. "Two nights before you stole her private phone, she and Dietz got in a terrible fight. Sarah had been drinking, and she told him she knew his secrets. That he had business dealings with a known pimp and more girls on the side. She threatened to sell them to the press if he didn't give her what she wanted."

"Which was?" Chris asked.

"Sam charged with stalking. She believed he'd crossed state lines to find her. She swore she'd seen him in the city. And she wanted Dietz to use his influence as a United States attorney to make her safe."

"I don't blame her," I said. "Sounds like it was the least he could do."

"Agreed," Coleman said. "She told him the information was on her phone, and he'd never find it as she didn't carry it with her. He promised to try with Sam."

"But the police, and therefore Dietz, know that your people erased the phone," I said. "So what's his issue?"

"Again," the senator said, "it's you. You have a reputation in the department, and he's heard it. He's likely convinced that you made a copy of the information before you gave it to me."

"I couldn't even get to it!"

"But I did," John said.

I jumped. I had forgotten about the informant standing at the door. I swiveled in my chair. "You didn't erase the SIM card?"

"I did, after I got the information off it."

"Why didn't you tell the police?" Chris demanded. "Lucy might not be a suspect if you had."

"There's nothing in that phone that will clear her. It's all code, and it's not even clear to me," John said. "But what is clear is that Dietz and Sarah had many lustful email conversations. She also had pictures of him entering motels and prostitutes following soon after."

"Was Preacher in any of them?" I asked.

"No." John sounded disappointed. "But both of them frequented Ward 8, so who knows?"

"Was Dietz messing with kids?" Chris asked.

"It doesn't look like it," Coleman said. "Which is why, when I spoke to him this morning, his agreement he will stop pressuring the police in this case was accepted."

"So you blackmailed him. Awesome," I said. "But the police are still after me." And his sudden eagerness to help me still didn't make sense.

"Not after I call the district attorney's office," the senator said. "You see, the district attorney handling Sarah's case is hoping to run for governor next fall."

"And that's why he's been so easily pressured," Chris said. "The help of a US attorney would go a long way."

"Exactly." Coleman nodded. "I plan on telling the district attorney both you and Sarah worked for me, that she was infiltrated in the ring in an effort to bring them down. I'll give them information on Preacher and his nasty habits. And I'll also let them know who Sarah was and that she believed her ex was back in town."

"That might not be enough to make them back off," I said.

"Did I mention it will be a conference call with US Attorney Dietz?" Coleman's smile made me feel dirty. "He will claim that in light of this information, the ADA needs to withdraw the charges and pursue a new investigative track."

"Why?" I asked. "Why are you helping me?"

"I'm helping Sarah," Coleman said. "I don't believe you killed her. She had many enemies, and for all I know, Dietz could have had it done. John's going to look into that for me. Whatever her flaws, she did not deserve this, and I want her real killer brought to justice."

Sounded great, except he'd already lied to both me and to the police. No reason to believe he wasn't doing it now. Still, this could work to my advantage. "And all I have to do is leave the trafficking ring to you?"

"Exactly. Don't taint our efforts."

"Or steal your thunder for your own re-election," Chris said.

The senator's smile was brittle.

"I agree," I said. "On one condition."

"I don't believe you're in the position to be making conditions, my dear," Coleman said.

"No, I'm not. This is more of a favor. And not for me."

"For whom, then?"

"Detective Todd Beckett," I said. "He started out as the lead investigator on the case, and he's just as invested in finding the real killer as you are. Please bring him in on the phone call. Do whatever it takes to get him reassigned."

"Isn't he the same one who believes you are, in fact, a killer?"

"The very one."

The senator stroked his chin. "You're an enigma, Lucy Kendall. But all right. In fairness to Detective Beckett, I'll do what I can."

"Thank you." Chris and I rose to leave.

"Remember our deal," Coleman said. "Leave the sex traffickers to me."

I nodded and followed Chris out of the posh house.

"You didn't tell him about the website Kelly found," Chris said.

"Nope."

"So you don't plan on keeping your end of the bargain."

"I haven't decided." I fastened my seatbelt. "I'm not convinced the senator is telling us everything, and I want to talk to Riley before I show my last good card."

TWENTY-NINE

"You're waiting in the car," I told Chris as he parked the Audi in the Motel North's pothole-filled lot.

He glared at me. "Why?"

"First, you really want to leave the car unattended in this place? Second, she remembers you as the pretty boy who threatened her."

"If I recall, didn't you scare the shit out of her last time you saw her?"

I knew telling him about my weak point with Riley was a mistake. But Chris had a way of sucking the truth out of me. "More like scared myself. I can handle her."

"What are you going to say? She's not going to believe Preacher just up and told you his life story."

I opened the car door, grateful for the icy wind in my face. The warmth of the car ride had me on the verge of falling asleep. "Undecided. Will you please wait here?"

"You're asking?" The cocky smirk I alternately loathed and loved appeared. "Helping you dispose of a body is all I had to do to earn that?"

Laughing was wrong. But I did it anyway. "Yes, I suppose

so. You've got your stripes now."

"Fine." He nodded toward the room Preacher said Riley occupied. "If she's still there, she might not be alone. And if she isn't, text me."

Riley tried to slam the door in my face. "I told you I can't help."

I jammed my foot in the door. "You don't have to be afraid of Preacher anymore."

"Right."

"He's gone." I waited. She stared at me through the space, calculating. This girl was street-smart and no stranger to violent crime. It didn't take her much to hazard an educated guess.

"Did you kill him like you did that truck driver?"

"I'm not on trial. But I'm here to help you. The senator told me about Sarah helping him. I think you knew about what she was doing, and you're afraid it got her killed."

Riley bit her lip. A tangled lock of black hair fell over her face. She swatted it away, and I took the opportunity to drop my shoulder and force the door open. She stumbled back.

The room was every bit as crappy as the one Preacher booked for us. "Are you alone?"

Wide-eyed, she nodded. She was scared of me. Smart girl.

I shut the door. The room smelled like day-old cigarette ashes, cheap booze, and sex. A crudely made pipe and fine white powder littered the junky side table.

"Preacher have you hooked on meth or coke?"

"Neither," she snapped. "Clients like the coke. Makes the sex better, so they think."

I believed her, and I understood why Riley couldn't go to the police about Preacher. She'd gone past the point of coercion and had all but accepted the lifestyle. She'd likely be charged.

I tossed her identification and cellphone at her. "Preacher gave this to me."

She looked at the items as if they were gold nuggets. "No, he didn't."

"They're yours, aren't they? I didn't even try to break your phone password."

"Who are you?"

"You know the main answer to that, and I'm not here to talk about me. Senator Coleman said Sarah was feeding him information on Preacher and trying to find out who was really running the show. And you knew that, right?"

She sank down on the bed, folding her thin legs beneath her equally malnourished body. "Sarah was stuck in a bad position, you know? Preacher had something on her, something that scared her. But she was trying to make it right."

"Did you guys spend a lot of time together?" I remained by the door, ready to fight if she tried to run.

"Preacher trusts me more than the others," she said. "He'd let me have an afternoon to myself. And I'd go to Sarah's. Then she'd take me to the library so I could take classes for my GED."

"How'd you get there? Did you take a bus? I know Preacher didn't give you much cash."

"Sarah took me. She never spent the money from him. She gave it back to me or kept it in her house. It was dirty money, she said." Riley rubbed her eyes.

The seed of admiration for Sarah that blossomed at the senator's place began to grow. She had guts. "Did she ever tell you about Sam?"

"No. Who's that?"

"An abusive ex-boyfriend," I said. "She was in hiding from him, and Preacher found out. That's what he had on her."

"I thought she came from a bad past," Riley said. "Like she didn't want to put down roots. Her place was never really decorated, and she didn't have a lot of clothes. Just enough to look professional at work. She always had a bag in her room, like she was getting ready to go somewhere."

"You never asked why?"

Riley shook her head. "She didn't have to tell me everything about her life. She was already doing enough."

More than Preacher ever did. I kept that thought to myself. "You mentioned keeping cash in her house. The police haven't found any kind of money, and there's virtually no financial trail. Her being in hiding explains it, but where's the cash? You think Preacher or whoever had her killed knew to take it?"

"No way," Riley said. "She had a little lockbox thing, hidden under the floorboards in her bedroom. That's where she kept it. Along with..." She chewed on her lip.

Sensing the turning point, I edged forward, fighting the urge to bully her. Now was not the time to show her how cruel I could be. "What?"

"Sarah kept information in there too. She had a notebook with everything she knew about Preacher's organization. It had all the names of any pimp she encountered, all the kids and where they came from—if she knew—and the people she thought might be running the real show."

My heart pounded. An entire list of suspects the police would have to acknowledge. "Why did she keep it in her house instead of with the senator? Did he know about it?"

"I don't think so. I gave her information, you know?" Riley picked at a patch of dry skin on her hand. "Whenever I found out something new. And when I'd ask what she was going to do with it, she'd talk about the timing and having a bargaining chip. She said the best way to get what you wanted in life was to always have something the other person wanted."

I sagged against the door. Sarah had planned to give the notebook of information to the US attorney in exchange for her silence on his dalliances and his help in bringing Sam to justice.

"So she said nothing to the senator about the notebook?"

Riley shook her head. "She wasn't sure she could trust him."

"Why?"

Riley dragged her hands through her messy hair. "One of the newer boys said he was inspected by a man whose cologne was so strong he sneezed in the man's face. The kid was blind-folded, but he remembered the fruity smell. And that he smelled it the entire car ride."

"The senator wears a fruity cologne," I said. "But Preacher claimed he didn't know who the boss was. If the boy was with the leader—"

"He wasn't brought in by Preacher," Riley cut me off. "He was delivered to an empty house by the man with the stinking cologne. Left tied up and cold and with wet pants. Preacher showed up hours later."

"Car ride?"

"'In a fancy car' was all the kid said. Soft leather and very quiet."

"And Sarah truly believed it could have been the senator and not just a coincidence?"

"I don't know," Riley said. "I just know she wasn't ready to bring that information to his office yet. That's what she said." Tears sprouted in her eyes. "Last time I saw her, actually. It took me a while to get the chance to see Sarah, and when I told her about the new kid and the cologne, she said she was going to look for the boy."

"We need to get that notebook," I said. "I just agreed to let the senator handle the sex ring investigation, and I might have played right into his hands."

"It's too late," Riley said. "She was worried Preacher was onto her, and he's got her locket."

"So?"

"The serial number on the locket was the code to her lock-box. He took it, probably the night he killed her. Whatever information she had is gone. Even if we get to the lockbox, it's useless."

The chain in my pocket seemed to burn. I reached inside

and brought out the shining necklace. The heart swung gently from side to side. Riley stared. "How did you get that?"

"That's for me to know, and you to not worry about," I said. "Preacher didn't know this had a code. He thought it was from her mother, and he took it to upset her."

"Maybe that's what he told you."

"Trust me, he was speaking the truth. He had no idea. Will you take me to Sarah's house?"

Riley stepped out into the bitter weather with her patented hunched over stature. "Where are you parked?"

"The Audi with the black rims."

"Jesus, you got some money."

"It's not mine."

She halted. "No way. No one else."

"You can trust him. He's the guy who showed up the night I found you at the Rattner, but I promise, he's good."

She snapped her head back and forth. I really didn't want to do this today. She was coming whether she wanted to or not, but I was bone-tired. I didn't feel like physically fighting with her.

"He knows more about me than anyone," I said. "Believe me, he could get me in a lot of trouble. But he won't, and we need him."

"You're going to get me killed."

I shook my head. "No chance."

I started for the Audi, but she remained rooted in place. "Look, you don't have to go," I called back over my shoulder. "I can find out where Sarah lived on my own. But don't you want to help the woman who did so much for you?"

"Preacher did stuff for me too, you know? I keep helping you, and either him or one of his boys will kill me."

"Is that what he told you when he took the little boy you were babysitting?"

She stilled. "What? I took him back to his mother after we talked."

I turned to face her, feeling as if I were caught up in the pivotal moment of a high-stakes film, when the music reaches a fervent peak and the final bomb is dropped. "Then Preacher took him after that. His picture is on a website advertising his services to the scum of the earth. Preacher provided his boss with it. What do you think of your big savior now?"

Fat tears squeezed out of Riley's eyes. "You telling the truth?"

"I'd never lie about something like that." At least that much was true.

Shoulders sagging, she slumped to the car. Her posture screamed defeat, and I knew she'd play by my rules now. *It's interesting just what exactly will break a person's will.*

I opened the back door and gave Chris a pointed look. "This is Riley. I've assured her you will be nice."

She slipped into the seat as if she expected it to open up and suck her into the fine leather.

"Hi." Chris turned around and flashed the smile I'd fully expected him to use.

Riley flushed and stared.

"What's going on?" Chris asked.

I quickly filled him in and then reached for his phone.

"Who are you calling?"

"Todd."

"What?" He snatched the phone from me.

"Todd? Who's Todd?" Riley said from the backseat. "You didn't mention anyone else."

I locked the doors and motioned for Chris to apply the child locks. "Detective Beckett isn't going to arrest you. He's trying to find Sarah's killer. That's all he cares about."

"Are you serious?" Riley burst out. "He's a cop! I thought we were going to get the notebook, maybe you'd take care of things yourself."

"I'm not sure what you mean."

"You killed people!"

I leveled an icy stare at her. Chris didn't turn around, but the tension crackled between us. He'd do whatever I needed him to do. "I think you're mistaken."

"Beckett isn't Vice," Chris said. "And you're a valuable witness. If all this information works out, you've got a lot to bargain with."

"And isn't that what Sarah taught you?" I said. "If you haven't learned it yet, you'd better start."

She looked between the two of us, anger and fear crawling over her skin. "You're going to get me killed." She fell back into her seat.

"Now explain to me why we're involving the guy who"—Chris glanced at Riley—"isn't always your fan."

"Because breaking into her house isn't going to do any good. Todd needs to go in himself."

"He won't have a warrant. We've already been through that scenario."

"Crime scene that's already been investigated," I said. "All he needs is the key. I'm hoping he still has it."

"And then what?"

"He finds the information, he brings the real deal down. The senator's cut out—if he's not the one we're after—and Todd gets the glory. Now how do you think he's going to see me after handing him that?"

Chris put the car in gear. "Well played."

In the backseat, Riley groaned. "I think you people might be scarier than Preacher."

I hid my smile.

THIRTY

Todd met us outside of Sarah's gated community. He punched in a code at the gate, and we followed him through the narrow, winding loops until he stopped in front of a small, cookie-cutter brick and tan house with a red front door.

"So," Todd said as we all got out of the car. "You've been doing your own investigation instead of lying low like I told you. Why am I not surprised?"

I grinned. "You know me well."

"More than I want to, I think." A moment passed between us, Justin's words echoing in my head. Did Todd want information instead of action? If he only wanted the knowledge that he was right, he'd likely have the answer some day. But if he wanted to get inside my head and understand why, he needed to squash that fantasy. He didn't need to see the true monster taking shape in my heart.

Chris cleared his throat and jerked his thumb over his shoulder. "This is Riley. She's the one who gave us the information."

Todd gave a quick nod of acknowledgment. His sharp gaze

remained on me. "Seems like the district attorney is rethinking things after Dietz and Coleman called. Imagine my surprise to be brought into that conversation."

"They owed you that much," I said.

"I don't want to know how you found out Dietz was pulling the strings or what the senator's got that made him back off," Todd said. "The important thing is the DA is looking at this Sam Townsend now."

"Is Lucy in the clear?" Chris asked.

"The DA is still deciding. But I think we'll hear something by the end of the day."

"What about Townsend?" I asked.

Todd fumbled a small notepad out of his pocket. "He quit his job in Columbus a month ago, and no one's heard from him in over two weeks. His bank said there was a major cash withdrawal around that time, and we're pulling his credit card records now. We've got his picture out to every station and agency in the area. Hopefully we'll get a hit." Todd toed the ground with his worn dress shoe. "Thanks for doing this mostly the right way, Lucy. You could have broken into this place like you did the storage locker, mucked things up. Instead you trusted me enough to call. I appreciate that."

Preacher's dead, frozen face with his flat eyes stared back at me. Only hours ago I killed a man. Not by poison this time, but by physical force. Brutally and without conscience. It was as if I'd been in a mind-altered state and suddenly everything snapped back into place. For the first time since Preacher died, I understood the reality of my actions. My knees buckled. Cold permeated my insides so forcefully I thought I'd never be warm again.

Chris's hand on my elbow—a gentle squeeze—was the only thing that steadied me. I cleared my throat. "Yeah, well, I'm hoping you won't forget it."

"Believe me, I won't." Todd had noticed my sudden switch.

He chewed the corner of his mouth, obviously aware something more was happening. Before he could ask questions, I retrieved the locket and handed it to him.

"The serial number is supposed to be the lockbox's combination."

"Where'd you get this?"

Sarah wore it at the time of death. I killed the man who took it from her. My prized ability to lie failed me, whether from exhaustion or guilt.

"I stole it." Riley spoke up and saved me. "Snuck in and got it out of Preacher's pants when he was passed out."

"Brave girl," Todd said. He seemed to believe her. "Where's the lockbox hidden?"

"Under the loose floorboards beneath her bed."

"All right." Todd looked straight at me. "Wait here."

He disappeared into the house. Chris moved to get back into the car, but I focused on Riley. "Why'd you lie for me?"

"Bargaining chips, remember?"

I laughed. "You'll be just fine."

Inside the car, I couldn't stop shivering. What happened to the confidence from an hour ago? The steely resolve that I'd done the absolute right thing? I felt like the new girl in school all over again, all the nosy eyes seeing past my bravado and figuring out exactly who and what I was.

Chris put his hand on my knee. I turned to explain, to flush my sins, but I caught sight of Riley in the backseat. Chris and I looked at one another for a long minute, the air between us loud with silent conversation. He finally nodded. He knew the crazy running around in my head.

"It's all right," he said. "It *was* right."

I sank back into the seat and tried to convince myself of exactly that.

. . .

Todd returned fifteen minutes later. His face was rosy with
excitement, his steps so quick he nearly slid down the sidewalk.
In his gloved hands was a plastic bag containing a large, red
notebook. "It's all here. Names, dates, just like she said. Some
are johns, some are the kids and where we can find them. Lots
of stuff about Preacher, which gives him motive. Ideas about
who his boss is. She makes a case for Dietz. Mentions him by
name."

"What about the senator?"

"Nothing. Maybe she wasn't certain enough to write about
it," Todd said. "I'll probably have to turn it over to Crimes
Against Persons/SVU. But this is big." He looked at Riley,
who'd shrunk into a mute ball in the backseat. "Listen, you're a
big witness for us. I don't want to take you in and stick you in a
cell to keep you from running. Would you be willing to stay at a
shelter I work with until I can find you a more permanent
place?"

She considered her options. "Yeah. All right."

"Good," Todd said. "You can ride with me. I'll drop you off
before I go into the station, I promise."

Looking wary, Riley exited the car. Todd still danced with
excitement.

I leaned over Chris to call out his open window. "Riley,
thank you. This is the right thing, you know."

Her dark hair framed her pale face, making her look like the
innocent child she should have been. "Yeah? Guess you and I
both need to believe that about ourselves."

I dropped back into my seat, hollow and spent. To hell with
that little girl.

"Oh, Lucy, I almost forgot." Todd leaned back down to our
level. "Got a text from the DA's office as I headed in to search.
The lab results came back. Fibers found with Sarah didn't

match your dress. He's officially taking you off the suspect list, and I guess I'm back on as lead investigator."

"You almost forgot?" I said. "How could you almost forget?"

His smile was almost as cocky as Chris's. "Maybe I didn't. Maybe I figured waiting another few minutes would even the score a bit."

THIRTY-ONE

Mousecop greeted me with a pained, drawn-out yowl. Contorting himself around my ankles as only cats can do, he followed me through the apartment. I dumped my stuff on the bed and scooped up the warm, fuzzy cat. He purred against my cheek, his paws resting against my neck. Still cradling him, I joined Chris in the kitchen.

"Thanks for feeding him," I said. Mousecop sauntered out of my arms and across the counter. He sat on the edge near Chris, flicking his bottlebrush tail in his direction.

Chris shoved the cat's tail out of his way. "You're welcome. What are you going to do now?"

I sat on the closest bar stool. "Sleep for a few hours. Or days."

"Me too."

"That's right." I rubbed my tired eyes. "You had a shift, and then you've been stuck with me. How do you do it?"

"Practice," he said. "Like anything else, you can train your body to go on very little sleep."

My body felt like liquid, and I was pretty sure if I didn't rest soon, I'd end up a puddle of flesh on the floor. And sleeping meant I could prolong the inevitable emotional slide over what I'd done to Preacher. "If you say so." A yawn cut through my throat. "Do you think Riley will tell Todd what I said about Preacher?"

"If she thinks she can benefit from it."

"Yeah. I guess I'll deal with that if it happens."

"Todd already thinks you're a killer." Chris shrugged. "What does it matter?"

"I don't want him looking into a new case." And I didn't want him to know about Preacher. He was different than the rest. If Todd found out what I'd done to him, he'd change his mind about me. He would see the real devil inside.

"Preacher's just gone missing," Chris said. "By the time he's found, it will take weeks to identify the body. Good luck with no identification."

"I hope we did a good enough job getting rid of it."

"It's all in the dump," Chris said. "Sprinkled over various mounds of trash. Fitting end for him, if you ask me."

"I didn't expect you to be so..." I searched for the right word "...complacent about this. I expected lots of battles of conscience."

"Didn't we discuss this?" He yawned, and then stretched his long arms high.

"You didn't panic because grisly death is nothing new. But this is the aftermath. This is when you're supposed to break down and think about what you've done."

"What good does that serve?"

"I think it reminds you that you're human." Sitting around in self-reflection had to serve some cause, or I'd wasted hours of my life.

"Did you feel that after you killed the truck driver? Or Preacher?"

"I felt it after I killed Brian Harrison. And when I realized what I'd done to Preacher, how far I'd gone..." I shuddered.

"But you don't feel it now."

"I'm too tired to feel anything."

His smile was flat. "No. It's your shadow side."

"Jung again."

"Because it's true," Chris said. "We've all got one. The inner part of us that wants to slap the jerk who cuts us off in traffic. Or chew out the person slowing up the checkout lane. We might even fantasize about what we'd say and how much we'd freak the person out."

"That's nothing but impatience and irritation speaking. People don't actually consider acting on those impulses."

"Except when their shadow side wins out," he countered. "Then you've got the douche fighting over a toy at Christmas. For most people, it's a one-time rage thing. But for some"—he spread his hands—"it becomes who they are."

"And you're saying that's what's happening to me? That my shadow side now governs my decisions?" I didn't want to be whittled down to fit into some scientific theory. I was more than that, full of complicated layers and inconsistencies. *We are all more than that.*

"Do you feel remorse?"

"I feel remorse for the victims," I clarified. "For friends and family who might mourn those people."

"But you feel no remorse for killing?"

"Right now? I feel nothing." Admitting the truth brought a wave of unexpected relief. Exhaustion might be driving my emotions, but there was no seed in the pit of my stomach, no flash of nausea when I thought of the dead trucker or Preacher's unseeing eyes. I felt nothing at all. Even the momentary panic in the car had gone. Without Todd as a reminder of consequence, I was calm.

"Do you think you're special?" Chris asked. "Like you're somehow genetically different?"

"Now what are you talking about?"

"You kill people and don't feel bad about it. My mother doesn't either. Neither did Bundy or countless others. Why is that? What makes it possible?"

My overwhelming tiredness was the only thing that kept me from coming off the stool and screaming at him. "First off, they're sociopaths. Psychopaths, actually—cold-blooded killers who get off on what they're doing. I'm nothing like them. I'm doing this for a reason, and it's got nothing to do with me."

"Sure it does. Every time you kill, you slice off a little of the guilt you feel over not being able to help your sister." His voice held no accusation, his eyes flatly calm.

"Fine," I said. "Because I'm about to keel over, I'll give you that one for now. But the people I kill hurt others. They don't need to be here. I'm solving a problem society can't. Or won't."

"You are," he agreed. "But you should still feel bad about taking a life. And you don't. Why?"

"I just told you why. These people shouldn't be allowed to breathe. Knowing that I'm saving kids is what keeps me going." My arms felt as if bugs were crawling over the fine hairs. Chris's ability to invade my subconscious and pluck out my specific demons was maddening. I knew I should feel some level of remorse for the men I killed, and I knew my lack of it meant something very bad. I just didn't want to acknowledge it. Not yet. Allowing the monster on my back to roam free in my head would be my undoing. So I kept him muzzled.

"That's all I can tell you," I said. "Take it or leave it."

"I'll take it, for now. But someday you'll have to stop dodging the truth about yourself."

"Why?"

"Facing it is the only thing that's going to keep you alive and out of jail."

My fingers went numb. I flexed them and waved Chris off. "Whatever. Too tired to think straight right now." I slid down off the stool. "We both need to sleep. Can you make it back to your place without passing out at the wheel, or do you need to crash on my couch?"

His glassy-eyed stare answered my question. I shuffled to my storage closet and retrieved an extra pillow and blanket. "Here." I tossed them on the couch. "Sleep for a while. If you wake up before I do and leave, lock the door."

I left him there before he could ask me any more questions, or before my mind could dwell on the sudden spark in his gaze and the pink flame in his cheeks. I wouldn't think about his sleeping fifteen feet away from me or how long it had been since I'd had sex or the way he made me feel accepted. Those thoughts would change our relationship, cheapen it.

I clung to that idea as I changed into an old T-shirt and then climbed into bed. Sex is a wonderful thing, and I'd had plenty of it. Given our strange connection and the way he understood me, sex with Chris would probably be incredible. But then what? How would it affect the bond we'd forged? Would he stop thinking rationally when it came to me? Would I become jealous and by extension, careless? Some relationships transcended sex. Physical intimacy wasn't always the pinnacle. Sometimes just knowing the person understood your darkest core and still wasn't going to walk away was enough,

I couldn't risk losing that. Because Chris was wrong. Accepting whatever power my shadow side had over me wouldn't keep me alive and out of jail.

His presence in my life—the only real anchor I'd ever had— was my saving grace.

THIRTY-TWO

Chris was gone when I woke up in the early morning hours. My eyes still blurry with sleep, I sat at the kitchen table and tried to reassess. The police now knew I hadn't killed Sarah and had a viable suspect. Figuring Sarah's murder out was no longer my problem. Preacher helped clear my name, and Todd had all the information Sarah had been gathering against the organization. Had she really suspected the senator of being involved?

I sipped on my coffee. The senator had resources. He'd arranged for Sarah to have a new identity. Hiding a perverted side would be relatively easy for him. His task force might even be a perfect cover-up, not to mention a perfect pool to fish for victims.

The idea still bothered me.

What about US Attorney Dietz? Had he simply been sweating the revelation of an affair and the loss of wealth? Or had Sarah discovered something far more sinister?

I didn't care for that idea, either.

What bothered me more than anything was how easily Dietz had caved to the senator. And the senator's offer to help me—why? Did he really want to get Sarah's true killer? Was I so jaded I couldn't believe someone actually did something good for the right reasons?

Entirely possible.

I wished I knew what Sarah's notes said.

My fingers edged toward my phone. Todd would tell me if I asked nicely. Maybe.

Common sense suggested I cut myself free of this entire mess. The sex trafficking was exposed, and Todd would make sure the information got into the right hands. But Sarah's hand-written information would only get them so far. I still had the information on the Candy Market. Todd could get that to the right people, and even if it took time, police could bring down the ring. Even if the leader got away, some of the johns could be found. Maybe the kids could be rescued. I couldn't do that all on my own.

I should do the right thing and move on, find a specific target.

A specific target. The one Chris had been hounding me about for weeks. We should find his mother and finish her.

How would that change Chris? Would he still be the same person? Or would he carry the same dark monster I did? After watching him dispose of Preacher, I had to wonder how close to the edge he was teetering. A push by me could ruin his chances at leading a fairly normal life.

Then again, being friends with me had already accomplished that.

I decided to call Todd.

He asked me over for dinner, which was the last thing I expected. I'd been in his apartment once before when Justin, Chris and I discovered the truth about their mother. Todd was ready to throttle me that night.

Todd's small kitchen had an eat-in nook, and he'd gone to

great lengths to make sure nothing about our dinner was romantic. All the lights were bright, Barry White wasn't playing, and he didn't bother to cook for me. Instead, he ordered pizza and served it on plastic plates.

I settled into the comfortable bench. The three bird feeders in his small yard were busy with hungry visitors. A nervous male cardinal flittered around the largest feeder, his ever-watchful eyes on his nearby mate. The female picked through the snow beneath the feeder, gorging on fallen seeds.

"I would never have taken you for a bird watcher."

He finished his slice of pizza. "It's calming. Especially when I have a particularly bad case. Sometimes I sit here and watch them, and I figure out what to do next."

"What are you going to do next?"

"Special Victims has Sarah's journal," he said. "That part of the case is in their hands now."

"Did you read it?"

"I did."

I picked off a slice of pepperoni. "And?"

"Telling you probably isn't a good idea."

"Neither was helping me hide from your colleagues."

He laughed. He needed to make that sound more often. "Point taken. Her journal—I don't know why I call it that, it's more like a case log—is full of potential johns. Unfortunately, this Preacher never gave her full names or identification information. But he did give initials and personal descriptions, along with the designated meeting places. Special Victims is going to start there."

"But we don't know the names of the kids? Or the clients?"

"We do know the names of some of the kids. Most of them were boys. Sarah didn't know where they stayed, and I suspect Preacher moved them around a lot, just like he did Riley. But three of them are missing kids from Ohio and New York. With Riley's help, we have some hope of finding their locations."

I took out the crumpled paper from my pocket. Kelly had given me the web address, username, and password with no argument. She was glad to be finished looking at the filth. "Here."

"What's this?" He eyed the crumpled paper as if it were about to explode.

Might as well get right to the point. "Preacher and his boss had an online site set up to sell kids. This is the address and your way into it."

"What? How did you find it?"

"A good friend," I said. "She knows how to use the software, and she spent hours searching. She's the one who made the connection."

He narrowed his eyes. "The same friend who found Kailey."

"Yes, and no, you're not getting her name, so don't ask. The Philadelphia connection is kind of brilliant." I explained about the historical names. "I've no doubt these kids are local, but who they're being sold to is anyone's guess. If Special Victims can get into the site—"

"They have a good shot at taking it down," he finished. "Finding the kids will be first priority. These users scatter like cockroaches. But we might be able to find a few. Thank you, Lucy. And thank your friend."

"One of the kids has a personal connection to Riley," I said. "Let her know he's got a chance at being saved."

"I will."

"What's she giving you?" I went back to my slice of pepperoni. It tasted bland and dry, like everything else.

"Preacher split his time with his mother in Strawberry Mansion and a decent apartment in North Philly," Todd said. "Riley gave us both addresses. Nothing at the mother's place—didn't expect there to be—but we've found enough at his apartment to book him on pandering and operating a house of prostitution. Our computer guys have his laptop. It's encrypted, of course, but we're hoping to get some information on clients and victims. If not the big boss."

"Riley said that Preacher didn't know who the boss was," I said. "You think he's lying?"

"I'm not sure." He pushed his plate aside. His demeanor changed. Nothing extreme but a subtle shift that warned me I wasn't going to care for his next line of thought. "What's more interesting to me is that we can't seem to locate him. Riley's given us the names of every known associate and location, and no one's seen or heard from him in more than twenty-four hours. His mother says he always checks in."

"He must have found out Riley smartened up and started talking to you."

"She hadn't heard from him, either. Hasn't seen him since she took that locket two days ago."

So Riley was sticking to that story. Smart girl. "You'll find him."

"Will we?"

The question hung between us. Maintaining eye contact was crucial in a lie. And lying to Todd should be easy. After all, I'd done it before.

I looked away and took a bite of pizza.

"Lucy, I don't know what you've done, which seems to be a running theme between us." He sighed. "But I don't think it's any coincidence that a prostitute known to be under Preacher's thumb for a long time is suddenly ratting him out. She doesn't seem to be afraid he'll retaliate."

I tried not to choke on the pizza or the rising gorge of my stomach. "She trusts you to keep her safe."

"Or she believes he's no longer a threat."

"Maybe he isn't. You think she's capable of hurting him?"

He rubbed his face. "No. I think you are."

I set down the slice. "There you go again. Why are you so

hell-bent on my being this terrible person? And if you really believe I am, why did you help me? Why am I here now?" I asked in my most gentle voice, even cocking my head so that I looked younger, more vulnerable. All a waste of time. Todd was better than that.

"I think you are incredibly damaged," he said. "Your sister's death, your years in CPS. My brother's case. I think you absorbed it all until it became too much, and your way of controlling the guilt and whatever other emotion you've manufactured is to lash out and eliminate threats."

I'd never thought of it that way, and now wasn't the time to start. "I don't feel threatened."

"Not threats to you. Threats to kids. All of whom represent your sister, of course."

My blood cooled. "You took a semester of psychology?"

"I've been studying."

"I suppose it could be a sound theory. If it were true."

He continued as if I hadn't denied it. "You asked why I help you despite my beliefs."

"Yes."

"Because as a citizen, as a person with normal human emotions, as someone who watched my little brother get screwed by this system, I understand what you're doing."

"You're not an average citizen, though." I tried to smile, but the effort made my face hurt. I was sick of pretending, sick of the game. I needed some time to be myself and not worry about saying the wrong thing. "Aren't you bound by the law to investigate me if you truly believe I'm doing these terrible things?"

"That's where the conflict is. I've got more cases than I can handle. Robberies and murders and rapes. True threats to society. I don't think you are. If I did, I wouldn't be so lenient."

"It's a good thing your theories are wrong." *Be done with this.* If he wasn't going to arrest me, why keep on? Did he think he could reach me? More importantly, if he understood why I did these things, why couldn't he just leave well enough alone?

Leave me alone.

My sweater stuck to my back, and I longed for the cold air outside. Coming here was a mistake.

"Preacher could have been an asset to us," he said. "Special Victims would like to speak with him. Imagine what trained detectives could have gotten out of him."

Likely not more than the ketamine. "I hope they find him."

"I can't always shield you," he said. "Preacher's their guy now. If he's found dead, I'm not going to be investigating it. Do you understand what I'm saying?"

I didn't care. What was done was done, and sitting around mulling over whether I'd pay the price or did the right thing was a waste of energy. Maybe Chris was right. "I do. And I think your intentions are admirable if not confusing. You don't need to worry about me."

His fingers inched across the table, their tips brushing against mine. I didn't move. Todd's hand slowly slipped over mine until our fingers were entwined. My body tensed, and for reasons I didn't understand, I squeezed his hand.

"Thank you for what you've done for me."

"I won't always be able to do it."

"I know."

"So you should stop while you're ahead."

I pulled my hand away and smiled. "Good thing this whole vigilante idea is just a figment of your imagination. Where is Riley now?"

"In a safe house of sorts. They're part of our children's advocacy group, and they'll work with her to get things straightened out. But they've got security."

"In case Preacher comes after her?"

Todd's mouth twitched. "Or his boys. He's got a few friends aware of the situation."

"I'm glad she's safe. Maybe she really can start fresh."

He shrugged. "We'll see."

"So let's get to the elephant in the room."

"Didn't we already do that?"

I laughed, some of my tension easing. "No, that's the elephant in your imagination. I'm talking about the senator. Riley thinks Sarah didn't trust him. Did you get that from Sarah's case log?"

"No. But her entries are very precise. They're not feelings. So if she didn't have any sort of concrete evidence, she probably didn't log it."

"Do you have any suspects for the ringleader?" I asked. "Riley said Sarah noted that."

"She did. In her code, which our people need to work out. Let them do it."

Todd's phone vibrated on the table. He swiped the screen and read the series of texts that beeped through.

"We found Sam Townsend in a morgue on the northwest side of town. Picture matched a John Doe. He was discovered dead in a motel room the day after Sarah's murder. Hung himself with a vague suicide note about killing his girlfriend." Todd glanced up at me. "He was wearing a green sweater."

"So that's it?" I sat back, waiting for the relief to come. "All of this, and Sarah wasn't even killed over her betrayal? It was her crazy ex?"

"Looks like it."

"I don't believe it," I said. "Riley said Preacher blackmailed her with Sam. He claimed to know where he was."

"You think Sam was tipped on her whereabouts so Preacher wouldn't get his hands dirty?"

"Makes sense," I said. "The senator helped hide her. I find it hard to believe he didn't do a good job."

"Except Preacher discovered her secret."

"That's part of his job. These guys work online now. When

your computer people get into his laptop, they'll find out exactly how sick the man was. Hopefully."

"Maybe," Todd said. "But I don't like it. Preacher's boss targeted Sarah because she had a weakness he could exploit. And no one but the senator knew that weakness."

"Riley said she didn't trust him." I still didn't like the idea. It didn't feel right.

Todd closed the pizza box. "It's still early enough for me to drop by the senator's office and have a chat. Do you mind?"

"Can I come?"

He rolled his eyes. "No."

"I mind that, but I'll see myself out."

He walked me to the door.

"Will you call me when you leave the senator's?"

"Again, that's information regarding an active case."

I folded my arms. He sighed, looking down at me as though he were humoring a toddler. "Maybe."

THIRTY-THREE

I didn't remember falling asleep on the couch, but the demanding shrill of my phone jolted me out of a foggy dream. Rubbing my eyes, I fumbled for the cell in my dark apartment, knocking off a coaster from the end table in the process. Finally, my fingers closed over the plastic case.

"Yeah."

"It's Riley." Her heady whisper brought me to full consciousness. The microwave's digital display said it was after midnight.

"What's going on?"

"I left that place your detective took me to, and now I'm in trouble."

"You what? Why would you do that? Those people actually want to help you." I sat up and tried to adjust to the lack of light.

"Those girls were gross. One of them was all messed up on drugs and trying to come down. She had the shakes and kept screaming. Another girl refused to take a bath and smelled like the toilet. I wanted a private room, but of course they don't have the space. I can do better on my own."

"You sound like it," I snapped. "You said you were in trouble."

Riley coughed. "I left my stuff in that hotel room. I don't have much, you know? I just wanted to get my clothes. When I got there, one of Preacher's friends was waiting for me."

"How badly are you hurt?"

"Not too bad. I kicked him in the nuts and ran. But now I'm on the street and lost."

"You don't know your way around?" Stupid girl. She knew better than this.

"Not everywhere. I ducked into some shithole bar at first, thinking I'd be all right if I stayed in a public place. They kicked me out for being underage. Now I'm at a laundromat hoping he doesn't think to look here."

"Did he run after you?"

"I heard him screaming at me, maybe running. I didn't look back." She started sniffling, followed by loud, gulping breaths.

"Tell me where you are, and I'll call you a cab."

"I can do that myself, but I don't want to go back to that place."

I wanted to scream. My patience for this kid was running thin. I'd practically handed her freedom on a silver platter. All she had to do was listen. "Riley, that's the best place for you."

"Can I come stay with you? Just for a couple of days? Preacher's buddies don't know where you live. And it's your fault I'm in this mess."

Helping her get her life on track was a mess. I gritted my teeth. "I don't have an extra bedroom."

"I can sleep on the couch."

"Detective Beckett will come looking for you. He'll check here." And I didn't need her watching me, digging her nose into my life.

"Fine," she said. "Then I'll go back. But can't I just have a day of peace? I don't want to go back to that screaming and fighting right now."

I dropped back onto the couch and stared up at the shadows created by the bright glow of my phone. My floor lamp looked like a giant scythe ready to slash me in two. "One night, and then I'm taking you back."

"Thank you so much. I promise, I won't fight leaving."

"I hope not. I'd have to call Detective Beckett and have him take you in." I gave her my address, told her to buzz me when she arrived, and dozed back off.

Caught in a lucid dream, I heard a distant rattling. I should wake up, but my body still hadn't caught up after my all-nighter with Preacher. A soft thud, followed by the slightest shake of my end table. And then the pattering footsteps of my fat cat.

"Leave stuff alone, Mouse."

"You'd be better off with a dog."

My eyes shot open. A face I recognized but couldn't place. How did he get inside? Why was he here? I raised my arms, intending to fight, but the sharp prick of a needle turned them into rolling sludge.

I barely had time to register the irony before I passed out.

THIRTY-FOUR

My senses came back to me in pieces. Smell first. Cologne. Sickeningly sweet and strong enough to taste. A hint of gasoline. My tongue felt thick. Throbbing pain tormented my arms and legs. My wrists burned. They were tied. Sweat burst over my forehead. Salty tears trickled onto my lips.

"You're waking up, I see." His voice could have belonged to any shy man on the street.

I forced my heavy eyelids open. "Jake."

My blurry vision allowed me to see Senator Coleman's aide sitting in a metal folding chair directly across from me.

I sat in a metal folding chair too.

White walls, gray floors. Tools hanging.

A garage. That's where he'd taken me.

"What did you give me?"

"Just a mild sedative. I'm sorry if you don't like needles, but it was really the quickest way."

I might have laughed, but the reality of my predicament snuffed out any humor. "Riley. Where is she?"

"Over here." The teenager's voice sent a new wave of shock through me. She stepped out of the shadows of the SUV sitting next to us. Her small hand rested on Jake's shoulder. Anger chipped away at the clouds in my head.

"The two of you are in this together."

She laughed. "You're the one who told me about bargaining. It worked like a charm on you."

I closed my eyes, fighting for my bearings. Opened them again. I needed to take stock of my surroundings. The tools on the back wall were basic: a hammer, shovel, nail gun, drill. I'd go for the hammer first. Or the shovel. It had a longer handle, and if I were lucky I could take them both out with one swing. Either way, I'd like to kill her first.

Once I got untied.

"How did you get into my building without my buzzing you up?"

She smiled, looking far sweeter than usual. "Come on, you know how easy it is to charm the right male. I just had to tell him I was visiting my aunt and forgot my code. I didn't want to wake her. Who's going to suspect anything else of this face?"

I hadn't given her nearly enough credit. "So you help get the kids, then?"

"Sometimes, if that's what Jake needs. It's not so hard, especially when they're little. Half of them have parents who don't know one day from another."

"What about the ones brought in from out of state?" My wrists were bound with zip ties tight enough to break the skin.

"I handle those," Jake said.

I licked my dry lips and looked at Riley. "You told me about Preacher, about other boys."

"I wanted you to stay on his trail," she said. "How did you kill him?"

"I didn't."

"And my driver," Jake said. "He was bringing that nice little black boy from Ohio. I figured he'd just had some kind of heart attack, but then you mentioned him to Riley, and I put it together. So you"—he trailed his hand on my knee—"have taken out two of my best people."

My ego had betrayed me. Don't cops say every criminal screws up? That their egos do them in?

"Don't bother denying it," Jake said.

"What about the senator?" I asked. "Is he involved?"

Jake's laugh was boisterous and cocky. "Please. He's too busy looking for political glory in all the wrong places. Everything's going on right under his nose, and I get to stay one step ahead of the task force. How brilliant is that?"

"Amazing," I said. "Is that how you got started?"

"Never mind that," he said. "Let's just say Preacher and I made a good team, and he introduced to me to little Riley here. Now I'll have to replace him, thanks to you."

Riley moaned. She looked like she wanted to cry, but those tears were likely nothing more than crocodile tears. I should have known there was more to this little girl. "He was good to me. Sometimes."

"He beat you," Jake said. "I'm the one who cares for you. Don't forget that. Preacher was just our pawn. We'll have to find another."

"What about Sarah?" I focused my attention on the black-haired girl. "I thought you were friends?"

"We were," Riley said. "Especially when she gave me money. But I couldn't let her get too close. I made sure she went in the wrong direction."

"Because of this piece of garbage?" I jerked my tied ankles toward Jake. "You're so in love with him you'll sacrifice friends? And the little kids you hurt, what about them? What about that little guy you were babysitting?"

Her mouth tightened, and she shook her head. So she didn't like to think about those things. Riley lived in survival mode. I could work with that.

"He's using you," I said. "For sex, for protection. Don't think for a minute he doesn't have a way to pin all of this on you and Preacher and walk off scot-free."

She looked at her feet. Stupid girl.

Jake's hand flashed out and connected with my face. My skin stung; I tasted blood. He'd pay for that. "You screwed up," he said. "Never should have told Riley you knew about that kid. You know how to access my website."

This time I did laugh. "So you're going to kill me, silence me forever?"

He shrugged.

I almost taunted him that I gave Todd the information but held my tongue. Jake could switch servers, alert his clients, move his kids.

"Whatever," I said. "But the police have Sarah's notebook. Which Riley led us to, by the way."

"I wanted the locket," she snapped. "I didn't think you'd involve the police since you just killed Preacher."

"You underestimated me." Just like she was doing right now.

"Doesn't matter," she said. "Sarah didn't have enough to bring Jake down."

"So how's it going to be?" I asked Jake. "You're way too delicate to have killed someone. If it needed to be done, you enlisted some other lackey. Except you can't this time, because only you and Riley can know. So you'll have to do it yourself." His darting gaze, shooting from me to Riley, and the burst of color on his cheeks told me I'd hit a very touchy nerve. "It's not easy to take someone's life. Even if you walk away before they die, you're still giving a part of your humanity to that death. You'll never be the same. Are you prepared for that?"

His grin reminded me of the eels tucked in the corner of the aquarium. Sinister and patient, and ever observant. His voice, stuffed full of forced bravado, betrayed him. "You surprise me," he said. "I expected you to beg. To name-drop your detective and your boyfriend. But instead you try to intimidate. Impressive."

I'd never beg. And I had little chance of Todd or Chris finding me. Riley had covered her bases very well.

"You have potential," I said to her. "Think of all the people you could help with me."

"But he's so much better than you are," she said. "He's not being watched by the police. And he's got money. What do you have?"

"Dignity."

"Not for long." The smirk on Jake's face sent a horrific chill through me. "To answer your question, no, I've never killed anyone before. I don't have to. If someone becomes a nuisance, I simply sell them. Or trade. Depending on the market and person in question." His eyes roamed over me. "You are worth a lot of money to a very interested client."

THIRTY-FIVE

They left me to wait. To my thoughts, I supposed. Expecting my imagination—powered by very real firsthand knowledge—to overwhelm me until I was at my weakest point, mentally and physically. I certainly could crumble into a thousand pieces of wasted ambition and dreams, but what would be the point? Had I really risked my own freedom, sacrificed my soul—if there even is such a thing as an afterlife—to end up as some cretin's bag of flesh to use whenever he wanted?

I'd make them kill me before that happened.

More black irony. My greatest fear would be a respite from what awaited me outside the garage.

Daylight slithered in beneath the door, giving me just enough light to take a better inventory of the tools on the wall. A skill saw that required electricity; two different-sized chisels that probably weren't sharp enough to slice a carotid; electrical cords that could be used to strangle, but I didn't have the strength against both of them. The shovel was still the easiest thing to incapacitate them with. The hammer would do the rest.

No chills of shame on my arms. The cold, methodical way I planned to kill two people would split me in two. The Lucy

Kendall that walked out of this garage would be a new person. *And I say person only because I would be the one still breathing. But I will be a brand new monster.*

Isn't it funny how far we will go for our own survival? Whether or not we actually deserve to live is irrelevant. Survival is a basic primal instinct, and the species who still walk this earth do so because they were willing to do whatever it took to stay alive. Less than two days ago, I thought I'd been ready to hand myself to the police, sign my life away. More lies to myself. I saw that now. Admitting defeat and turning myself in would have made me feel like a martyr, alleviating the guilt of Todd and Justin and even Chris's involvement. Stuck in a prison cell and then probably death row, I would have consoled myself with my personal sacrifice.

I started to laugh. I'd fooled myself quite well. Which meant it shouldn't be too difficult to trick the weakest link in this duo.

Stupid little girl. I'd kill her first.

Escaping the zip ties around my wrists and ankles was impossible. Riley would have to cut me free, or I'd have to bank on them cutting them off during the transport to the buyer. Too risky. Playing Riley was easier.

I started to scream.

As expected, she slammed out of the door that connected to the house. She stunk of sex, and her sweater was gone, leaving her in a skimpy tank top that showed off her perky breasts. "What do you want?"

"Where's Jake?"

"He's taking a nap." She smiled, and I wondered why I'd ever thought she was pretty. "He's taking you to the buyer himself, and it's a long drive. He needs his rest."

"After you serviced him."

No response.

"Why are doing this?"

She shrugged. "Why not?"

"No." I shook my head. "I don't know how you got involved in this, but it's not too late for you. Let me go, and we'll turn Jake in."

Riley snorted, making her even more ugly. "Please. I have no skills. I'm a prostitute. Even if I didn't get charged because I helped, where do I go after this? Not to my parents. Right back to the streets giving blowjobs to dirty old men who think ten bucks is a fair price. No thanks. Jake's making real money, and I'm not walking away from him."

"You don't love him."

"What's love, anyway? I'm happy and fed, and he doesn't make me do shit I don't want to do. That's good enough for me."

Old Lucy would have felt sorry for this poor girl who'd been so used and abused she'd lost all self-worth and hope. New Lucy saw nothing but an obstacle and a waste of space.

"You're not going to change your mind."

She shook her head.

I let my chin fall to my chest, summoning my worst memory —the one I'd stored in the vault decades ago. Not finding my sister dead or hearing my mother call Lily a liar. The memory occurred two nights earlier, when my mother went out with friends, and her boyfriend slipped into bed with Lily in the next room. Usually he waited until I was asleep, until the middle of the night, she'd said later. But that night he was drinking and feeling brave. He stole into her room and made her scream so badly I wet the bed. I thought of that scream now, of her begging him to stop, of her pleading with him not to make her do *that*. He sodomized her and left her bleeding into the toilet while he passed out in the bed he shared with our mother.

Ashamed that I'd been too terrified to get up and do some-thing to stop it, my underwear soaked with my own urine, I went to the bathroom and cleaned both of us up. That's when she told me how long it had been going on, and I convinced her to tell Mom. I truly believed she would listen and make him go away. But Mom didn't, and Lily killed herself.

I wondered about the role I played in her death. What if I'd kept my mouth shut, and Lily had simply endured until she outgrew his interest? He might have moved on to me, but she might be alive. Our mother's disbelief is what made Lily take her own life.

When I tasted the hot, salty tears, I raised my head and looked at Riley. She stood with her skinny hip cocked to the side, arms folded over her chest. Smug little shit.

"What's wrong, Lucy? Finally realizing you're not calling the shots?"

A perfectly round tear rolled down my cheek and dripped onto the floor. "Who's buying me?"

"Some big, sweaty guy in Jersey and his new wife." Her laugh sounded like a braying horse. "They can't wait to get you."

"So Jake's been planning this?"

"Ever since the wife contacted him, yeah. She asked for you by name."

Through my tears and the bad light, I stared at the babbling brat. Everything in the garage became crystal clear, as though I'd just managed to focus a microscope after fiddling with the lens. "Why would a woman contact Jake about me specifically?"

"She bought a girl from us before, so she knew Jake had good product. Said she was looking for you. Jake couldn't believe the timing because you'd become a big problem." Another braying laugh. "I liked her better when she was distrusting and quiet. "Talk about luck."

"Her name is Mary?"

"Very good." Riley clapped her hands and danced on her

toes. "You must have really pissed her off. Did you kill someone she loved?"

"No."

Mary was looking for me, not her sons. How did she know of my connection to Chris and Justin? When the news first broke about Mary Weston being Martha Beckett, Chris's personal history had been dragged through the papers. Had I been mentioned in those articles? I couldn't remember.

Riley picked at her fingernails. "And just so you know, I recognized you from the street right away. Your face is pretty memorable, even with the wig and nerdy glasses. I hoped you'd find Preacher. How did you kill him? Tell me, please? I'm sure he deserved it."

So she wanted to share secrets. Bond. Dumb girl, playing right into my hands. "An overdose of ketamine."

She threw her head back and bellowed. "Oh, I hope he suffered. Did he?"

"Yes. And he begged for his life. Peed his pants."

She ate it up, and I layered more on. "I could have turned him in, but I killed him for beating you. He treated you like a piece of garbage. And that's why I killed him. For you, Riley."

For the first time, uncertainty flickered in her dark eyes. "Really?"

"Yes. But I guess it doesn't matter now." I summoned more tears and said a silent apology to my dead sister. "I know you're not going to let me go, but can you at least let me go to the bathroom?"

"I'd have to take you into the house. Jake would freak."

"I'll be quiet, I promise." More tears dripped onto the floor. "Mary is a monster, and the things she's got planned for me are nightmarish. Please don't send me to her on a full bladder. I don't want to piss myself. Give me some dignity, like I did for you by killing Preacher."

She debated, clearly enjoying seeing me beg. Let her. "You won't try anything?"

"Like what? I kill with poison. I don't know any other way. And I'm done, kid. Done trying to hide and pretend to be something I'm not. Let Mary have me. But let me go my way, just a little."

"Well, I guess you don't have anything on you that could hurt me." She took a step forward and then balked. "And I've been on the streets a long time. I know how to fight."

Of course she did. And she was too stupid to think about the wall of weapons behind her. "I know."

She dug out a pocketknife from her jeans and slowly approached. A three-inch, curved blade. Enough to work with. "This probably can't kill you, but it would hurt. So don't be stupid."

Foolish girl.

I promised I wouldn't. Carefully, her dark eyes never wavering from mine, she cut the ties that anchored my feet to the chair. "I'm not cutting your hands free."

"That's fine."

"Stand up."

I did, slowly, letting my legs adjust after being in the same position for too long. Faking a dizzy spell, I stumbled and clasped the metal chair to keep from falling. With my wrists still tied, I wouldn't get the same leverage, but I could stun her enough to make it to the hammer. "Woozy," I mumbled. "Guess whatever he gave me hasn't quite worn off."

"Don't fall and hurt yourself. I don't want Jake finding out I let you up."

Still clutching the metal chair, I tried to step forward and failed. "I'm not sure I can walk on my own. Can you help me?"

Her youth made her overconfident, and my supposed weakness gave her a false sense of security. She'd been taken care of by Preacher and Jake long enough she'd forgotten how to survive on the streets.

Riley stuck her knife back in her pocket and stepped forward. In one motion I planted my feet for leverage and then yanked the chair up, hard and fast. The metal seat caught her chin, making her neck snap back. Too shocked to even utter a word, she staggered sideways. I swung the chair around and slammed it into her temple. She dropped to her knees. I jammed the chair onto the back of her head and then tossed it aside, rooting for the pocketknife.

I sawed quickly at my bonds as Riley rolled around, trying to call Jake's name. My wrists twisted awkwardly, I kept hacking at the zip tie and kicked her in the face. Blood gushed from her mouth. The sight of it seemed to pull her back from the edge of consciousness and give her new energy. She grabbed my leg and yanked me down hard. My ass and right elbow hit the concrete, and a lightning streak of pain ascended up my arm, but the velocity was enough to cut the last plastic thread of the zip tie. My hands were free, and Riley was coming right at me.

Scrambling on her hands and knees, she reached for the chair and brought it over her head to slam it down onto mine.

I shoved the blade into her stomach just as the connecting door opened.

THIRTY-SIX

Riley dropped to her knees; the chair clattered to the floor. Blood oozed through her shirt. If I remembered my anatomy, I'd at least nicked her spleen. I planned to go for the hammer next, but Jake's rushing form ruined that plan.

Shirtless and shouting, his pale chest reminding me of a hairless corpse, he charged. I dodged, barely, swinging the knife at blank air. Now he stood between a moaning Riley and me, his glittering eyes darting between the bleeding girl he supposedly cared about and the one who was going to ruin his life.

"You bitch." Spittle flew from his lips.

I stepped back, edging toward the tools. If only the keys were in the SUV. As it stood, when I brought Jake down, I'd have two options: hit the garage door opener and run into the freezing afternoon and hope I wasn't in the country, or dart into an unfamiliar house and search for a phone. Neither were appealing.

Riley screamed. The wound in her stomach was gushing blood. "Please, Jake, help me. Call an ambulance."

"I can't." He sounded like the pathetic, unsure boy he was. "What about her?"

"Kill her!"

"I cut her spleen," I said. "Look at how dirty this floor is. If she doesn't bleed out by the time you get her to safety, an infection is pretty much guaranteed. And if you don't treat that quickly, with high-powered antibiotics, it will kill her slowly." Better than the hammer.

Riley sobbed, rolling around and making it worse and soaking up even more dirt. "Please, Jake."

"You could run," I said. "Find someone to take care of her, leave me be. My word against yours."

"Or I can kill you."

My turn for the creepy eel smile. The difference was I would back up mine. "You're too inexperienced. You have no weapon. I have plenty behind me. And I have no fear." I let my eyes roam his shivering, half-naked body. "You're terrified."

"I'm not leaving here."

I gestured to Riley with the knife. "You're just going to let her die? After all she did for you? That's cold, Jake. Even I have a better moral code than that."

He glanced down at the girl staring up at him with bone-chilling fear and the slightest hint of rage. She latched on to his leg and half pulled herself into a sitting position. Blood squirted from her wound. "You're not going to let me die, are you?"

This girl who might be able to survive on the streets but had no idea how to fight monsters was again playing right into my hands. "He was never going to let you live."

Her head slowly angled toward mine. Pale skin, dilated pupils. She'd pass out soon. "What?"

"You served his purpose until you didn't. Now you're a liability." I shrugged, waving the knife. "Now, he probably would have had Preacher kill you because this guy isn't getting his hands dirty. I bet he's happy I've done it for him."

She gazed up at Jake. "Is that true?"

As I'd banked on, Jake wasn't so good at face-to-face

confrontation. His particular villainy worked best behind the safety of the Internet. He dragged his hands through his hair. "I... don't know."

"That's a yes," I said. "He sells little kids to be raped, Riley." My harsh voice echoed in the small garage. "You think you mean anything?"

"Shut up!" Jake screamed at me. He stepped forward, but a clinging Riley halted his progress. I brandished the knife. What a coward and a pathetic excuse for a foe. "All I know is I'm not going to jail." He looked down at Riley. "I'm sorry, but taking you anywhere is a risk. I'll try to stop the blood, make some calls. But I gotta deal with her first."

"I'm dying!" Riley's voice was an owlish screech. "I don't have that much time."

Jake's patience cracked. "You'll just have to wait, bitch. Jesus, haven't I done enough for you?"

The girl recoiled in defeat, but I saw the fury ripple over her face. As I reached for the shovel, Riley, with whatever strength she had left, brought her arms up and punched Jake in the genitals with both fists. He doubled over like every man does, and I swung the shovel around until it connected with his head. Once, twice, three times I hit him until he was down. On the floor now, slithering like the snake he was, I realized I'd cut off the head of the serpent exactly as I'd set out to do. Not literally, but close enough.

Riley was crying now, gurgling Jake's name between sobs. He was stunned and trying to recover, slipping around on hands and knees.

I turned the shovel around and drove the round handle into his temple as hard as I could. Jake fell flat and went silent. Blood trickled from his left nostril. Riley screamed. Her eyes were the size of the old silver dollars Mac liked to collect.

My knees popped as I knelt down to check for a pulse. He was gone.

Good riddance.

Gazing at Riley, I contemplated my problem. I'd admitted to her I killed Preacher. She would tell everyone if I let her live. But letting her die wouldn't look much like self-defense.

Widening the wound was an option. I could jam the knife in again, jerk it up and down and inch or two. But a good pathologist might be able to figure me out.

"Please don't let me die," she said. "I won't tell about Preacher."

"I don't believe you." I looked at the tip of the bloody knife. "You've lied to me so many times already."

She squeezed her eyes shut. Snot and tears drained onto the floor beneath her cheek. "I'm only fifteen. I swear. I didn't know what else to do. I thought he loved me."

"That's no excuse. Not for what you did to other kids." I waved the knife in the air, and Riley's hazy eyes followed its jagged path. "To yourself? I get it. Young and dumb. Mistakes are a rite of passage, and in your case, you had a messed-up start. Jake was a predator. But you didn't have to help little kids suffer. How could you do that? Killing you is really a generous act. Otherwise you'll have to live with those kids' faces in your memory. And with Jake being dead, you'll get the brunt of the state's fury."

"I didn't know what else to do." Fear pitched her words into another octave.

"Self-preservation? Is that what you're telling me? That you could do nothing else but take the easy way out?"

Lily was cold by the time I found her. I instantly knew what she'd done, and mixed in with the shock and panic was a cancerous anger. Her pain had been more than I could imagine, but how could she leave me like this? To deal with our mother and the fallout of Lily's death? Of all the selfish things to do.

Lily in the pink casket she would have hated. My mother preening for attention. Everyone staring at me while they whis-

pered the rumor—had Lily really been sexually abused, or was I just a liar? My mother wanted everything kept quiet, her boyfriend was gone, and I'd be safe. She never confirmed the story. Lily's death was about my mother's personal loss and embarrassment. I was left behind to heal myself in the best way possible.

Lily left me with that woman, for her own self-preservation. The easy way out.

The sudden shift in Riley's eyes snapped me from the memory. Their color had faded to a listless, watery gray, her skin crystalline and pale.

She's not breathing.

I dove forward, trying to resuscitate her, trying to stop the bleeding. Smelling Riley's blood and sweat and my own guilt, I fought for her life. She was a liability, but she was also a child. Standing by while she died made me the kind of monster I'd sworn I'd never become.

But it was too late. I couldn't save her any more than I could have saved my sister.

What would happen to me now?

Jake was dead. It was my word against their silence.

Using my shirt, I wiped the knife handle clean of my prints, and then shoved it into his hands. If the police dusted for prints, I might have a problem, but staging the scene would go a long way to proving self-defense.

It was the only option I had left.

THIRTY-SEVEN

Todd arrived first with two ambulances. Paramedics quickly pronounced Jake and Riley dead and began loading them for transport to the morgue. Todd took my statement in the living room of the nearly empty house. There was a couch and two chairs, with a laptop tossed causally aside. Since Jake's wallet was right next to it, Todd and I both knew it was his, and if we had any luck, it was the one he ran the sex ring from.

Before I called Todd, I'd found some gloves and spent a few minutes in Jake's email.

I told Todd everything in full, omitting only my confession to Riley about Preacher. "He stabbed Riley when she started to argue with him. The little boy she'd been taking care of appeared on Jake's trafficking site, and she lost it when I told her. He wasn't interested. I tried to save her, but by the time I took care of Jake, she was gone." I shivered, crossing my arms over my chest.

"I can't believe you got out of this," Todd said. He'd just led me out of the house and hovered protectively.

"I didn't want to die." There was nothing more to it. I used my considerable skills at reading and manipulating people and did what I had to do. Survival of the fittest.

Todd wrapped me in his big coat as we walked to his car. "I'm glad you didn't."

I'd made a wise choice not to run. Todd said we were at least five miles from civilization, as he put it, just west of Philadelphia. Without a coat, I'd have ended up with hypothermia.

The Audi with the black rims squealed to a halt just before I was ready to collapse into Todd's modest sedan. Chris left the engine running and burst through paramedics to get to me. I let him take me into his arms, breathing in the warm, safe scent that was decidedly him. He grabbed my face with both hands. "Are you all right?"

"Yes," I said. "It was Jake, the senator's aide. And Riley. He killed her, and I hit him with the shovel. I had to."

His eyes searched mine, and then he pulled me close again. "As long as you're safe."

Todd cleared his throat. "Listen, I need to take her in and get her statement."

"Whatever happened was self-defense," Chris said. His grip around me tightened. I felt like I was melting into him, exhaustion turning my limbs into jelly.

"Of course it is," Todd said. "But we need to get an official statement."

Todd gestured for me to get into the car. "Chris, you can meet us at the station, be there with her when she gives the statement." He cleared his throat again and glanced at me. "If that's what she wants."

"It is," I said. "But can you give us a minute?"

A flash of disappointment in Todd's eyes, followed by a hard nod. "Hurry. It's cold."

I waited until he'd gotten behind the wheel and shut the car door before I looked up at Chris. He hugged me tighter.

"What is it?"

"They were going to sell me to a couple."

Icy blue eyes stared down at me. He dipped his head toward mine so only I could hear him. "You did the right thing."

"I know, but we have a bigger problem, and I don't plan on telling Todd about it."

He waited, staring at me as if I held all the secrets of the world. "Your mother was the buyer. She bought from Jake before, and she was looking for me."

Chris pressed his lips together. His jaw clenched, a muscle in his right cheek flexing. "You know what this means."

"I do. I have the information we'll need."

It was time to take care of Mother Mary.

THIRTY-EIGHT

Unknown

"Three blind fools, See them run. The blond was in the way; The redhead is learning her place; The last one will soon go away. Three blind fools, See them run..."

He singsongs the silly rhyme he's made up, tottering around his spotless kitchen. Dawn is breaking, and National Public Radio is talking about the massive child sex trafficking ring discovered by the Philadelphia police.

Pouring freshly squeezed orange juice, he scoffs. Detective Todd Beckett, a joke.

Beckett couldn't even figure out Sam Townsend was the perfect patsy. It had been easy enough to fake Townsend's suicide by hanging, a simple trick of wearing gloves and providing the right leverage. Sarah had been harder, more willing to fight.

Killing her was fun.

He laughs now, cleaning his single morning dish. Todd Beckett getting the glory for that case was a damned shame.

He'd had it all handed to him by the woman with the power to destroy them all.

He's confident she's learning her place, but this latest stunt makes him wonder.

He doesn't want to fight the redhead. She's too useful.

But if it comes to that, he will do what is necessary.

He always has.

A LETTER FROM STACY

Dear reader,

Thank you so much for reading *Little Lost Souls*! I had a lot of fun researching and writing the entire Lucy Kendall series despite the dark overtones. If you read and enjoyed the book and want to get updates on the next release in the series, just sign up at the following link. Your email address will never be shared, and you can unsubscribe at any time.

www.bookouture.com/stacy-green

As always, the best part of writing is the reaction from readers. If you loved Lucy and Chris as much as I do, I would love it if you could leave a short review. Getting feedback from readers is amazing and helps encourage new readers to try my books for the very first time.

Thank you so much for reading,

Stacy Green

KEEP IN TOUCH WITH STACY

www.stacygreenauthor.com

facebook.com/StacyGreenAuthor

twitter.com/StacyGreen26

instagram.com/authorstacygreen

ACKNOWLEDGMENTS

Writing the Lucy Kendall series was rewarding but also an exhaustive endeavor that has challenged my confidence and my heart. Without the help of several experts and a very patient support group, I'd have curled up in a ball with my dogs and given up. Many thanks to Dr. D.P. Lyle (*Howdunit Forensics: A Guide for Writers*) for his patience and willingness to volley murder scenarios back and forth. His suggestion of the ketamine resulted in a scene I loved writing and sent Lucy down a fresh path. Thanks to the late William Simon for his expertise in computer programming and police procedure, and thank you to Heather Cathrall for being my virtual eyes and ears to the city of Philadelphia. Thanks to Chief of Police Scott Silvarii for his assistance in making sure my character's interrogation and investigation were going in the right direction.

Little Lost Souls takes Lucy into very real and very dark territory. Sex trafficking of minors is happening every day in this country. As a mother, it is a sobering and terrifying reality, and as a writer, it means doing my research. Thanks to Detective Caroline Holliday of the Greensboro, North Carolina Police Department for her frank answers my endless questions about the exploitation of minors. Thank you to Staca Shehan, Director of Case Analysis Division at the National Center of Missing and Exploited Children. Staca's explanation of how the trafficking rings work and what her organization does for law enforcement gave the book a much-needed extra layer.

To Kristine Kelly, my line editor and dear friend, thanks so much for your constant support of my writing. To Annetta Ribken, I'm forever grateful for your tough love and belief in my abilities and in Lucy. To my readers who have fallen in love with Lucy despite her many faults, thank you! I am so happy you're on this journey with me. Finally, to my family, especially my ever-supportive husband: thank you for encouraging me to follow my dreams. It means the world to me.

Made in United States
Orlando, FL
03 May 2023

32720465R10176